GW01396258

The Kindness of Strangers

By the same author

Fiction
Once in a New Moon
Death without Trace

Non-fiction
The Year of Disappearances
(Political Killings in Cork 1921-1922)

The Kindness of Strangers

A Novel

Gerard Murphy

CreateSpace

First published 2013

© Gerard Murphy 2013

Gerard Murphy has asserted his moral right to be identified as author of this work.

All rights reserved. No part of this book may be reprinted or reproduced or utilized in any form or by any electronic, mechanical or other means, now known or thereafter invented, including photocopying and recording or in any information storage or retrieval system, without the permission in writing of the author.

ISBN: 9781484822142

Prologue

Many years ago, a young man on a creaking cart was making his way slowly up a lane. The lane was winding, narrow and ran under clumps of alders by a tiny stream. His shoulders were hunched, his head disappeared into an old brown coat and he looked like a half-filled sack tied to a crooked piece of ash. The cart was pulled by a grey mare and the young man flicked the mare's rump and she moved faster for a step or two before slowing again. An occasional spark came off the stones under the mare's shoes and her hooves were covered with rough hair encrusted in mud, so they moved like dancing strawmen.

It was gloomy in the lane and the only colour was the track of grass along the centre that was lit by an unexpected trail of half-opened daisies. In this damp glen there was only moss and a clinging fog that hooked itself onto the trees and dripped everywhere. And because there was no wind, the stream on one side of the lane was singing loudly as it fell blindly over the cold stones.

But there were three other men here who would never again hear the stream sing or listen to the wind blowing. They lay under brown sacks on the floor of the cart and, though they were still warm, they wore bullet holes like wet carnations on their foreheads and their blood ran along the floor of the cart and dripped onto the daisied grass like the scarlet trail of geese being killed for Christmas.

But this was no Christmas, and the young man knew that no Christ could ever smile down on this. For this was the Devil's work and there were some who said that there are times when the Devil's work must be done, when the ways of Christ were not enough. But the young man was beginning to have his doubts about this and he knew that doubts are where trouble starts. And he was in enough trouble already without questioning why he was here, or doing what he was doing, and going the way he was going, or ending the lives he was ending.

He tried to banish these doubts from his mind and made an effort to think only one thought and that was the hope that rain would come and wash away the drips of blood he was leaving in his wake and perhaps keep the bloodhounds off his trail.

'Go on there, Doll,' he said to the mare. 'Good girl. Only another mile to go.'

The boy lived with his parents and brother and sister, in a small house under a hill at the top of the lane, near a twisted ash tree and three pines that had been combed into slanted plains by the relentless winds. Today, because there was no wind, a thin plume of smoke walked straight up from the chimney to the sky, a fragile string that in those times was humanity's only bind to heaven. He knew that this was no sign of rain. But there were other contradictory signs: he heard a curlew's call and the late starlings were flying low and the sound of the river was clear in the distance.

He would pray for rain, but felt that no God would listen to his prayers, unless he was a contrary God indeed. Instead, he merely prodded the mare again and willed her on her way to the mountain beyond the house.

When he reached his destination, he took a shovel from the cart and began to dig. The earth was hard and clumpy, the shovel pummelling into heather roots like a child's fist against a bed of cushions. I'll make no progress like this, he thought. So he tied the mare to a furze root and made his way back down to his long low homestead where he found an old pickaxe, loose in its handle like a cheap trinket.

He hammered a washer into the shaft of the pickaxe and walked back up the mountain until he reached again the place where the mare was tethered. He resumed his work, alternately picking and shovelling and pulling big stones out of the grave with his hands. It was hard work and he rested every few minutes, straightening his back and putting his hands on his hips and gazing at the fog across the valley.

The same sequence of thoughts entered his mind every time he rested. First his mind would go blank, then a longing for the vastness of the valley would come with the moving fog. Then would come the realization of what that fog might bring and his ears would strain to catch the first sound of lorries. When he was satisfied he could hear no such sound, he would go back to his digging until he resembled a small factory with steam rising from his shirt, sweat dripping onto his boots and the skin of his forearms got chaffed from rubbing the corduroy of his thigh with every shovelful.

After two hours, he was satisfied that the hole was big enough, so he untethered the mare and, taking the reins by her jaw, reversed the cart a few yards to the edge of the crumbling grave, the axle creaking and the cart juddering on the rough ground.

'Good girl, Doll. Another bit, another bit. Whoa, whoa, hold it. Good girl.'

The mare stopped, snorted and shook herself. He opened the tailboard of the cart and lined up the corpses feet first. He lifted the shafts off the traces and tipped up the cart. The dead men, one of them a middle-aged man, the other two almost youngsters, slid together in a singular embrace and fell with a soft clump like aborted calves into the grave. Then he himself got into the grave and straightened them out along the bottom so that they would lie together, one on top of the other, for all the eternity of the mountain.

When he climbed out, he tackled the mare to the cart again and feverishly began to shovel the earth in on top of the bodies. He did not look into the grave again. Instead, he focused on the soil in front of him, which he saw now as the new enemy to be got rid of as cleanly and as completely as possible. When he had finished, he went to a nearby ditch and, with a slash hook, cut the largest hawthorn he could find and dragged it back to conceal the mound of earth and stones.

By the time he had finished, there were no lights to be seen in the valley for miles around. The fog had not lifted. He knew it would be dark in half an hour. Even so, he went on his knees beside the grave and said slow silent prayers for the souls of the men he had interred.

'Thou, O Lord, wilt open my lips...'

As he said a decade of the Rosary, the bog water seeped into his knees and by the time he stood up his trousers were sodden. Without looking back and with that cold damp stain on his knees, he sat up on the cart behind the mare and, legs swinging sideways against the wheel band, spoke quietly to the mare to 'gee up'. The cart shuddered and the wheels, with small creaks, ground stones into the mud of the mountain. The mare moved into the darkness and found her own way home over the hillocky ground. To the young man's surprise and relief, it began to rain; soft spring-like rain, fine silent drops like damp gossamer. 'Thanks be to God,' he said, for he knew that the rain would make his journey difficult to trace.

The eye of the world was closing down. He was glad to be out of there and relieved to be alive, but he would never want to look upon that part of the mountain again, though he knew that in the nature of things he probably would, again and again, until something intervened to end the murderous cycle that was going on. Unless, and that was very unlikely, he could do something about it himself.

1

The spring of 1920 found Dinny Fitzgibbon, for that was the young man's name, ploughing stubbles in a high field with only crows and gulls for company. The ground was soft and the plough threw the sod clean on its back in long brown lines. The gulls and crows lined up behind him, queuing for fresh worms. He stumbled in the furrows so that dirt filled his boots; every so often he would have to stop and empty them of small stones. The frost had crumbled the ground. A week earlier, it would have been like trying to plough iron and the plough board would have skidded off the shale. Now the earth turned willingly and ploughing was a form of joy, happiness in the opening of the new year.

Dinny, as was the custom of that time, wore hobnailed boots, brown corduroy trousers and a black, worn waistcoat. He had removed his jacket and hung it on a gatepost. He lived with his family at the edge of the upland area known as the Rea, which formed a triangle of furze and rushes in the middle of East Cork, a few miles from the villages of Knockraha and Watergrasshill. The land he was ploughing was poor, cold land, hard won from the hills by men who had lived before the Famine, who surrounded it with high stone walls of shale and red sandstone.

He was nineteen years old and apprenticed to a carpenter, but demand for carpentry had effectively come to a standstill, with the country in upheaval and poverty rampant since the end of the Great War. So, instead of knocking joists together, making windows and hanging doors, he was back at one of his favourite occupations, ploughing. For you did not shirk hard work in a high place like this. The proximity of hunger both in time and reality ensured that complacency was not a fault found in those who lived in the high country, with rushes all around and cold gales coming from all corners of the land. Dinny was also a Volunteer in the local IRA Company. He was a private in an amateur army, a part-time player in the fight to free Ireland from British rule. He worked all day, saving his country in his spare time.

It was a local schoolteacher called Tadhg Manley who had got him interested in revolution in the first place. Tadhg Manley was an idealist and a visionary, the only great man Dinny had ever met. Manley had picked up the language of revolution while working in Midleton as a teacher, where he shared lodgings with Diarmuid Hurley, the leader of the East Cork IRA, and he was only too willing to pass on his ideals to younger lads like Dinny Fitzgibbon. All the youngsters wanted to get involved, particularly during 1918 and the Conscription Crisis. As Dinny saw it, everyone had to do his or her bit for Ireland. The others were too old and crabbed, too fond of money – what little of it there was around – or security. The revolution was in the hands of the young.

'We are the small and poor of Ireland,' Manley had said, 'and we are powerless. We are the sons of small farmers and artisans and we have no future. We should have no qualms about the methods we use, because the enemy is far more powerful than we are.' And yet when it came to arithmetic and spelling and doing the two-times-tables, this same man was as kind and helpful to the weakest students in his classes as he was to the bright ones. Now in the spring of 1920, Manley had gone back to Midleton, where he got involved in the earliest ambushes and attacks on RIC barracks, striking a blow for the Republic.

Dinny wiped the sweat off his brow and began to sing as he walked in the furrow, shaking hands with the plough as it shuddered from stone to stone. He looked around. A miracle of seagulls had exploded behind the plough. He sang out loud, at the top of his voice, for the simple joy that he found in the world.

By the sea of Odessa, I rambled one night,
The moon it was shining quite clear.
For no reason at all, I heard someone call.
It was Abdul the Bulbul Amir.

People are different, he thought. Some men love the camaraderie of the pub and the lofts where dances are held and like nothing more than to make foolish talk in groups after Mass. But Dinny loved the solitude of the high fields and the sense of the immensity of the world that they gave him. He looked north towards the distant blue hills of the Galtees and east to the Knockmealdowns, blue sleeping giants snoozing on the horizon. County Waterford. He had never been there. He had no idea what kind of people lived there either, though he had heard they were rich, that they had big farms; that the landlords there owned the fishing rights of all the rivers and could get you jailed for poaching.

Then in the tomb's shadow,
There rose from the grave
The form of a Russian hussar.
My skin nearly peeled as he stood there revealed
It was Ivan Skivinski Skivaar.

He stopped the horses for a few seconds, rubbed the sweat off his brow with the sleeve of his shirt before stumbling back into the furrows again. The earth smelt as fresh as air. In the brown ditches small buds hopped between the hawthorns. Spring light found clusters of primroses and violets. High clouds marched in a line like goslings across the sky. There would be no rain for at least a week. Dinny took out his pocket watch and looked at it. It was ten minutes to one.

'Come on, Doll and Sonny,' he said to the mare and the roan gelding, ''tis time for a bite of grub.'

He flicked their rumps with the reins and brought them over to the headland where he untackled the plough and walked them through three bawn fields to the stables for water and buckets of oats. Then he went into the house for his dinner.

2

'They're going to save Ireland, are they? By Christ, I'd say they are too. If Parnell couldn't save Ireland, I doubt these fellows will.'

Dinny Fitzgibbon's father was hunched over his dinner. He had just been reading about the shooting of policemen in the Cork Examiner and had folded the newspaper in front of him. He began peeling potatoes, distractedly letting the skins fall in a small pile by his plate.

'Ah, the hoors. Murdering peelers from behind stone walls. Brave men.'

He grunted and spat, his shoulders rounded like a small hill from years of physical work, his thick eyebrows watching his plate as if it held some form of prey that might escape at any minute. He was a hardy old fellow with hair growing in tufts out of his ears and down his nose and was well known in the area for having strong opinions on everything. He was nicknamed 'Tim Healy', after the well-known barrister and MP, a tribute to his opinionated erudition. Once he started talking, you couldn't stop him.

'That is, of course, if Ireland wants to be saved.' He raised his fork and stabbed the air with it. He cut a slice of bacon, popped it into his mouth and began to chew it in a circular motion with what was left of his teeth, like a cow chewing the cud. He was a firm supporter of the Irish Nationalist Party, the party of Parnell and Redmond. He was a Home Ruler and had no time for the republican movement led by Sinn Féin.

'There was a man below here one time and do you know what he said to me? He said of all the outfits going the road that the Volunteers are the most dangerous. Young fellows! Sure what do young fellows know? You see, this is politics at the point of a gun. Didn't I see them myself, for the love of God, over in Ballynoe one Sunday after Mass. You would have thought the ranting and raving of the lad inside would be enough for us for one day. But not at all. The Sinn Féiners don't just drill and march; they have their sermons too.'

Dinny's mother threw her eyes up to heaven. What self-opinionated raiméis, she thought. He was like a train going under a bridge; there would be no silence until long after the caboose was gone out of sight. The only thing for it was to let him talk.

'That fella MacSwiney was arrested after it, a complete fanatic, if you ask me. As for the sister! But he wasn't the worst, by Jaysus you should have seen the lads he had around him. I tell ya something, they were the toughest crew I've ever seen, and I've seen a fair few in my time. Peggy Flaherty's twins were small at the time. The two dotiest little pets you ever saw in your life. I watched that crowd troop down past Peggy Flaherty and the twins, and not one of them as much as looked twice at those babies. Ye see,' he shook his fork, 'those lads don't see people as human beings, I reckon. I said to myself, if fellas like that ever get hold of the country, what are we in for? And wasn't I right, hah? Look what's happening now.'

Dinny knew what his father was up to. The old bastard was trying to stir up an argument. Dinny was furious with his father's outdated ideas but resolved not to rise to the bait. There was nothing Dinny's father liked more than a good row during mealtimes and Dinny wouldn't give him the satisfaction of stirring it up.

'Whether you like it or not, you'll have to admit,' Dinny's older brother, Bill, said, 'that the people voted for Sinn Féin the last time out.'

Bill had a rim of milk around his mouth and was scooping up cabbage from his plate. He was a man of few words, a big fellow with an easy grin, interested just now in extracting a little entertainment from his father.

'They did too. But they didn't vote for murdering fellas coming out of Mass. If they believed their precious Sinn Féin was going to do that, I doubt that we'd have had the same result in 1918. I'll tell you what it is now. I'll tell you.'

He half-closed one eye and gesticulated again with his fork for emphasis. (This was no ordinary fork. This was his own personal fork, which had been in the family for generations and which by now had shrunk to a short stump on a worn piece of bone.)

'War. That's the thing. War is the only man for the farmer. By Christ, we had four mighty years during the Great War. What a pity it had to end, hah! What a pity them bleddy old hoors of Germans couldn't keep up the fight a bit longer.' The old man was in despair at the collapse of the price of farm produce since the end of the war.

'I'll tell you what it is. Tis all rack and ruin now. Four years ago, oats was making ten shillings a hundredweight, hay was five pounds a ton and potatoes nine pence a stone. Now you couldn't give 'em away.' He gritted his teeth and took a deep intake of breath. 'War is the man for the farmer, mark my words. No doubt about it. But not this type of war. Burning creameries is not war.'

'So long as he doesn't have to fight in it,' Dinny's mother muttered as she emptied the last of the potatoes out of the pot onto a dish in the middle of the table and sat down to eat her own dinner. She was twenty years younger than her husband and lived, wedged in a generation gap between him and their sons. They had one daughter, Bina. Today, Bina was in Cork, buying curtain material. There were two factions within the family: the three men muttering at each other in a grumpy, benign sort of way, and Bina and herself, both quiet, more like sisters than mother and daughter. She observed her sons with a shrewd gaze. She had no fears for Bill – he was as solid as a gatepost – but sometimes she worried about Dinny. He was sensitive and malleable as a pig-skin purse and a bit too idealistic for his own good. He was just the kind of lad who was attracted to the Volunteers. A boy like Dinny could get in with a dangerous crowd and could very easily find himself in Cork Jail or worse.

'Ah, what do women know?' Dinny's father said, as if it was perfectly self-evident to anybody with even the slightest shred of intelligence that there was no way on earth a woman could possibly understand something as well as a man.

'I have it on good authority that the first shots in 1916 were fired by a woman – Countess Markievicz,' Bill said, still trying to get a rise out of his father.

'Is it any wonder, looking at Mary MacSwiney? I'm not surprised, another daffer. And where, may I ask, did that get them? That de Valera is a bad egg. I heard he was only spared from execution because his mother was able to prove he was an American.'

'de Valera is a fine man,' Dinny's mother said.

'Yerra, maybe he is. Maybe he's not. Can't a man have his own opinions in his own house?'

'You mean to say you're against Irish freedom?' Dinny finally blurted out. This was a cliché, but, in Dinny's view, clichés were called clichés because they were true. He knew his father's political views and normally he wouldn't challenge him. But, because he had been sworn in as a Volunteer in his local Company the previous week and because of his new-found hope for the future, he did not want to let his father get away with this rant.

'Irish freedom! For the love of God, boy, what use would Irish freedom be to any of us? Do you think they'd make a better job of running the show than John Redmond? By Jaysus, I'd say they'd be a whole lot worse. Imagine that de Valera fella as king. Imagine a crown on his tussely oul nut!'

'There will be no crown on the future heads of Ireland. What we want now is a republic.'

'We? Who's we, may I ask?'

'Well, the Irish People. The Republicans.'

'A republic! Could you tell me the difference between a republic and Home Rule? Could you tell me that now, hah?'

'There would be no king or queen, for a start. Parliament would be answerable to the people,' Dinny shot back.

His father waved his fork about like an ageing Poseidon waving a tiny trident. 'The people! For the love of God, man, would you have a titter of wit. I'll tell you about the people now and the kind of lads we're going to have working for the people.'

'What are you?' Dinny asked in a fit of uncharacteristic anger and boldness.

'What kind of a question is that to ask your father? What do you mean "what am I"?'

'Just answer it.'

'What am I? Christ. I'm a farmer and a father of two lazy ludramáns of sons, that's what I am.'

'You're a subject.'

'I'm a subject? Am I? What the hell does that mean?'

'You're a subject of the Crown, of the King of England.'

'So? We're all the subjects of The Man Above.' He pointed to the ceiling.

'What Sinn Féin wants is to make people citizens, not subjects. You get rid of the King of England and you have citizens, you have equality for all.'

Dinny's father laughed at this.

'Equality, me eye.' He shoved a forkful of cabbage into his mouth.

'Fanatics, that's what they are. You think Ireland gives a rat's arse? Take Dan Donohoe, our parish Napoleon. He's a fine specimen now and he should be old enough to have a bit more sense.'

Dan Donohoe was the local IRA captain. A long-time republican, he had been sent, it was believed, by the city men to kick the parish into shape. He was nominally a captain, but in the parish his rank went all the way to brigadier or even dictator. Stubborn as a charging bull, he was a little man with a tight jaw, an uncompromising master of colourful language and fierce hatreds, who would do anything for the cause.

'If he's the kind of bird you're hoping will save Ireland, then God help us. He's been out with the Fenians for years. I've watched him in his cocked hat and galoshes. He came to this parish to drum up a bit of support I suppose because he thought we were a bit mountainy. Well, if I had my way, he'd be well and truly run out of the country.'

'Maybe it's just as well you don't have your way.'

'By Christ, there's a nice way to speak to your father.'

'Well...'

'During the election two years ago,' the fork was flying again, 'and this is no word of a lie – I was there myself – wasn't the hoor below at the polling station all day and he wouldn't let people vote inside. "Mark your vote out here in public" he said to me, "and don't go into the polling booth. 'Tis too much of this British secrecy we have, and the sooner we get away from it, the better." And he had all the local lads impersonating the gentry who were afraid to go to the polling station. "How are you, Colonel Murphy?" the Presiding Officer said to Mick Foley, "and how are things going in the brewing business?" "Apart from the bad harvest, things are going very well in the brewing business," Mick said. If Mick Foley had half as much money as Colonel Murphy, he wouldn't need to pull stunts like that at the polling station.' The fork was flying again.

'Dan Donohoe put Foley up to it. There's your democracy now for you, boy, there's your republic. These are the lads we'll have running the country if the Fenians get their way.'

Dinny always got really annoyed at his father's insistence on referring to the IRA and Sinn Fein as Fenians.

'That's not true.'

'It's true all right. And if this kind of thing was general all over the country, then it's no surprise that the Irish Party got only six seats.' Dinny's father had never forgiven Sinn Féin for defeating his party so totally in the 1918 general election and

14

for 'the way they treated that decent man John Dillon' as he put it.

'The whole country is shagged. Do you know what I saw the other day?' Neither the boys nor their mother replied. They didn't need to; they were going to hear the answer anyway.

'I saw Foley's son Con going down through the village with what looked like a revolver sticking out of his pocket, bold as brass in the middle of the day. Who do they think they are – cowboys and Indians? Now, if that kind of carry-on is going to start around here, we're all banjaxed. I mean has he any idea what would happen to him if he was caught? Maybe he's just an innocent fooleen, but, if you ask me, I think Dan Donohoe is coddin' him up to his eyeballs.'

Dinny blushed and kept his head down, eating with concentration and staring into his plate. If his father had any idea that he was a sworn-in member of an IRA battalion, he would have been run out of the house. He was lucky though. He had to swear a vow of allegiance to the Republic and part of the vow was that he had to keep his activities secret, even from close family members. It wasn't easy. He was so filled with enthusiasm, he wanted to tell everybody how he was going to save Ireland. He was even prepared to die for Ireland like the men of 1916, if it came to that. His father was all bluff and banter, all bull and no balls. There was nothing behind it, Dinny knew, only fear of change.

Saving Ireland was a secret business, to be done only by those who could be trusted. Hadn't all the previous rebellions been defeated by spies and informers? The country, if Dan Donohoe was to be believed, was alive with them. Sometimes Dinny thought the Irish didn't deserve to be set free.

And so the Fitzgibbon family finished their meal, like trains pulled up at the same station, but heading off on tracks leading them in completely different directions.

3

A week later, the last week of March, a meeting of the Company was convened in the snug of Corrigan's public house in Knockraha. About a dozen men turned up. It was presided over by Dan Donohoe, a wiry man of about thirty with a thick moustache and peculiar flap-like ears that reminded Dinny of the leaves of winter cabbage that had been burnt by frost. He wore thick-soled boots to make himself look taller and, when standing, stuck out his chest like a bantam cock. Today, he was even more serious-looking than usual. In fact, he was white-faced with rage.

The country was abuzz with rumour: that the British were going to send in more troops; that the RIC was going to be reinforced with thugs and ruffians from the jails of England; that the country was going to be overrun with the scum of the Empire.

Donohoe had a map opened in front of him and was fidgeting with a pen and noting things on a sheet of paper. He placed his revolver on the table in front of him as the snug was filled with the sound of stools being scraped into position. His eyes were small and there were pebbles of remorseless anger in them. He cleared his throat and stood up and raised his hand for silence.

'Ye all know why we're here, don't ye?' He took several deep breaths, as if trying to calm himself. The men stared at him. They mostly ranged in age from fifteen to twenty-three, none of them brave enough to contradict a man of thirty, particularly someone who carried the authority Donohoe did. The only exception was Ned Murphy, the blacksmith, who was himself over thirty, a broad man with a sooty face who guarded the door, letting in those he knew to be trustworthy and refusing entry to anyone not interested in the cause of Ireland.

In fact, they didn't know why they were there; their parish was small and quiet and seemed to be pretty irrelevant to the saving of Ireland.

'If you've read the papers in the last day or two, then you'll know what I'm here to tell you.' Most of the men kept on staring, cradling their lemonade and beer glasses in their hands. Most of them looked down.

'As you may know, the bastards murdered the Lord Mayor on Sunday night.' He paused for effect. Tomás MacCurtain, the Sinn Féin Lord Mayor of Cork, had been shot dead in his bed the previous weekend and the country was awash with rumours as to who had done it.

'They had their faces painted black, but we know they were RIC men. This is the kind of country we're living in now.'

What Donohoe didn't remind them of was that the murder of Tomás MacCurtain was in response to the murder of RIC men up and down the country over the previous few months and that the police had merely joined their enemies in the politics of assassination. What mattered to Donohoe was that MacCurtain was dead, an elected Lord Mayor, murdered by forces of the Crown. He banged the table for emphasis and took another deep breath before going on.

'In front of his wife and little children, the RIC broke into his home in the middle of the night and shot Tomás MacCurtain dead. I have to tell you that Terence MacSwiney has assumed the role of O/C of the Brigade, as well as the Lord Mayorship, and Seán Ó'Hegarty is to be vice O/C. But that's not the point. The question is, what are we going to do about it?'

There was more uncomfortable silence in the room and a dozen pairs of eyes searched the floorboards for things they had not lost.

'Now, they might have had blackened faces but they're not fooling us. We know who did it.' He tapped the table. 'Swanzy is the DI and he's behind it. He went after us in riot gear in 1918, and since. Well, he won't go after us for too long more. He's vanished from Cork but, don't worry, we'll get him, if we have to chase the shagger to the farthest corners of the earth.'

Donohoe picked up his revolver, waved it around before slamming it down on the table again. 'Here, in this part of Cork, we have our work to do, and part of that work is to get every last one of the bastards who helped or had any hand, act or part in that murder. If it takes us ten years, we'll get those hoors.'

There was silence in the room again.

'This means there may be some pretty grim jobs needing to be carried out. I want anybody who is not interested in doing this work to leave the room immediately.'

The men, the boys, looked at each other but nobody moved.

'I take that as meaning that you're all with us then?'

They all nodded and assumed serious grown-up expressions.

'Right. That's settled. Now down to business.' He poked the Ordnance Survey map in front of him with his forefinger.

'There's a vault here, I believe, in one of the graveyards of this area. Is that right?'

'I know where it is,' Ned Murphy answered. It was a half a mile outside the village and local rumour had it that it had been used in the nineteenth century to store dead bodies, to prevent them from being stolen by body-snatchers.

'Is it suitable for holding prisoners?'

'Well, it's ten feet underground and it's got a solid stone wall. I would think so, yes.'

'It was used to stop the corpses from trying to escape,' Con Foley a whey-faced runt of a fellow said, smirking at his own joke.

'Maybe it will be used to stop the corpses from trying to escape again,' Dan Donohoe muttered. There was an odd silence in the room, as if the boys did not know whether to laugh or not. 'Do you think you could open it up for me?'

Ned Murphy cleared his throat. 'All it'll take is a slasher for the briars and a few slaps of the hammer to open it up. Nobody's been in there for years.'

'Well, they will now. Terry MacSwiney has given us authorization to use whatever means we have to hold spies and interrogate them and do whatever is necessary. We are to be set up as a Special Operations Unit, a detention centre, to guard this vault and to be under arms at all times,' Donohoe said officiously.

Dinny thought he detected a note of triumph in Donohoe's voice, as if this was the moment he had been waiting for all his life and MacCurtain's death was some sort of excuse to set him up in business, a justification for greater things to come.

'There are other reasons why we have been singled out for this very important task by the Brigade. There are no Protestants here, no loyalists and no lackeys of the Crown, at least none we know of. This is an ideal spot for what we have to do. And we are near enough to Cork. We have looked at this in some detail and we have no doubt that this is the best place in the vicinity of Cork city for holding spies and prisoners of war.' So, Dinny thought, this is the mysterious reason why the parish had been honoured with an outsider as captain: it was seen as a safe area.

'Can anyone think of any reasons why this may not be the case. For, if there are good reasons, spit 'em out now.' He spread his hands over the map in front of him.

Again the floorboards were searched and searched again and nothing was found.

'I needn't tell you that total secrecy has to be maintained at all times, not only from people in this locality but even from people within our own movement. While we are technically under the command of the Cobh battalion, on the matter of prisoners we are answerable only to the O/C of the Brigade and his vice O/C. We take our orders from Seán O'Hegarty and nobody else. Is that clear?'

The men nodded in unison. Unlike Tomás MacCurtain, the dead Lord Mayor, who was familiar to them from his visits to feiseanna in the area, Terence MacSwiney and Sean O'Hegarty were near mythical characters, distant city men of vague importance to the lads in the snug, their very distance giving them added authority. Besides, revenge for MacCurtain's murder seemed a good enough reason for any of them to be involved.

'This is the ASU that doesn't exist, if you get my drift. Do you all understand what I mean?'

ASU stood for Active Service Unit. They nodded in unison.

'One more thing. The O/C has decreed that there be no more overt military activity in this area. That means no ambushes, no tree-felling and no trench-digging. And no more drilling or marching or wearing uniforms either. We'll have to hide our uniforms. We'll be doing work of the utmost importance. On no account are we to attract the attentions of the military to this area. This is going to be the quietest place in County Cork from now on. Is that understood?'

'What if they get suspicious because the place is so quiet?' Con Foley asked.

'The belief of the O/C is that the British move where they think the action is. They're like young fellas playing hurling; they play out of position, all rushing around after the same ball. There is no police barracks here, so the RIC has no ears or eyes. This is blind man's bluff. As regards the military,' Dan Donohoe smiled, 'we have informants at the very highest level. We know what the military will do even before the military itself gets its orders.'

Donohoe allowed himself a little smile. 'Put it like this: in Cork, our Intelligence is a lot more intelligent than the British. We can buy and sell them. There are people sleeping in their beds tonight and they think they have got away with this. Well, by Christ, they haven't, and time will prove that they haven't.'

4

It was a fine April morning a few days later, the sky scrubbed by high cloud; fields looked flung against the distant hills as if they were drying out in the breeze. A cuckoo sang out of the blue distance of Watergrasshill. Dinny and Ned Murphy were on their way into the graveyard to open up the vault.

The graveyard, half-hidden on a bush-covered knoll outside the village, was surrounded by four fields, each of which sloped off towards a pair of narrow thicket-filled comars. Though the cemetery wore a crown of stone and had a moss-covered gravel path, it was in a state of perpetual neglect. The hands of weeds reached up the faces of headstones, as if the living had forgotten about their dead and were not too worried about the state of things in the next life.

'I'll tell you a good one now,' Ned Murphy said, as he climbed over the style into the graveyard and handed his bag of blacksmith's tools over the wall to Dinny who already had his own tools – a bill hook, a pitchfork, a slasher and a whetstone – on the grass beside him. 'And this is no word of a lie. Con Foley's father was digging a grave in here one time and he had a bottle of whiskey inside of him. Didn't the bleddy fella fall into the grave after he dug it. He was so drunk, the hoor had trouble getting out. I tell ye, he never touched a drop after that. Father Mathew should have thought of that when he wanted to turn lads into teetotallers.'

'That would wake 'em up alright, I should imagine,' Dinny said, smiling. He was glad to be out working with Ned, whom he looked up to, for he considered Ned to be wise in a way that most people were not.

'The things people come up with! I was at a Stations over in Forde's last week and do you know what the subject was at the men's table? Fast and slow graveyards, would you believe it?'

'Fast and slow graveyards?'

'Apparently, there are fast and slow graveyards, depending on the rate the bodies rot. It seems it's all to do with the soil. When the soil is sandy, then corpses rot far quicker. Wet soil, it's slower.'

'A lovely topic after Mass,' Dinny said.

'Well, that's the kind of thing they talk about down in the Room. Baloney. They can't talk dirty in front of the priest, So it's graveyards and funerals and the like. Very optimistic stuff.'

They picked up their tools and made their way across the graveyard. The ground was uneven and dry underfoot. Birds sang. Bushes sagged here and there. Briars reached in from the overgrown hedges to the graves, patches of dead nettles leaned like bundles of dry stalks. The sun was not yet directly over their heads.

'What do you think of this idea of using sacred ground for the holding of prisoners?' Dinny asked.

'If it's safe enough, it's good enough. Sure, prisoners have to be kept somewhere.'

'The priest might have something to say about it, though.'

'The new priest will keep his mouth shut, so I'm told.'

'And you'll have no problem minding people here? What about ghosts?'

'Ghosts? Sure, there's no such thing as ghosts.'

'So you'd stay here, in the middle of the night?'

'In the middle of the day, in the middle of the night. It'd make no difference to me. Nobody in there is going to do me any harm.' He waved a dismissive hand around him at the graveyard, a tumble-down shantytown of the dead, headstones lichened with age. Daisies and dandelions covered the knolls, ash trees waved in the breeze. 'There isn't much of a kick left in these lads now, I can tell ye,' Ned said.

Dinny laughed.

'There she is, over there, boy, right in the middle. See that mound of earth? It's right under those briars.' Ned pointed to a high thicket of brambles in the middle of the cemetery. 'My father told me about it many years ago, well before you were born. It was built to stop the bodysnatchers.'

'We'll have one hell of a job rooting down through that lot.'

'No, we won't. I know where the door is. We'll be in there in twenty minutes.'

Dinny took off his coat, hung it on a headstone and rolled up his sleeves. He sharpened his slasher using the whetstone and began hacking at the edge of the mound. Soon he was flailing left and right, making a hole for himself in the undergrowth until piles of briars thick as saplings sagged down on him like an unsupported roof, while Ned forked out the cut undergrowth. Clouds of wasps and insects rose around him as if he was signalling the end of their world. He stopped occasionally, mopping his forehead to avoid getting sweat and weed sap and creepy crawlies into his eyes.

''Tis is a right hoor in here. These briars would take your eye out if you weren't careful.'

'Come on, you'd swear you never did a bit of scouring in your life. Mind the briars.' Ned lifted a pile of briars and an ambitiously tall but dead thistle out of the way with the pitchfork.

After a while Dinny was able to make out a few steps littered with dead leaves and the shape of some kind of doorway half-hidden by the cast-iron palisade around the tomb of some long-forgotten parishioner.

'I tell you one thing. It might be all right to go in here dead, but I wouldn't like to have to go in here alive,' Dinny said, spitting on his palms to hold the slasher tighter.

'Did you ever hear of The Midnight Court?' Ned asked.

'The what?'

'The Midnight Court, a big long poem in Irish, written by a Clareman, I believe, about a fellow who wakes up in the middle of a graveyard one night, surrounded by naked women.'

'Naked women? I never thought there were any naked women in the Irish.'

'Naked as the day they came into the world. I swear to God. They wanted him to ride 'em, but he wasn't up to it. The hoor had no lead in his pencil.'

'I didn't think there was much riding in those days.'

'Much riding? Sure the Irish were a holy terror for riding in the days before the Famine. The old Famine knocked the spunk out of 'em, in more ways than one, I can tell you. They were no good for the oul bit of riding after that. A man said to me one time that singing and laughter went out the door and the riding went out with it.'

'That was before your time, Ned?'

'Oh, a long time before that. But my father remembered it and fellows dying at the side of the road all the way to Watergrasshill and the poor bastards not even able to get to the priest's house. They were dying so fast, neither priest nor doctor could get around to 'em quick enough. And then there was the fever. That got the rest of 'em. I remember my father telling me there were twenty-two houses between here and the main road. There's only one now and Pat Hackett won't be around much longer.'

Pat Hackett was an elderly neighbour who was no longer able to look after his own farm. Dinny used to do a lot of work for him when he was a youngster. They were friendly in the way that men separated by two generations can be friendly. Dinny would clean out the outhouses and water and feed Pat's old mare. He would put on the kettle and make a cup of tea for Pat and get a shilling or two for his trouble. It was the only pocket money Dinny ever got when he was young. Pat never said much but he was a kindly old fellow.

Dinny thought anyone over fifty was really ancient.

'What age is Pat now?' he asked.

'Sure he must be going on ninety. Now there's a man who'd remember the Famine. Not that he'd tell you, of course. Pat was always the kind of fellow if you asked him the time, he'd be wondering that you were trying to get something out of him. You'd get more information out of that headstone over there.'

'There's iron down here, Ned. Listen.' Dinny got the pitchfork and tapped through the dead briars at the bottom of the hole. There was a hollow sound. 'I hope it's not a bloody coffin.'

'Don't worry. There's no coffin down there. I know. I was down there when I was a young fellow. Now it's my turn.'

Dinny scraped about again with the pitchfork. He cleared away the brown dead briars and suddenly there it was, right at the foot of the series of stone steps: a rusted iron door covered with dead leaves.

'There you go. We'll never open that,' he said.

'We'll open it all right. I've all the gear here. It's what's inside that I'd be more worried about.'

'God almighty, Ned, what could be inside? I hope we don't find skeletons. I'd hate to find a skeleton.'

'We'll soon find out, won't we?'

Dinny got out of the cave of undergrowth he had made and shook a variety of insects, earwigs and beetles from his hair. Then Ned lowered his big frame between the walls of cut brambles and got into the hole. He got a crowbar under the iron door and leaned on it. Slowly, creakingly, with the falling of a shower of rust, the door opened. A smell of mould and rot came out to greet them. Ned turned on his bicycle lamp and shone it inside.

The vault was a dark musty cavern about six feet high and twenty feet long. It was lined with brick and stone and dripped from roof to floor. There were no skeletons in it and no traces of coffins. Dinny was relieved. There was nothing on the earthen floor, apart from mud and one or two half-rotten planks. Stalactites hung from the ceiling like winter icicles from a leaky tank.

'May the Lord have mercy on us all. We're the opposite to Lazarus now, whatever that makes us, going into the tomb. Nobody's been in here for a hundred years, I'd say.'

Ned picked up one of the planks. It fell to brown powder in his hands. 'These aren't going to be much use to us, anyway,' he said as handfuls of rotten wood fell around his feet.

'What could a place like this be for, Ned? Who could have built it?'

''Twas used for storing dead bodies, so far as I know.' Ned went into the chamber, knocking stalactites off with his head.

'What in the name of God did they want to store dead bodies for?'

'To keep the grave robbers from getting their hands on them. To let 'em rot a bit first before burying 'em.' Ned Murphy's voice boomed in the narrow confines of the vault.

'And what did they want to do that for?'

'To make sure they wouldn't sell the parts while the bodies were still fresh.'

'The parts? What parts? Like spares?'

'Yea. There was a trade in spares in those days, boy.'

'Cripes.'

Suddenly the leaves moved and a rat, like a hunchbacked Jack Russell, scuttled out of the doorway and was gone in a flash past Ned's heel and up and out between Dinny's legs.

Dinny felt the hair stand on the back of his head.

'They're quick bastards, aren't they?'

'They're the lads for the speed, alright, boy. I'd say he's delighted to see us. That lad hadn't had much living company for a long time, I'd imagine.' Ned Murphy said with a laugh.

'He gave me the fright of my life.'

'If the rat is the worst thing you'll see here over the next few months, Dinny, you'll be a lucky boy.' Ned tapped the walls of the vault with his crowbar. 'Bejapers, those are mighty walls. This will make a great spot for holding spies, all the same. For one thing is sure: nobody's going to get out of here in a hurry.'

'Where do you think the spies will come from, Ned? I mean I don't know anybody who's a spy.'

'But you wouldn't, would you? Isn't that the whole point of being a spy: nobody knows what you're doing? That's why this place was selected. Isn't that what Donohoe said? Because there are no spies around here, no loyalists.'

'So, where will they find them?'

'In the city, of course. The city is an awful nest of spies. Donohoe says the place is alive with the bastards. Did you not know that?'

'No.'

'They're everywhere. The place is infested with them. The city is a big snakepit full of spies and touts and informers, low fellas with VD and the likes.'

'What's VD, Ned?'

'It's something like the soldiers get. It's when your nuts begin to rot off you. Your tackle turns black and you get the shakes and so on. It's from going with hoors and the likes.'

'Are you sure about all them spies?'

'Well, if you were to believe Mick Twomey and the boys in town, up around the army barracks is walking with them and around the RIC barracks too. And down Cove Street, full of hoors. Of course, they'll be tried. We'll have to go through proper procedure. GHQ will have to sanction everything we do. That's why we'll have to hold them here to wait for senior officers to try them. If they're innocent, they'll be released. If not, boom.' Ned put an imaginary gun to his head and pulled an imaginary trigger.

'You think so?'

'What else would we do with them – keep running to them with the dinner till the end of time?'

'We?'

'Who else? This is a war, boy. We're the army. This is to be our responsibility. And a very important job it is too.'

'Jesus, that sounds desperate altogether.'

'What did you expect? That we'd just have them over for the turkey at Christmas?'

'No, but...'

'There's no buts now, boy. We're in this up to our oxters. We've no choice but to do this for the city boys. These are bad people, criminals. Pass me that.' Ned Murphy pointed to a cog wheel drill that he had left on a headstone behind Dinny's back. Dinny passed it to him. Ned got the drill, and kneeling over the heavy iron door, slowly and patiently drilled half a dozen holes in it.

'The hoors will need to breathe,' he said, sweating with the pressure against the door.

By noon they had the vault cleared out. The sun was high in the sky and the mist was rising. Smoke escaped from chimneys of the village and climbed straight up like ladders into the sky; a sure sign of good weather to come. The Angelus bell rang from the chapel and Ned and Dinny took off their caps, blessed themselves, bowed their heads and prayed in silence.

A man passed by on a horse and cart and waved at them. It was Con Foley.

'How are things in Sing Sing?' he shouted from the road.

'Things are great in Sing Sing,' Dinny replied. 'All we need now are a few prisoners.'

Con Foley stood to attention against the cribs of his cart and saluted Ned officiously. 'You'll be Governor of Cork Prison yet, Ned.'

'Keep your voice down, ye little bollix,' Ned shouted back at him. 'Do you want the whole country to know our business?'

Foley only laughed. He hit his horse a crack of the reins and headed off down the road in the direction of the village.

Dinny and Ned went back to piling up the weeds until they had a big heap of brambles at the bottom of the graveyard. Then, with a bottle of paraffin and some rags, they began to burn them. The smoke rose slowly in the midday air, dense as cream, carrying the smells of burnt stems and holly leaves. It spoke of normality, of necessary, if unpleasant work; that of tending to the already dead, not of preparing for the dead of the future.

'I'll be glad to get away from here,' Dinny said when he was finished.

'Maybe it won't be as bad as you think. Maybe they'll get no spies anyway. Sure we're miles from anywhere and we all know what kind of an blowhole Dan Donohoe is.'

'I hope so. One thing is sure, though: I don't think we'll be seeing any naked women around here.'

'More's the pity.'

By one o'clock Dinny was back at home, eating his dinner and getting ready to tackle his horses to go opening drills for potatoes. His father was, as usual, embedded in the Cork Examiner. Nobody commented on the smell of smoke from Dinny's clothes. When he had his dinner eaten, he was relieved get out of the house again.

5

A week after he and Ned had opened up the vault, Dinny was lying in bed with his clothes still on, waiting for the household to fall asleep before he went out to join the Company. He listened to the sounds of the spring night and gave his mother ten minutes to get settled in bed. Then he let himself out the window and scrambled down the drainpipe into the darkness.

It was cool in the yard. A cow shuffled; a dog barked in the distance. The stars were high in the roof of the night, like so many snowflakes, surprisingly unmelting. Dinny was delighted to be out of the house as he made his way across the fields to the village.

It was now an almost nightly routine for him to leave the house as soon as it was dark to do some work for the Company and get back in the small hours of the morning. This night involved running around with dispatches, messages from one Company to another or building bunkers for hiding guns or felling trees or calling to farmers' houses to 'borrow' shotguns. So far, his parents did not appear to notice that he was missing, though his dreaminess during the day confirmed his father's belief that young people were naturally lazy, 'useless bostoons', who needed everything done for them. 'What will become of the world at all when the next generation takes over?' was his father's endless refrain.

Dinny realized something different to the normal routine was afoot when he reached Ned Murphy's house. All the lights were out. He knocked on the door.

'Who is it?' came the voice from inside.

'Dinny Fitz.'

There was a rattle of locks and the eye bolt popped up. A group of men were gathered in the kitchen, including Dan Donohoe, Con Foley, his brother Mick and two or three lads from Cork city whose faces he vaguely recognized. Ned Murphy was sitting under the hearth, turning the fire machine. He had a long unhappy face on him. Con Foley had a pillow in one hand and a pair of shears in the other. A curious smell, something like Rito or burning pitch, filled the room.

'What's going on?' Dinny whispered.

'Tell him what's happening, Con.' Dan Donohoe said. 'Make it fast.' Con Foley stuck out his chest and declared in a voice as solemn as a judge's. 'We're doing a tarring. The prisoner's an informer with the enemy.'

So the curious smell was tar, which Ned was heating in the tin can over the fire. It bubbled black on the hob like molten lava, the occasional splash flaring up when it spattered on the red spreece beneath.

'The prisoner is above in Sing Sing.' Dan Donohoe said. 'First, I want you all to wear these.' He handed out hoods made from what looked like cut-up pillowcases.

'I wonder whose head was on that?' Con Foley smirked.

Dan Donohoe gave him a blank look. Instead of responding, he went on: 'While the prisoner will be blindfolded and shouldn't see us, she just might get a look, all the same. And just remember this; if she sees us, we'll have to plug her and that will be on your heads.'

'It's a woman?' Dinny was surprised. Women were not normally picked up by the Brigade, even when they did consort with the enemy.

'A woman can be an informer, just as easily as a man,' Dan Donohoe replied. 'Sometimes they can be a lot more dangerous because they can get closer to the enemy. Pillow talk is the most deadly talk of all. But we don't want to have to kill her. Shooting a woman prisoner would only turn the people against us. Our aim is to frighten those who are friendly with the enemy. So we have to be careful. When you put those masks on, keep them on, okay?'

The men nodded with faces serious as pall bearers.

So this was it. The first blow. They were heading into a graveyard to do some work for Ireland. Dinny tried to rationalize it to himself. There was, he supposed, some method in their madness and tarring was a small, though probably important part of the terror campaign. The principal aim of the IRA campaign was to target the offices of the Crown, the police and the military and, to a lesser extent, coastguard and marine stations. It was partly to acquire guns and ammunition and partly to deliver a blow for freedom.

But it was equally necessary to terrorize the people into giving no succour to the enemy. It had been drilled into them. If a policeman was shot in Cork city, just because he might be a Mass-going Catholic was no reason to come to his assistance. The gunman should be able to melt into the crowd, and the authorities should get the impression that the whole country was against them. It was necessary to sway public opinion by creating fear. You forced people to take sides. The way of fear was the way to go.

'Now Con and Mick and you three,' he pointed to the lads from Cork city, 'you go down to Dunkettle Bridge and hide behind the ditch. Bring the poster and the pillow and shears with you and, for the love of God, make sure that the tar is still hot when you get there. There's nothing as ridiculous as trying to pour tar that's already solid. Ned and Dinny, you're to come with me to Sing Sing. Just remember all of you: what we're doing tonight is dangerous. Dunkettle Bridge is a very public place. Once we get there, we move fast, we tie her to the gate and we get the job done quickly. No hanging around to admire our handiwork, you understand?'

They all nodded. Con Foley's eyes were bright and shiny and full of fervour and concentrated like lumps of hot coal.

Dinny, Ned and Dan Donohoe went out into the night and made their way to the graveyard to get the prisoner. Ned was big and broad and shuffling from one side to another like an overbalanced haycock. Donohoe was like a ferret beside him. Dinny was nervous. This was his most important assignment to date and he was fearful. But he believed himself to be a soldier, and a soldier has to take his orders and obey them.

When they got to the graveyard, it stuck Dinny that it was the loneliest place in the world in the middle of the night. Crosses and the shadows of headstones swayed drunkenly across the weeds and hillocks. Yews cast shadows like big trowels on the stones. Dan Donohoe half-tripped, kicked a funeral wreath out of his way and muttered a curse. He had no respect, Dinny thought, for the living or the dead.

The girl to be tarred, he was told, was a well-off young woman from Cork. Her crime, like that of a lot of Cork girls, was to have walked out with an officer from Victoria Barracks. Girls who went out with soldiers were now to be uniformly classed as spies and informers. While it was not exactly proven that she had passed on information to the authorities, it was the kind of behaviour that should be discouraged and, in a tradition that went back to the time of the land agitation and, beyond, to the Whiteboys, the way to do it was by a very public humiliation.

Ned Murphy went down the three steps to the vault door and, after spending almost a minute looking for the right key, swung the iron door open. The others stood in a semi-circle around the vault where they could not be seen.

'Miss Margaret.' They could hear Ned speak softly to the prisoner. 'Miss Margaret, are you awake?' The sound of sneezing came from the vault.

This Margaret girl was Ned's first prisoner and, from a combination of gallantry, nervousness and respect, he didn't seem to know what to say to her. He had treated her well; Dinny knew he had brought her bags of straw to sleep on and an old chamber pot his mother had given him. He even had the place thoroughly cleaned out before she arrived so as to make the damp cave as inoffensive as possible.

'I'm awake.' She had been there for three days and nights and would hardly know what time of night or day it was. 'I feel awful. I think I'm coming down with something.' They could hear her words echoing clearly in the vault.

'Miss Margaret, we're going to take you away from here now,' Ned whispered from the darkness at the bottom of the steps. There was a poorly disguised tenderness in his voice, as if he would have much preferred to be in a position to set her free. That would not go down well with Donohoe, Dinny thought.

'You mean, the Sinn Féiners are going to kill me, I suppose.' She sounded terrified.

'No, they're not going to kill you.'

She sneezed again. 'I've been praying non-stop that I wouldn't be shot since those terrible men picked me up in the Grand Parade. At least they left me with my beads.' There was the rustling of Rosary beads in the vault.

'You'll have to put this on,' Ned passed the blindfold to her, 'and I'm sorry but I'm going to have to tie your hands as well'.

'To listen to him, you'd swear she was his mother,' Dan Donohoe muttered outside. 'This is a waste of bloody time, I swear to Christ. Niceties. A bullet to the back of the head would solve the problem a lot quicker.'

Suddenly, there was fear in the young woman's voice again. 'Are there others outside? I hear whispering.'

'There are always others outside,' Dan Donohoe said sharply as he pulled the hood over his head and marched down the steps into the vault. If he had his way, there would be no need for masks because no convicted prisoner would ever live to recognize him. However, he had his orders and was still inclined to obey them.

'I'm afraid you'll be used as an example,' Dan Donohoe said aloud. 'Now get a move on here. We haven't got all night.'

'Who ... who are you?' The girl now sounded even more terrified, if that were possible.

34

'I'm a Captain in the Irish Republican Army.'

'What do you... mean, "an example"?'

'You have been court-martialled by the Irish Republican Army and have been found guilty of fraternizing with the enemy. This puts you technically in the category of spy. However, because you are a woman, you will escape the fate normally meted out to spies, which is execution. You have been sentenced to be publicly humiliated for your crimes. Now, come on, get her out of there. Make sure she's gagged and blindfolded. We've got to get moving.'

'But..'

'Maybe you can thank your beads for this, though it's no thanks to the Rosary or to Danny Boy that you're not going to be executed.'

'Danny Boy' was Bishop Daniel Cohalan, the Bishop of Cork, who had spoken out regularly against the IRA's campaign and was their greatest enemy in Cork besides the British. Dan Donohoe had suggested that the bishop should be hanged, but calmer heads prevailed when it was realized the damage this would do to public opinion in Cork.

Ned and Dan Donohoe came out of the vault with the girl between them. She was hooded but wore good shoes and her clothes were fancy, as if she had been headed for a dress dance when she was picked up. There was just the faintest smell of perfume from her, oddly feminine in that malevolent place.

'Where are you taking me?' She lurched into Ned.

'We're taking you where you'll be found,' Dan Donohoe said. 'Now, one more word and you'll die on the spot. Do you understand?'

'You're not going to harm me? I'd prefer to be dead than to be mutilated.'

'We're not going to harm you, Miss Margaret,' Ned said.

'Silence now,' Dan Donohoe said.

'God have mercy on me,' she whispered. 'Can I have my beads again?' Ned Murphy reached into the pocket of her dress and placed the beads in her handcuffed hands. She began to recite the Rosary quietly to herself as she fingered them. Dan Donohoe motioned with his revolver to Dinny to walk ahead, while Ned closed the vault.

The pony and trap was tethered in the laneway, out of sight of the road that led to the village. Dinny held the pony while the others got into the trap. Ned guided the girl gently to her bench.

'Here, put the pillow under her cardigan,' Dan Donohoe said to Ned and, when Ned didn't do it fast enough, Donohoe grabbed her cardigan and stuffed the pillow up under it. 'If we're stopped, hide the masks. We'll say you're expecting a child and we're taking you to the midwife. Here.' He handed Dinny his revolver. 'Now you guard her. Make sure she doesn't get up to any funny business. If she tries anything, plug her. You stay behind,' he indicated to Ned.

Ned stepped down off the trap and closed the tail board. He knew his job. He would have to get Sing Sing ready for the next prisoner. He gazed forlornly at the girl like a big lovesick farm-hand.

Dinny sat beside the girl in the trap and felt her tense beside him. He was fearful of the weapon in his hand and prayed she wouldn't do something stupid. She was so close, he could feel the softness of her body as, mindful of Donohoe's instructions to be quiet, she did her best to suppress her coughs and sneezes. Dinny cradled the revolver in his hands, careful to ensure that it was not cocked. It was an ugly brute of a thing, probably stolen from an RIC man somewhere, heavy as a ploughshare and as cold as the bed of a stream.

'Do as you are told and you'll be all right.'

The road was a tunnel of trees. The wind whistled through the branches and ash boughs brushed their faces. They drove south for half an hour. He didn't want to worry her unduly, but warned her that on no account should she try to remove the blindfold, for that would mean certain death.

'Is that a river I hear?' she whispered.

'Sheesh. You're better off not speaking, Miss,' Dinny muttered. 'Pretend nothing, hear nothing, know nothing. It's the best way – it's the only way.'

'Are you sure they're not going to shoot me?'

'You're not going to be killed, but you must stay quiet, for the love of God, or you might be.'

The softness of the girl's body and the rocking of the trap combined to give Dinny an involuntary erection. He wasn't used to being this near to young women. To Dinny, girls were another world, spaces into which to shine beams of idealistic speculation. He dreamed about being in love. He wondered what it would be like to be really in love, but the world was too upside down now to contemplate how to go looking for love. Anyway, he couldn't imagine a girl like her ever fancying him; a mere carpenter's apprentice, a small farmer's son with nothing to his name. He was full of vague yearnings and inarticulate longings. Girls like her were out of his reach and belonged to the world of the city; of gaiety, of parties, of fine manners and musical evenings by the piano. She might marry a solicitor, a doctor or a professor at the university. He was embarrassed at what had grown between his legs and, coughing to cover his unease, moved an inch or two away from her.

And yet she was fool enough to give her heart to an English officer, or at least Dinny presumed he was an officer. She would hardly be knocking around with a mere Tommy. Then again, maybe she might. There was no understanding the ways of women sometimes, just as there was no understanding the lives of those who played cricket or rugby or collaborated with the enemy.

When they reached the main road on the Midleton side of Dunkettle, the others came out from behind the hedges to join them. Mick Foley held the box of tar and a blow lamp which he had been using to keep the tar molten. He pumped it a few times and it a roared a blue flame in the darkness like a firework ready for take-off. Dan Donohoe pulled up the pony by a gateway leading into a field. One of the Cork boys grabbed the pony by the bridle and held it. The others gathered around, curious to see what goods had been brought from Sing Sing.

'Get her down,' Donohoe ordered.

Dinny helped the girl down from the trap and took the pillow from her. She stumbled like a blind person into the men who stood around her wondering what they should do next. Mick Foley handed Dinny the tin of tar, which he placed on the ground to cool it.

'Turn off that blowlamp. It'll be seen a mile away,' Donohoe said. 'Now move fast. Tie her to the gate. Make sure yeer all covered up before taking off her hood.'

Dinny put on his mask and could feel his own breath hot on his face. The girl said nothing as Foley eagerly tied her arms and legs to the bars. He was rough with the knots, tying her tightly. She winced with pain. 'Take it easy, sure she's only a girl' Dinny said, to which Con Foley replied that all informers deserved to be harshly treated and that Ireland would have been freed years ago were it were not for informers. When he had finished, Donohoe went to the girl's side to check the knots.

'Here, for the love of Jesus, boy, what are you trying to do, cut off her blood supply?'

He loosened the knots a little, took off her hood and tied a gag around her mouth. 'Now, that'll do. She won't get too far away anyway.'

Even in the darkness, through the holes in the mask, Dinny could see that the girl was quite pretty, though she looked from one to the other of the masked strangers around her with haunted fear in her eyes.

'Can I do the clipping?' Con Foley asked. 'I was always a good man with the shears.'

'You'll do no such thing, boy. I wouldn't trust you not to cut the ears clean off her. Give me the shears.' One of the Cork boys handed the shears to Donohoe and he began to pull the pins out of the young woman's hair until it fell in pale tresses around her shoulders.

She started sobbing into the gag.

That hair is so lovely,' one of the Cork boys said; 'it's a pity to cut it all off.'

'It'll grow again,' Donohoe said quickly, as he caught fistfuls of her hair and began to hack it off. He knew what he was doing – he had sheared enough sheep in his day. He cut quickly and efficiently.

And indeed it was just like sheep-shearing time. Dinny was appalled at the casual matter-of-fact cruelty of it. Ringlets of the girl's hair fell to the ground until she was completely shorn and she stood shivering before them like a famished boy, vulnerable and robbed of her femininity, standing on a pile of her blonde tresses. 'Now the tar. You pour it,' Dan Donohoe indicated to Dinny. 'Don't let any get on your hands. Tar is easy to see and a hoor to get off.'

Dinny hesitated. He knew Donohoe had asked him to do this to test him. He touched the base of the tin and delayed as long as he could to let it cool. Reluctantly, he moved nearer the girl and held the tin over her head, a hesitant priest administering a pitch-like baptism.

'What's keeping you, for the love of God, man?' Donohoe said. 'What are you waiting for, a funt up the hole? Do I have to do everything around here? What a crowd of lúberas I've been saddled with.'

Before anyone could move, Con Foley snatched the tar tin out of Dinny's hands and poured it quickly over the girl's head. She let out a muffled groan under her gag and twisted against the bars of the gate.

The tar ran down her face like warm treacle, down the back of her head and under her collar. It dripped on her shoulders, and she squirmed and moaned inside her gag, trying to kick the gate as if she were a tethered calf crammed into the face of a cattle crush. The tar stuck to her cardigan and dripped as slow as snails down her blouse and onto her dress. It solidified on the pale base of her skull, on her outstretched arms and dribbled down the bars of the gate, raining black drops on the blonde curls at her feet. It congealed into coal-like diamonds and glistened in the moonlight, smooth as marbles, covering the area around the gate like old clotted blood. She cried because her skin was burning and, after a minute she fell silent and passed out, collapsing against the gate as if in a black modern crucifixion, a sudden exposure and mortification.

She was now transformed by this trickling baptism of hate. She was no longer feminine, no longer human, she was not Margaret whatever her name was, but a mere rag doll, a thing that looked as if it existed merely to be abused. Dinny realized that he was profoundly ashamed to be involved in this kind of behaviour. Though he knew she was not that badly burnt since the tin had not been that hot when he held it.

Still, he was appalled and transfixed at the same time. He couldn't believe that this could go on in what had been a civilized country, and that he was a part of it. He tried to speculate on what would happen to the young woman now. Would she be marked for life? If so, would she have to leave Cork and maybe even Ireland? The mark of tar is the mark of the traitor. It was a terrible thing to do, to take a slip of a girl and inflict such a torture on her. Dinny wanted to get as far away from Dunkettle as he possibly could.

Dan Donohoe then picked up the pillow, slit the end of it with the shears and poured the down over the girl's head. The feathers stuck to the tar all over her so that she looked like an outsized goose that had been half-plucked and rolled in her own plumage.

'Now you hang the sign around her neck,' Dan Donohoe said, handing Dinny a piece of cardboard on a length of binder twine. It read, clear in the moonlight, in big capital letters; Spies and Informers Beware, signed the IRA. 'At least do something right this time.'

Feeling nothing but shame, Dinny put the twine around the girl's neck. The sign hung crooked on her breast as if she were some kind of scarecrow which she was now, at least in political terms.

As they were getting ready to leave, Con Foley made a move towards the limp form of the girl spreadeagled across the gate. He went down on one knee and, full of lascivious curiosity, began lifting her dress to paw her thighs.

'What the fuck are you doing?' Donohoe caught Foley by the shoulder and spun him around.

'I...I... was just going to search her, you know, in case she might have a weapon concealed under her frock.' Foley replied sheepishly. 'You can never trust an informer.'

Donohoe cocked his revolver. 'Lay one more finger on her, ya little prick,' he said with a low growl, 'and I'll blow your fuckin' brains out. Just remember, you could very easily look like a dead informer yourself.' And Foley knew he meant every word of it.

Foley backed off; his leer vanished and he hunched his shoulders like a skulking cur that had just been kicked away from its food bowl. Disappointment and resentment clouded his eyes as he gathered up the shears and the pillowcase.

'We're not barbarians and we don't want the Cork Examiner tomorrow labelling us as such. Now gather up everything and let's get out of here.'

Con Foley picked up the empty tar tin.

'Leave that. Just take the shears and the blowlamp.'

With that, the boys and men each went their separate ways, leaving the unconscious girl where she was, slumped like a ragged scarecrow on the gate.

She would be found the next morning by passers by and returned to her family. Yet nobody would go to the police. And it would not make the newspapers. Everyone was by now too frightened to report this sort of thing.

Meanwhile, the boys went home through fields they knew as well as they knew their own kitchens, to climb up drainpipes to the empty bedrooms in the homes of their disapproving parents, to sleep and dream, nightmares to some and lewd and glamorous dreams to others. Only Dan Donohoe had more plans to make before he got to bed that night. Only Donohoe knew that even more terrible deeds were being planned.

6

On the other side of Cork city, Edward Mills had a different set of problems. He stared out the window of the Munster Insititute where he worked and let out a long slow sigh. Then with four drawing pins, he carefully pinned a note to the inside wall of the garden shed that he used as his office. 'Thou shalt not try to be all things to all people,' it read. He stood back and looked at it. It fitted into the symmetry of the office, where everything was neatly in its place.

Mills was forty-five years old and a horticultural instructor. He was exhausted from involvement in too many committees: gardening, cultural, sporting. He had been running from pillar to post for years, organizing this, arranging that, for groups where no one was putting in as much effort as he was.

Mills was right in the middle of middle age, the busy years, the years of giving to wives, children, colleagues, ageing parents, the general community. You love your neighbour as yourself. You returned to society what you received as a youngster. If you were lucky, you might get it back when you were old.

Of course, he knew he was drawing it all on himself with his willingness to do favours for people. But one thing was certain; he would never see fifty if he continued the way he was going. He was doing more than people twenty years younger and was getting occasional palpitations in his chest. Already he had an ulcer. He felt he was being squeezed on all sides. His doctor, Dr O'Connor, an outgoing Roman Catholic with a florid face and a fierce moustache, had warned him.

'You'll get a whacker of a heart attack one of these days, Ted, if you don't slow down. Do you want to see fifty? It's a decision you've got to make, and there's nobody to make it but yourself.'

So, at the start of 1920, Mills made a New Year's resolution to slow down, to cut what he could out of his life, to make more time for his family and indeed for himself. And the only way to do that was to simplify the way he was living.

Of course, the level of pressure was inevitable, given the circumstances under which he had begun his career in Cork. When he took over the nursery ten years earlier at the Munster Institute on the Model Farm Road, it was far from being the Model Farm the road was called after. In fact, it was a shambles. Good manpower was draining off, first to emigration, then to the killing fields of the Western Front. John O'Loughlin, Mills's predecessor, had allowed the place fall to pieces. Nobody tended the beds, planting out wasn't done properly, watering was cursory and left largely to the showers coming in on the west wind over Ballincollig. When Mills took over the nursery, shrubs grew scrawny on thin stems and blew over easily in the wind, roses and clematis and even specimen beeches drooped down under a fluff of greenfly. It was enough to make a grown man weep.

As if he had not done enough weeping already himself, with a younger brother lost at the Somme and several cousins and friends missing or buried in the mud of Flanders. There was only one thing to do during the Great War when you are too old to serve your country: use work to lever your way out of the misery that the world had become. So Cork was the Good Lord's gift to Mills: it was a path to get him out of himself. It was his Cross, his personal Calvary, the road to redemption. He was perhaps running away from his grief, covering it up by getting involved in as many committees as possible, but at least he was now turning his heartbreak into something positive.

Being a good-living member of the Church of Ireland, when he originally left his native Braemor Road in Dublin to bring the much-needed knowledge of horticulture to Cork, Mills felt a sense of mission, a duty to pass on what he had learned at the Royal Horticultural Society at Kew and at the Royal Botanic Gardens in Glasnevin. He would be a sort of St Patrick, bringing the message of good husbandry to the people of the south.

He also believed that his enthusiasm could be passed on; that when people saw what he was doing, they would be impressed and would aspire to doing the same. And, by and large, that was true: people wanted to emulate success. Corkmen (and women) wanted things of beauty: magnolia, camellia, azalea, spectacular Himalayan rhododendron, poppy trees. They wanted blight-free potatoes, good vegetables and crisp apples; those with sheltered gardens and high walls wanted pears and plums. Mills's dream, one he had never quite achieved, was to design a south-facing and sheltered garden in such a way that figs would ripen out of doors over an Irish summer.

It had taken him ten years to get the Model Farm into shape. He had to do a lot of the work himself. He begged the Institute for technical assistance, but all they gave him was an old gardener with a wooden leg and a wheezy chest. Sometimes Mills would get young lads from the surrounding farms to help him, particularly when manure was delivered but, even then, he was left trying to bend the rules to find a way to pay them and sometimes even had to do so out of his own pocket.

Still, he felt himself lucky to be alive, when a lot of his generation were not. He had the stoicism of his creed. He believed in hard work and still had just about enough of his youth left to do any physical tasks that were required to be done.

And he loved being out on the Model Farm. It was bright and airy, and good dry land. He could straighten his back on a fine day in May and look across the river to Kerry Pike at the hawthorn hedges laden with blossom; he would thank the Lord for allowing him to work in such a place.

For twenty years Mills had been gardening, and hundreds of times he had found himself amazed at what he had produced. The excitement of new colour never seemed to wear thin. Gardening was the one great consolation for growing old. With the sweat of your brow, and the Good Lord of the Earth to help you, you could make a full aesthetic out of very little.

For the civilization of a country could be measured by its gardens. Gardeners were the composers and artists of the soil. England had great arboretums and Ireland wasn't far behind. In fact, Mills was of the view that the great gardens of Ireland – Powerscourt, Anne's Grove, Westport House and Fota – were among the finest anywhere. They were something of which the country could be justly proud.

And County Cork had its share; Fota itself, Convamore and Castle Mary, and the Townshend holdings in the far west. The Edwardian heyday was the best time to be alive in the whole history of Ireland. The modern world. Every weekend in spring and early summer brought 5,000 visitors to the Royal Botanic Gardens in Glasnevin. Even Edward VII himself had visited Convamore and Mills had been responsible for getting the place into shape for the visit, even if he was still living in Dublin at that stage. It was the proudest moment of his life; His Majesty gazing at the work of one of his more humble servants.

Ireland was never more British than in those early years of the twentieth century. The country was becoming prosperous. The Catholic middle class was gradually taking over from the old Ascendancy. With the arrival of William O'Brien's party in Cork, there was hope for all. Catholic and Protestant, rebel and dissenter, all striving for a better future. Suddenly it seemed as if the future envisaged by Sir Horace Plunkett, the greatest Irishman of his generation, might be possible. The All-for-Ireland League, the only political party for which Mills had ever felt any affiliation suddenly made it seem as if the sterile divisions of old might finally be abandoned. Home Rule but with England's support. The farmers effectively owned their own land anyway, which was more than could be said of farmers in England. In fact, Ireland was now a land of small farmers, peasants who no longer wanted to be called peasants. These days, Mills spent most of his time teaching horticulture to the sons and sometimes the daughters of the rising Catholic farming classes. There was work for anyone with specialist knowledge. The horticulturist, the nursery man and the landscape gardener had never had it so good.

Proof of the cordial relations between Ireland and England was the fact that over a 100,000 Irish Catholics had volunteered to fight in the Great War in 1914. At thirty-nine, Mills was too old to go to war but his younger brothers did and that was when the torment began. For 1914 changed everything.

For Mills personally, 1916 and the Somme stood out as huge traumas in a litany of suffering. In the summer of 1916, the Royal Ulster Regiment was almost wiped out, his brother Jeremy among them. He could never forgive the Irish rebels that very same year for stabbing England in the back and rising up against the government at the very time when the country was at its greatest peril. For the first time in his life, he was ashamed to be called an Irishman.

The fall-out from the War was a general disillusionment. There were strikes everywhere, soviets being set up in Scotland and the North of England, dockers and coal miners refusing to work. These disturbances were at their worst in Ireland. The country had slipped badly since the Edwardian days. The military made a mad and ill-informed decision in 1916 to execute the leaders of the Easter Rebellion. Even Carson, Ulster's hero, had spoken out against the executions in the House of Commons. You make martyrs, they pay you back. The Irish love their dead. An Irish patriot is worth a lot more dead than alive. The republicans were now trying to grab power in the uncertainty created by the end of war and they were bringing very little in the way of refinement or culture with them.

Which was why, when Mills saw three men in cloth caps and fairly presentable suits stroll with pointed arrogance up the avenue to his office at the nursery, he knew they would get nothing from him. They were Sinn Féiners, the new men, young men, hungry for power, canvassing for the local government elections. He recognized one of them, a big red-necked fellow called Mahony; he had failed him once in a horticulture exam. All three had sheets of paper, notepads and pencils in their hands. Mahony was full of self-importance.

They looked busy, determined, as if they couldn't wait to get their hands on the country and run it the way they wanted, probably into the ground.

'Are you canvassing?' Mills asked. 'Because if you are, we're non-political here. There are no votes for you in this establishment.'

'We're not asking for your vote, Mr Mills. We just want to put up these posters around the place for the benefit of your staff.'

'Go ahead.'

'You are a very popular man, Mr Mills,' Mahony said. 'You know all about lime and planting potatoes.'

'A very popular man indeed,' the smallest of the three smiled. 'You've taught the children of half the country all about the gardening and that's no bad thing. The people of Cork are indebted to you, no doubt about it. The people need to know how to grow food. The country will need men like you, Mr Mills, in the future, if it's to stand on its own two feet. We need men with get-up-and-go, who are prepared to put their shoulders to the wheel.'

'Which wheel?'

'The wheel of the Irish Republic,' Mahony said.

Mills said nothing. The day was fine, there was watering to be done, rows of plants to be pruned, notes to be put together for the practical class in grafting he was going to give that afternoon. He had better things to do than spend the day talking about the future of a vague and euphemistic republic.

'We are also collecting for the Irish Republican Army's arms fund. We were wondering if you would be interested in making a contribution?'

The effrontery of these men to come looking for a contribution to buy guns for an illegal rabble bent on kicking out the King's forces from Ireland! The sheer cheek of it. Mills tried to bite his tongue.

'Not particularly. I've nothing against you, you understand. It's just that I don't subscribe to your views, I'm afraid.' He tried to say it as nicely as possible, but he also wanted to state clearly where he stood. He was not going to be intimidated by three uncouth men in cloth caps, even if they were wearing new suits.

'That's a pity, Mr Mills. We were rather hoping you might be on our side.'

Mills looked at the three men in their Sunday best and their air of self-importance. He realized he would rather dig trenches or weed a thousand acres on his knees for the rest of his life than help buy guns that would be used against the police and the government of the land.

'There are other, more practical ways of being patriotic,' he said. 'We all do it in our own way.'

'Still and all, it might be in your interest to at least give a little something,' the small one muttered, and there was just a slight edge in his voice.

'In my interest? Are you threatening me?'

'Do you know a John Lynch, Mr Mills, a John Sullivan Lynch?'

'Yes, he works for me sometimes. He's a clerk at the railway station in Carrigrohane.'

'Just to let you know, he might not be in for work this week.'

'Is he ill?'

'He's ill, all right.' The two other men looked at each other and one of them smiled.

'Listen, if you fellows are threatening me, I'll call the police.' Mills was suddenly angry. He wanted to run these interlopers right off his land.

'That would not be a good idea, Mr Mills.'

'Please, get off this property this instant. I've a day's work to do. And take your posters with you.'

'Fair enough, then. We can see where you stand.' The men looked at each other again and turned around to walk back out the drive. Mahony looked at him with big calm eyes. Mills felt that if he ever had authority in the community, he had now lost it. As they were shuffling out of the yard, the leader shouted back. 'Just be careful. Your popularity may not always protect you.'

Mills went back to work. He was shaken by the encounter and annoyed with himself for losing his temper. As he saw it, these men were the ominous edge of an advancing movement, the breaking waves of a rising tide. They should be placated. The sensible thing would have been to give them something, if only a few shillings. But in that split second he just couldn't bring himself to do it. The thought of giving money to backstabbers made his blood boil.

But he had too much to do to continue worrying about them for very long. John Lynch had not turned up to work that morning. An ex-soldier and a part-time railwayman, he helped Mills out around the yard from time to time. But he would never help him again, for, though Mills did not know it, Lynch had been taken from his house the night before in a dispute over a back garden and he would never be seen alive in Ballincollig again.

A week later, Mills was driving his motor car to work from his home in Blackrock. He had begun to sort out the things in his life that needed sorting and was starting to feel good about himself. As he drove up Wilton and emerged into the countryside, he spotted white smoke rising and drifting away in the still morning air.

50

His nursery was on fire! Flames leaped everywhere like wild men doing a mad pagan dance against the sky. The fire brigade was doing its best but its efforts were to no avail. So the firemen confined themselves to spraying water on the limestone buildings of the Institute to prevent it from going up as well. The nursery was ruined. Whoever had set it alight had done a thorough job. They had brought in a cartload of straw and scattered it all over the beds. The evergreens had gone up first in a rush of crackling and the fields were filled with the smell of burning pines. When the flames died down, there was nothing left but the charred remains of his prize trees and shrubs, and smoke still rising from the camellias where the fire had crept. The men who wanted to claim the future had wiped out ten year's work, the legacy of one man's life, in a single night. Mills was on the verge of tears.

7

It was late April and there was a full moon. A cold damp wind was blowing up Cork harbour. A gabhareen roe bleated in a bog like a tethered goat and demented trees shook on the ditches like the inmates of some forgotten bedlam.

Dinny was on his way to the graveyard with Ned Murphy. By now Sing Sing was well established as a place for holding prisoners and Ned Murphy was unofficially designated as the 'Governer of Sing Sing'. They each had in their arms a gabhal of hay for making sugáns.

They reached the graveyard at midnight. Dinny had heard that there had been several prisoners held there since the girl called Margaret. Each had been kept for a number of nights before being taken away to God knows where. Now there was just one prisoner in the vault: a Sergeant Lehane of the RIC. He had been picked up one evening by the Cobh Company while patrolling the town, bundled into a car and taken to the vault to await his fate. Fourteen RIC men had been shot by the IRA across the country during the previous months without any significant retaliation by the police, apart from the killing of Tomás MacCurtain, and Dinny was sure Sergeant Lehane would soon join their number. So he was more than surprised to be told that a court martial had decided that Lehane would not be executed but would be released after being held for a time for tactical reasons.

'This is a bad old business, you know,' Ned said, 'and mark my words, it'll get worse. Wait till the British start to hit back. So far, they've been going around like headless chickens. It won't always be like that. Then it'll get very hot around here.

I'll be glad to see the end of it. There's a lot of our lads, though, who don't think like I do – lads who'll be sorry when this is over. Some of the boys in this game would fight with their grandmothers. It's the only thing they have in their lives.'

Dinny wasn't sure whom Ned was talking about but he assumed it was men like Dan Donohoe.

'I didn't like that business of the girl.' Dinny said. 'I thought she was a nice little young one.'

'She was that, boy.' Ned Murphy nodded philosophically in the moonlight. 'She was all that.'

'You've still seen no ghosts in there, Ned?'

'Ghosts? Devil a one. I've been coming to this graveyard every night for weeks, sometimes two or three times a night, sitting on tombstones, watching while they ate inside and cleaning out the bucket and I've never seen as much as a trace of a ghost.'

'But the lads inside? The spies. What do they say? Do they see ghosts?'

'Now that's a very curious thing. None of them spies have any way of knowing where they are, yet I've heard several of them say "wherever we are, we're among the dead". How do they know that, now I ask you? They're blindfolded when they're brought here and they always arrive in the middle of the night. One man said that he could feel the sensation of dead people all round him. Another believed that the dead were trying to murder him all night. Maybe there are ghosts after all, but I reckon the whole thing just gets in on their nerves.'

'I'd go cracked in there. The dripping alone would get to me.' Dinny shivered at the thought of being locked up in the vault. He had gone in there once on his own and closed the heavy door behind him just to see how it felt. He couldn't wait to get out.

'It's rough all right. But it wouldn't be too bad if there were three or four of them in there together: they'd keep each other company. But they're nearly always on their own and a fella on

53

his own in there would go mad. Except for the Sergeant, of course. The Sergeant would put up with anything.'

Lehane was a big genial man of about fifty. His six feet in height made him look like a lumbering giant in the confines of the vault. He was religious and prayed a lot and, perhaps because he got on well with his captors, he believed he was safe. While other prisoners were terrified of the darkness and the rats, and were demented and annoyed by the constant dripping water and sometimes screamed in terror, Lehane managed to remain calm. He tried to relax in the wretched confines of the vault and had made a pet of one of the rats that visited him through a vent in the wall. There was a rumour that he was to be spared because he had agreed to pass information to the IRA once released, though he didn't seem to be the type to get involved in such duplicity.

In any case, he was not facing execution and he had been told this, so the main concern of his jailers was to ensure he would have no idea where he was being held. When the time came for his release, they said, he would be moved to one or two safe houses and taken by car and released several parishes away.

'Jesus', Ned said, 'that wind would cut you in two. The poor hoor will be frozen alive.'

The Sergeant had bad circulation. During his confinement he had developed cramps in his legs because there was no space to exercise. He was sometimes in terrible pain and complained that the cold and damp were freezing the blood in his feet. The gabhal of hay Dinny and Ned had brought with them was to make sugáns to wrap around the Sergeant's legs to keep out the cold. (Although Dinny didn't know it, only prisoners awaiting execution were allowed out to exercise; they would not be in a position to spill the beans later about where they had been incarcerated. Those being released were, ironically, treated worse and got no exercise at all, being confined day and night in the vault.)

They climbed down the steps and opened the vault. The Sergeant, though still wearing his uniform, was now dishevelled and bearded because of his confinement. He was on first-name terms with the Volunteers, though this was completely against Brigade rules and would not have been tolerated if Dan Donohoe had been around.

'Is that you, boys?' came the booming voice of this Lazarus from the tomb.

''Tis me, Sergeant.'   Ned insisted on addressing the policeman as 'Sergeant', even though Lehane had asked him to call him 'Paddy'. It was partly out of respect and partly because he felt awkward calling an RIC man 'Paddy'.

'We brought the hay, Sergeant.'   Ned handed his shotgun to Dinny.

'Ah, good lads. Me legs are killing me.'

They shone the light inside. Sergeant Lehane was lying on one of the planks with his head resting on a pile of crushed straw. He looked up and squinted like an Old Testament prophet in the guise of a policeman. He had gaiters on his shins and his bottle green tunic was buttoned up to the neck to ward off the cold. He was shivering. The shadow of his head moved on the walls in the torchlight like a monster from a Punch and Judy show.

Dinny stood by the door, reluctantly pointing the shotgun in the general direction of the Sergeant.

'I brought you the paper, Sergeant,' Ned said.

'Ah, good man. I can read it tomorrow, when there's a bit of light. During the daytime enough light comes in through the crack in the doorway for you to read – just about. I was wondering to myself how things were in Upper Silesia.'   The Sergeant smiled.

'They're a lot better there than they are here, Sergeant.' Ned handed the policeman a copy of the Cork Examiner.

'Myself, I don't blame the Poles for wanting a bit of Germany. There's a lot of coal there.'

'Everybody wants a bit of everything, Sergeant,' Ned said.

'I hope ye get me out of here soon, lads. This place is fierce cold altogether.' He looked at Dinny. 'There's no need to keep that shotgun pointed at me at this stage, young fella. It just makes me nervous. I don't think I could get far on these legs.'

Embarrassed, Dinny lowered the gun.

'We'll get you out as soon as we can,' Ned said. 'But we've no say over what goes on. We're just doing our job. We leave the decisions to the officers.'

'I know you don't. I tried to tidy the place up today while there was still some light.' And indeed the vault was a little cleaner and tidier-looking than usual.

'There was a woman here, wasn't there?' the Sergeant asked.

'How do you know?'

'I found this.' The Sergeant held up a locket.

The men looked at it but said nothing.

'I hope ye didn't harm her.'

'She wasn't killed. She was tied to a gate. I'm sure she's back in Cork with her family now.'

'That's good. Ye should never harm a woman, whatever else ye do. Here.' The Sergeant handed Ned the plate, cup and spoon – knives and forks were banned in the vault.

Ned took the kitchen ware and placed it by the door. 'Now you and I, Sergeant, can make the sugáns. My colleague will stand guard by the door. Move the bucket, Volunteer.' Dinny picked up the slop bucket and placed it outside the door. Then he sat on the bottom flag, idly holding the shotgun, while Ned and the Sergeant pulled the hay from the bags and gradually, with a lot of twisting, began to make ropes out of it.

'Leave the bags. They'd make good pillows when I'll get around to filling them with straw. A pillow can keep a fellow as warm as a blanket.'

'You're welcome to them, Sergeant.'

'Do you know something' – the Sergeant had a strange faraway look in his eyes – 'the oddest thing happened to me here last night.'

'Funny things would happen to all of us, if we were locked up here, Sergeant.'

'Believe me, it did, lads. Believe me it did.' The Sergeant's eyes brightened. He squinted into the light of the storm lamp.

'You know, I've often said to you, I've nothing to fear. I don't fear death, though I don't suppose I'd like to be tortured.'

'Nobody would ever do that to you, Sergeant.'

'I know you wouldn't.' The Sergeant coughed. 'But I also know there's others who might. But I say my prayers and, if I go to meet my Maker, I know I'm prepared. I've nothing on my conscience. But the strangest thing happened, I swear to God. May I be struck down.' The Sergeant took has hands off the sugán and blessed himself. 'This is no word of a lie. As true as God, this beautiful lady came right in through that door last night. She was tall and dressed in blue and white. And this light was shining behind her so that she was sort of in silhouette. She just kind of slid right in, as if the door wasn't there. An iron door.' The Sergeant shook his head. 'An iron door with a big lock.'

'As I say, she was dressed all in white and blue and she hovered round the room, moving slowly from side to side. A feeling of great love came from her. The only way I can describe it is that I knew I was in the presence of love. Can you understand that?'

'That sounds like some kind of miracle,' Ned said. 'Like Lourdes or Fatima.' An apparition at the mouth of hell, more likely, Dinny thought.

'She was here for maybe five minutes and smiling at me all the time. Then she just vanished out through the wall – just like that – and was gone. First, I thought she was a messenger from the Other Side, but I wasn't afraid. The more I think about it, the more I believe she was the Blessed Virgin, come to tell me I had nothing to fear. That's what I think, lads. She didn't even ask me to pray, unlike the little children in Fatima. She just smiled at me.'

'I'd say she figured you were praying enough as it was, Sergeant.'

'If I live a thousand years, I'll never forget that smile and, as I say, I'll never fear death. Not now, not ever again. So I guess the Sinn Féiners can do what they like with me now. I know I'll be safe.'

'Our understanding is that you'll be safe anyway, Sergeant.'

'Maybe I should go for the religious life if ever I get out of here alive.'

'Maybe you should do that, Sergeant.'

When the sugáns were made, the policeman began to wrap them around his legs and feet. They made his shins look elephantine in the half-light.

'You've no idea the difference this will make to me, lads. Sometimes, over the past days I was afraid my toes would fall off with the cold. This will keep the heat in them now, with the help of God.'

Just then the hum of a car engine came from the road at the other side of the glen. Dinny cocked the shotgun. The Sergeant looked up from his sugán and listened. The sound of the car was quite clear, coming closer, grinding gears as it approached the bridge and crunching gravel as it took the bend over the river. Then it dropped to a low gear and chugged a little as it climbed the hill outside the graveyard. Ned said nothing. The car passed by the graveyard gate and headed north in the direction of the Rea. They heard it stop and a minute or two later revolver shots rang out. A dog barked at the echo across the valley and then there was silence again.

The Sergeant shuddered with fright and blessed himself.

'God between us and all harm,' he said.

A few minutes later the car came back down the hill. It took the corner at the bridge and went back up the twisting country road in the general direction of the city. Men in black cars did black deeds on black nights, Dinny thought, and nobody knew who they were. Ned and Dinny looked at each other but said nothing, though the Sergeant was visibly shaken.

'These are terrible times we live in, boys, terrible times.' He sat down again.

Neither Ned nor Dinny had the heart to say anything but sat in embarrassed silence, staring at the vault's grey walls. Then Ned went back to twisting a few more sugáns, in case the Sergeant should need them. Eventually he said; 'As I say, our information is that you'll be all right, Sergeant, that you'll be taken far away from here and released.'

'I hope you're right, and I know you sincerely believe it. But I'm not so sure about it myself. Still, as I say, I've said my prayers and I know I'll be fine.'

8

The political situation in Cork deteriorated rapidly during the summer of 1920. The police, whose numbers had decreased because of IRA intimidation, started to recruit, and the new recruits, the Black and Tans, at last began to hit back. However, because their knowledge of the country was poor and they were hated by everyone, their reprisals were usually directed at the population as a whole. Cork city was exposed to a long campaign of arson; in the country at large shops, creameries and business premises went up in flames, which simply resulted in increasing support for the republicans among the ordinary people.

Very few of the gunmen were taken out of circulation and of those who were, most, like Dan Donohoe, were released again after a few weeks' hunger strike. The authorities seemed to be paralysed in the face of rebel activity. Then, gradually, the wheel of conflict began to gather speed. The military started to become involved, though their local intelligence was even worse than that of the police and they were deeply suspicious of the police. The Black and Tans had carte blanche to fight terror with terror, arson with arson, and murder with murder. The RIC, which had borne the brunt of the IRA campaign, now began to return fire and the country descended into a hell of random shootings from which it would not emerge for another three years.

And nowhere was the anarchy worse than in Cork. Murders were occurring with greater and greater frequency, as if killing had become a habit that nobody could abandon. In the city, death squads roamed the streets or hid in alleyways, or walked out casually among the people, strolling in cloth caps or broad-rimmed hats, like accidental out-of-town tourists. Then from under their coats a Mauser or a Webley – for the British had their own 'civilian' death squads – would suddenly spring and start spitting fire and lead, and an ex-soldier or a plain clothes policeman, or in the case of British murders someone with the same name as a prominent IRA man would fall over clutching his chest, his eyes open in amazement to find himself suddenly coughing blood. Some were dead before they hit the ground, their blood seeping from flagstone pavement to horse-dunged street. Others howled for mercy, and mercy would come quickly from the calm hand of the gunman placed to the back of the skull and a second shot would ring out and the twitching would stop and never, ever would the onlookers come to help.

The gunman would turn but, no matter which side he was on, he would have no need to run, for fear had crept into the hearts of the people and they were afraid of the IRA and the British alike. There were alleys and safe houses and thousands of terrified people to act as human camouflage. The authorities began to look like fools, their reprisals blundering and incompetent, and nearly always ill-conceived as they vented their frustration on the innocent in yet another round of revenge killing and burning that served only to swell support for the gunmen of the Republic.

By late 1920, it looked as if the only way to operate was by bartering death on both sides. Killing was the sole currency and the men of the IRA and their enemies were like players in a poker game aiming for ever higher stakes. Death was the certain outcome for the first to blink.

The trade in murder in Cork city was practised by fewer than a score of men on either side, yet this was more than enough, for they practised it with care and an economy of scale, and they doled it out while they saved on bullets like thrifty shopkeepers. They were known on the IRA side as 'Hegarty's Men', from their leader, Seán O'Hegarty – called 'the Joker' because he rarely smiled – who took over command of the brigade when the new Lord Mayor, Terence MacSwiney, was arrested and died in October 1920 after seventy-four days on hunger strike.

Their enemies, undercover RIC men and Black and Tans, as well as military hit squads who dressed in civilian clothes and operated at night during curfew hours, traded under a variety of names, of which the best known was the Anti-Sinn Féin League. This Anti-Sinn Féin League issued threats of dire consequence to the populace in the newspapers and on notices hung on lamp-posts around the streets in a malevolant imitation of electioneering publicity. They sometimes labelled the people they murdered just like the IRA did. And the population knew that these threats would be followed through with bomb and bullet.

By the winter the city had become a nest of intrigue, with killings and counter-killings, with information leaking from barracks and police stations like water from a sieve, for the IRA had moles everywhere. This atmosphere made for a strange intimacy between friend and foe. The killers in many cases knew their targets well, for they often worked for them, cleaning their rooms or shining their shoes or servicing their cars and changing the oil in their engines.

And in the midst of all this terror there was only one place in the vicinity of the city that was as quiet as a churchyard, and that was Knockraha and the surrounding countryside. If the police and the army had been able to use their multitudinous and incompetent intelligence systems, they should have been suspicious of a place where nothing seemed to happen. But such was the chaos all over the county that every parish seemed equally black and full of rebels. The result of this was that the area of Sing Sing and the Rea had the least amount of enemy activity in the entire county during 1920 and 1921. So it was to become, from November 1920 right to the Truce in July 1921 and afterwards, the private charnel house of the campaign, a human dumping ground, the quiet abattoir where Dan Donohoe went about his nightly work.

9

Late June found Dinny on his hands and knees with his brother, father and sister, thinning mangolds in the Well Field beside the house. The drills rose dizzily like rails to the low horizon and Dinny's father cursed when he accidentally grasped a hemp nettle and it stung him on the inside of his wrist.

'God blast it! I've been meaning to buy a hoe for ages. But do you think I'd remember?' he asked the drills in front of him and any of his offspring who were within earshot. 'Of course, I did think of it and then the hoors of Tans came and burned down the creamery, so I never got the chance.'

Dinny's brother and sister were ahead of him, up the drills like burrowing animals, pulling up fistfuls of weeds and mangold seedlings and leaving plants at six-inch intervals like wilted drooping feathers. Tomorrow they would be upright, today they just looked sad. Like Ireland, Dinny thought: poor, sad, wilted Ireland.

Three siblings in the one field. It wouldn't happen in normal circumstances. Either Bill or himself or Bina would be gone to England, America or the colonies. But emigration had been banned, first by the government on account of the Great War and then by Sinn Féin which wanted to keep everyone at home; the human powder in the powder keg. The country was awash with young people. There would be no Sinn Féin if it weren't for them; and probably no revolution either.

However, this morning Dinny Fitzgibbon was truly sick of the revolution. For this was the worst day of his life. He had witnessed his first execution the night before and he hadn't slept a wink as a result of it. The drills looked blurred and vague, as if the whole world was swimming under a layer of water. He felt he would never be the same again, never go out and look at a spring morning in the same way as he had done heretofore. He would never again be able to look in the same light at the Rea, where the execution had taken place and where he had hunted with his father as a youngster. Dinny wished he could unlive the previous twenty-four hours or turn into somebody other than himself. Everything – places, names, people – was now cast in a new and sinister light.

He had been out thinning mangolds in the same field the previous evening when the word came via a runner that Dan Donohoe wanted him to dig a grave in the Rea for a spy who was about to be shot. Donohoe had been released from jail, after spending time on hunger strike. He was full of renewed patriotic fervour and mad for action.

Dinny picked up a shovel and pick and headed across the fields to the Rea and there, beside a clump of stunted sally bushes, he began to dig. It took him three hours. Sweat ran down the inside of his shirt. His back ached. New welts began to grow under the old welts on his hands. By the time he had finished, in a hum of insects and late birdsong, the sun was sinking northwest over the Nagle mountains and shadows were climbing the hill to replace the orange evening across the bog.

He was hoping he would get away and not have to witness the execution and the filling of the grave. He was tempted to leave his shovel by the hole and slip back to the house. But his instructions had been to bring a storm lamp and stay until the execution party arrived.

So he just sat down on the pile of earth in the middle of the Rea and waited for the approach of car headlights from the direction of the city. He would have to light the storm lamp and wave it to indicate to the men exactly where the grave was. Then, if he was lucky, he could go home.

Dinny thought about Dan Donohoe as darkness filled in the hollows of the mountain. He had spent a week in Crumlin Road jail in Belfast and then ten days on hunger strike in Wormwood Scrubs prison in England before being released. He had been badly treated, he said, having had a bucket of cold water thrown over him every day as he got dizzy and weak from lack of food. When he was released, he immediately went on the run and his home was searched regularly by the military and the police in a vain attempt to find him. There were rumours in the area that, since coming out of jail, Donohoe and the city men were doing terrible things in the name of Ireland. There was no way of proving whether these stories were true or not, but they added to the fear and, in some quarters, the regard in which Donohoe was now held.

It was getting dark when Dinny noticed the headlights of a car moving in his direction along an bóthar úaigneach, as the old people called it, the narrow lane that crossed the moor from the south-east.

The car stopped at the side of the Rea half a mile away and the headlights went off. It was an unusual car, a brick red American Buick the colour of haysheds. The city boys had commandeered it from some toff in Montenotte and were now using it to spirit away someone they suspected of helping the enemy. (Dinny had heard of other phantom cars: a gold Rolls-Royce, a hearse and several Fords, driven by various murder gangs – mostly British – which emerged at night from garages like vampires for sessions of bloodletting.)

Dinny's hands were shaking as he searched his pockets for a box of matches. He lit the storm lamp, raised it over his head and waved it back and forth. Another storm lamp was lit beside the Buick and waved back.

Dinny watched the occupants of the car make their way slowly, with many stops and starts, across the bog in his direction. There were five of them: Dan Donohoe, Con Foley, Daithi O'Brien from Cobh, the prisoner and a light-footed fellow in a cloth cap with a cigarette hanging out of the corner of his mouth whom Dinny believed to be one of the Blake brothers who ran a garage in Cork and were drivers for the city battalion of the IRA.

Donohoe had grown thin, gaunt and demented-looking from his hunger strike. He was swinging his storm lamp in front of him like a priest's thurible. The prisoner, just as thin, was a man in his thirties with a slight limp. He was shuffling along in dusty blue workman's overalls, his head bowed and hands tied behind his back. There was a noose around his neck and Con Foley was driving him from behind with an ashplant. The others were walking in a semi-circle around him, trying to avoid falling over clumps of heather or getting their feet wet in the bog water. This eerie procession was like a nocturnal Corpus Christi heading towards Dinny, with the prisoner as celebrant, surrounded by his death-dealing acolytes.

The prisoner could see where he was going, for he was neither blindfolded nor gagged. There was no need to blindfold him now, for he would not be reporting back from the Rea. When he spotted the grave, he stopped, staggered and looked as if he was about to get sick. Then as he got closer, for a moment that seemed like an eternity, he stared at Dinny. It was a big-eyed stare of terror and pleading. What those eyes seemed to say was 'please save me, for you are the only one here like me, the only one who is not a madman filled with hate.' It was as if he had some kind of instinct, a knowledge that Dinny was not fully compliant in all this. Dinny felt the prisoner's stare go right through him, reverberating like a kick on the bottom of a barrel.

Dinny knew he would never forget that look for the rest of his life. He had dug a grave for this man who was a stranger, yet his stare seemed familiar. It was as if they had known each other all their lives and shared some form of mutual understanding, some kind of hopeless hope. Those petrified eyes said 'you are to blame; you can save me and you will not'.

When the entourage reached the pile of wet mud and flattened heather where Dinny was standing, Donohoe handed his storm lamp to Con Foley. Then he said to the prisoner: 'Are you Thomas Deveney?'

The prisoner staggered again and swayed over the grave and Dinny thought he was going to collapse, but Con Foley gave him a poke in the back with the ashplant and somehow he was persuaded to move nearer the last place he would see on earth.

The prisoner replied in an almost inaudible whisper, 'I am.'

'You are a carpenter in the Victoria Barracks in Cork? Is that right?'

The prisoner said nothing.

'Answer me, boy. Either you are or you aren't.'

'I am.'

'Why do you work for the enemy?'

'Where else was I supposed to get work?'

'But you are more than that, aren't you? You are the chairman of the Discharged Soldiers and Sailors Federation?'

'I am, and proud of it.'

'Do you realize that by taking a job in the Barracks you're doing something that a soldier could be doing?' Dan Donohoe asked.

The prisoner said nothing.

'Answer me when I'm talking to you, goddamit.' Donohoe slapped the man across the face.

'I...I suppose so.'

'You suppose so? Do you realize that the implications of that are that there is at least one more soldier on the street. That's one more soldier against the Republic. That makes you the equivalent of an enemy officer. What do you say to that?'

'I never looked at it like that. I just wanted a job to help rear my family. '

'No doubt you have been using this "job" to pass on information to the enemy about our men.'

'I know nothing about that, sir, nothing at all. I never told anybody anything. I know nothing about Sinn Féin people, nothing at all.'

'Are you going to deny that you used your position to pass on information to the British?'

'As I say, how could I pass on information when I know nothing more than what I read in the papers?'

'You're wasting your time talking to the likes of him,' Daithi O'Brien said. 'Get it over with.'

'Would you agree that your position in the Barracks is supporting the British war effort against the Republic?'

The prisoner was puzzled and said nothing for a few seconds. Then he said, 'I suppose it is.'

'If you tell us who the other spies are, we'll put fifty pounds in your pocket and put you on the boat for England,' Daithi O'Brien said.

'What spies? I know nothing about spies. And what would I be doing going to England? I know nobody in England' He started to cough. 'I don't know what you're talking about.'

'Listen Deveney, we know you're a stoolie. One night you were heard admitting in a pub that you had something to do with the Anti-Sinn Féin League. Isn't that right?'

'I don't know what you're talking about. What's the Anti-Sinn Féin League?'

'You know damn well what we're talking about. The Anti-Sinn Féin League, the group of Black and Tans who are burning and bombing all around them in Cork city and raping women and dragging innocent civilians out of their beds and shooting them dead in the street.'

'I know nothing about that.'

'So how do they know where to go? How do they know the people to target? They can do it because they're getting help from fellas like you. They recruit in the ex-soldiers federation, isn't that right?'

'Those people never go next or near the Discharged Soldiers Federation. Didn't they attack us last summer and shoot two of our lads.'

'They do, and you know it.'

'They've got him completely corrupted. I'm tired from saying it,' Daithi O'Brien said. 'He'll tell us nothing.'

'Well, we're going to have to execute you so,' Dan Donohoe said in a deliberately matter of fact tone.

'Please don't execute me. I'll tell you anything you want.'

By now he was swaying on his feet as if his legs were melting wax and he was about to slide to the ground in a faint.

'Okay. Talk.'

And he gave them a list of names who he said were contacts, none of whom meant anything to Dinny.

'Who is your contact, your intelligence officer in the Barracks?'

The man thought for a while and began again his terrified stare at Dinny.

'Captain Kelley.'

'Spell his name' Jim Blake said.

'KELLEY.'

'That's it – that's the way the hoor spells his name,' said Con Foley. 'We've got our man.'

'So Kelley is the intelligence officer? Well, that's good progress now. Do you have fifty quid on you, Daithi?'

'Indeed then I have.'

Donohoe took a tie out of his pocket and handed it to Dinny.

'Dinny, put this man's tie back on him. We have to have you looking respectable now, don't we, Mr Deveney.'

Dinny, relieved that it looked like the man was about to be released, put the tie around his collar and tied a knot and straightened it up under his chin.

'Right so. We'll have to get this lad down to Queenstown to the boat. Of course, we'll have to blindfold you now, Deveney. Otherwise, you'd know where we are and where we're been holding you.'

'That's alright. Blindfold me away.'

Jim Blake tied a red oil rag around the prisoner's head and Deveney sighed with relief, thinking he was going to be taken to Queenstown.

'Say a prayer now, boy, and thank God you've been spared.'

Deveney stood upright with relief and made the Sign of the Cross and his lips began to move as he muttered prayers quietly to himself. Con Foley looked away as Donohoe took his revolver from his pocket, cocked it silently under his sleeve and lifted it to within three inches of the man's head. As he fired, Deveney moved, and the bullet missed him. It whizzed past Dinny's shoulder and crashed through the sally bushes behind him. Birds screeched and a scatter of snipe and moorhen rose from the scrub as the shot echoed around the bogs.

'Cursed bastard,' Dan Donohoe muttered.

'What are you doing?' Deveney cried. 'I thought you were going ...'

Dan Donohoe didn't miss the second time. He fired through the back of the man's skull; the front of his face was blown out and a hole as big as a saucer opened in his forehead. Dinny winced as he watched the gush of blood and grey matter and bits of bone splash over several square yards of heather. He felt he was going to get sick. The man's knees crumpled under him and he fell forward into the bushes. His legs twitched and kicked for a while like those of a slaughtered calf and his jaw opened and closed a few times, as if he had to chew his last breath. Donohoe lifted the gun again to finish him off.

'Don't waste another bullet on him, Dan,' Daithi O'Brien said. 'He's as dead as he'll ever be. He'll stop jerking after a while. Come on, lads, move him. We'd better skeet.'

'You got those names, Jim?' Dan Donohoe said to Blake.

'I got 'em. Kelley is the intelligence officer alright inside at the Barracks, and we've three touts.'

'That's enough about it then. Bastard'n spies,' Donohoe spat. 'The city boys will be delighted. That'll be a few more of them off the streets. A few more for the Rea.'

Jim Blake and Daithi O'Brien waited for Deveney to stop twitching. Then they picked him up and threw him into the grave. He flopped in, flaccid as a bag of water.

'This'll save you a job, boy.' Blake said to Dinny with a crooked smile. 'The first one is always the worst. After a while you just pop 'em off and it's as easy as drowning kittens.'

'Cover him up there now, Dinny. Cover him up well and make sure to put a few bushes over the grave so that the whole country doesn't know he's there. And wash up that.' Dan Donohoe pointed to the blood and brains that was smearing the bushes to his right. 'Fire a sup of Jeyes Fluid on it, or the dogs of the country will be here by morning.'

The bog had settled into silence again as if the shots had never been fired. But, to Dinny, it was not the same silence as before. This was a new silence, the dark side of summer; it was as if a cloud of change, a layer of horror, had descended on his own familiar stomping ground.

'We've got to skedaddle now. You know your job, Dinny,' Dan Donohoe said. 'And we know our job. We'll have to plant a lot more of these fuckers before Ireland is saved.' The men left him with his shovel and his pick and his storm lamp to fill in the grave.

As he watched them move away towards the car, laughing and talking as if they were staggering home from the pub, he felt hollow inside, as though something had been gouged out of him and he felt lessened and more shrunken, squeezed of the life that he had lived up until then. He could hear Jim Blake in the distance whistling 'The Maid of Aughrim'. Jim Blake, happy as Larry, delighted with his night's work. He watched the Buick turn with difficulty in the narrow lane and drive away towards the city.

He thought about the position in which he now found himself. He was out of his depth. Fellows like Jim Blake and Daithi O'Brien were fierce and dangerous men who seemed to enjoy their work; they had no consciences but rather were equipped with a daring and savage bravery. Dan Donohoe was a hundred times more dangerous still, for he had a cunning that the others did not have. He was the leader, the executioner, the master of his own patch. Dinny's father had been right all along, he realized. Donohoe could buy and sell city man and country man, Irishman and Englishman alike. He was craftier than a hayshed rat in a nest of rat poison.

What was wrong with himself that he couldn't be like that, be decisive and believe that he was just doing his duty? What was it about them, with their fearless distilled hate, their pure extremism? Why could he not be like that? He had some kind of soft centre, like that of a sickly calf. He would never make a real gunman. There was no two ways about it: he was a something of a coward.

Dinny turned back towards the grave and looked down at the man inside it. He looked at him for a long time as the last light drained from the mountain. For no one else would ever look at him again and he felt that he deserved one last, small act of respect. Dinny supposed that the man's family would report him missing, but his body would never be found. For the Rea would never yield up its secrets, though the killers would live, in many cases, to a ripe old age.

Dinny thought about the killing system that could eliminate Thomas Deveney from the city with a calm and sudden efficiency. And 'eliminate' was the right word. There were rumours of lists. Deveney had been on a list somewhere. Now he was struck off it, the account of terror debited by one. There were a lot of spaces opening up in people's lives. Nobody would ever fill in the gaps.

And so what if Deveney was working for the British? Wasn't half the country in the pay of England in one way or another? That could easily have been himself in Deveney's position. A decision one way or another, often born out of necessity. The country hadn't exactly been overrun with jobs since the end of the Great War. Ex-soldiers had nothing. You could be a carpenter for the British Army or working as an employee in one capacity or another in the Barracks and that would have drawn the hand of suspicion down upon you.

Deveney had given the men a list of names. Who were they? Donohoe would remember them with all the efficiency of his devil's memory. The IRA would pick them up over the coming months and there would be another collection of unmarked graves in the high country stretching all the way from Watergrasshill to Rylane. He said Captain Kelley was the intelligence officer in the Barracks. There was a Captain Kelley; he was the most wanted man on the IRA lists. Deveney wouldn't have to be a spy to know who he was, just a desperate man who would say anything to save his skin.

So Dinny stood in for mother and father, for brother and sister, for the grieving relatives who would go to their own graves not knowing where their son was buried. And something he wasn't able to define, something like grief and loss, but worse, began to seep like the bog water into him.

It was getting chilly. A sharp breeze stirred the mist up from the hollows to the east. He knelt on the pile of peaty earth and said a decade of the Rosary for the repose of the soul of Thomas Deveney and, for reasons that he couldn't understand, tears began to come into his eyes, tears for the dead and the helpless dead, for victims on both sides, for victims everywhere.

Dinny tore at the blood-spattered bushes and pulled the gory marsh grass out of the ground and threw it into the grave that was already seeping, its sides falling in on Deveney's soiled overalls. Eventually he got his shovel and reluctantly began to fill in the hole, doing it gently at first, as if he would hurt the corpse inside. Then he began to work furiously. When he had it done, the mound was taller than he had expected, so he cut down a few bushes to camouflage the grave. Thomas Deveney had vanished forever.

Then Dinny went home through the fields, crept into an outhouse, got a tin of Jeyes Fluid and went back to the Rea and doused the blood-stained bushes with its tar-like odour. It was after midnight when he got home again. He washed his hands and went to bed. He tried to sleep but, instead, he lay tossing and turning, replaying the execution a thousand times over in his mind.

10

His mother had come into his room in the small hours of the morning. Dawn had just broken through the window, the dawn of the first of the days of his life that would never be the same as the days which had gone before.

'What ails you, a stóir?' she asked. 'You've been tossing and turning all night. And you came home very late.'

'Just a bad dream. I was out with the lads.'

'You're out with the Volunteers at night, aren't you?' she said with a frown. 'This is all very sinful, you know that, don't you? You'll just have to stop whatever it is you're doing. It's as simple as that.'

'I wish it was.'

He turned to the wall. She might be worried, but if she knew what was actually going on, she would have been out of her mind. It didn't bear thinking about; ordinary decent people involved in the killing of nameless though not, certainly not, faceless strangers.

'You'll have to try or we'll all be in trouble. And your poor father working all the hours that God sends. You know what can happen to people now that these Black and Tans are on the go. Have you been to Confession?'

Dinny swallowed.

'No.'

'You'll have to go to Confession.'

'Confession is no place to be going now. You know what the Bishop says about the IRA, and many of his priests agree with him.'

'Still, you'll have to go to Confession.'

'If I can get a priest to hear me, that is. The Bishop is no friend of the IRA. Listen, Mother, there are terrible things happening, right under people's noses, things you'd never suspect in a month of Sundays.' Dinny stared up at the cracks in the ceiling. 'I can't tell you what they are, because I'm sworn to secrecy and my life wouldn't be worth a thrawneen if I did.' His mother made the Sign of the Cross.

'Just for my sake, Mother, please don't ask me questions. I promise you one thing: I'll not get you or father or Bina or Bill into trouble. I swear on that. Just go easy on me, no questions, all right?'

'No questions. Just promise me you'll go to confession.'

'I will.'

It was a relief to know that she knew that he was going out with 'the boys'. At least that was now out in the open. For one of the biggest problems up till now had been the secrecy and the strain all this put him under.

'How long have you known that I'm going out with the boys'? he asked.

'It's easy enough to put two and two together.'

'Does himself know?'

'Your father is such a heavy sleeper. I think he suspects nothing.'

'Don't tell him, so.'

'I won't. But what's going to happen to you, Din'? Where will you end up? Saving Ireland? A lot of good Ireland will ever be to you. You could end up in Cork jail or on hunger strike like those foolish boys or, God between us and all harm, you could end up dead, thrown like a rag on the side of the road.' His mother whispered in the light of the candle.

'Pearse and Connolly died for Ireland. The least we can do is help set her free. We have do do our bit. Besides, the hunger strikes have been the best weapon we ever had.'

'That may be the case. But don't have anything bad on your conscience on Ireland's account. It's not worth that. Nothing is.'

'I won't, Mother.'

His mother went back to her room. The light to the hall shrank to a rectangle and then went out. She was no fool; she understood him. His mother was, as always, comforting, civilized, decent, qualities which were now in short supply in the world.

Two days later he was still thinning the mangolds with his father, Bina and Bill, and if anything, his mental state was even worse. The previous night the Rea had claimed its next victim. He was a middle-aged man in a good suit, a well-spoken city type. His name was McManus and, Dinny gathered from the men, he worked in the War Pensions Office in Cork. He went on his knees. Dinny handed him his Rosary beads; he said his prayers and went down without a murmur. You could tell a lot about a man from the way he faced his death. McManus was resigned and prayed the entire time before his execution. It must be very hard, Dinny thought, for a non-believer to face death. McManus believed this was not the end, that he would go on to meet his Lord. It was leaving their loved ones that seemed to be the worst part of it for most people.

He gave Dinny his watch before he died and asked him to pass it on to his wife - he even gave him his address in Cork. Dinny promised he would do so but, after the execution, Dan Donohoe took the watch from him and flung it into the middle of Carroll's Pond, the little lake not far from the Rea.

'She won't need that. Our instructions are that spies are to vanish without trace. Nothing is to be known about them. We don't want that watch turning up. We don't want families learning that they have informers in their midst. That would be a terrible shame on a family. These people are best forgotten about, you understand? It's cleaner that way and easier on everyone.'

For better or worse, that was how it was going to be. Dinny looked up from his work. The day shimmered like old windows. The drills swayed in front of him as if they had melted and were flowing down the field.

He looked at his hands and was surprised to see them shaking; he was powerless to stop them.

'That's a terrible state you're in, Dinny,' Bina said from the second drill next to him.

'That's just from lack of sleep, three nights in a row.'

Suddenly there was a shout from the headland.

'You're going very slow this morning, Din,' his father called. 'What's ails you at all, man? Bill and Bina have already three drills done. You're only on your second.'

'I don't feel so good.'

'Then pull yourself together, man. We won't be out of here by the middle of August at this go.'

Dinny wiped his brow and went back to yanking up the weeds and mangolds, and teasing out the weak seedlings, his nails black with earth and his hands stained with sap. The ground smelled of redshank.

He thought about his mother and Bina. It was a funny thing: the women were more understanding of the cause of Ireland than the men. Mothers and sisters provided safe houses all over the country. Mothers were more flexible, more open to change. Sisters smuggled revolvers in prams and under shawls. Fathers never seemed to understand. Old men were like old railway engines, stuck in a siding in some rarely used station where the weeds grew high, and going nowhere.

There was only one conclusion to come to now, and that was that killing was part of what they had become. Killing had become part of the lexicon of life. And of course it happened on the other side too. The Black and Tans could murder anyone for simply having the wrong surname. Con Foley said that at least four Twomeys had been murdered in Cork city by the authorities trying to get their hands on Mick Twomey, commander of one of the city battalions of the IRA and one of Cork's most wanted men. It was a matter of ignorance and madness. Since the breakdown of law and order, people could do exactly what they liked. It was a bad time to have the wrong name or to be in the wrong place at the wrong time. Survival was all a matter of luck.

He thinned on up the hill towards the top of the drill, pulling fistfuls of redshank and betony and hemp nettle. Then he heard the long call, the shrill peep-peep of his mother's whistle for the dinner. He stood up, and swaying uncontrollably, opened the binder twines tied around his knees and took off the lengths of sacking from around his knees. Then he joined the others and they stumbled across the half-flattened drills towards the house. His mother was standing with her arms folded by the door. She gazed at him as he passed into the kitchen. She seemed distant and foreign and her eyes were blank pages upon which to write the history of care.

11

July found Dinny cutting hay, bouncing up and down on the cast iron seat of the mowing machine as Doll pulled it round and round the Big Field. He was shaving lengths off the hayfield as a barber shaves a face, a charioteer in his own circus, giving Doll an odd whack on the rump with the reins, moving through the world in a cloud of pollen. It was one of those blue-skied days when the memory of all other kinds of weather seems just a dream, the shadow of an entirely different world. All his life he had loved doing this. Now he did not love it anymore, for it gave him too much time to think.

All summer, the IRA had been picking up spies in Cork city on the basis of information extracted from other spies: Captain Kelley was losing his informants one or two at a time. They were abducted on the streets of Cork, moved to Sing Sing, interrogated, executed and buried in the Rea. Hardly a single week passed but one or two such men were shot. Dinny dug the graves for most of them. He had dug five graves in the five weeks since Deveney's execution.

He looked up from the row of hay in front of him and saw Bina coming across the field with a basket containing his dinner.

'Whoa!' he said to Doll and the mowing machine came to a shuddering stop, the clicking of its mechanics stopping in unison with the drive wheels. He lifted the mowing bar from the sward and untackled Doll from the mower and led her to the water trough in the corner of the field. When he got back to the mowing machine he found Bina laying out his dinner on the frame of the mower. He sat down, his back to the iron wheel of the machine, as Bina took the teacloth off his plate and handed it to him.

'Thanks B',' he said.

Bina said nothing. Like most rural families, when there was no need to talk, they didn't talk. He avoided eye contact with her and kept his head down and started eating.

'Do you mind my saying something, Din?' she said after a while.

'Fire away.' He tried to focus on his food. Normally, he loved eating out of doors; it brought him back to his childhood in the days when men with their sleeves rolled up saved hay with forks before horse-drawn hayrakes were invented and the air was heavy with meadowsweet and a lens of heat shimmered over every field. A season of bounty was always on the land in the middle of July. As a child he used to love to play among the cocks as the adults piled the hay high into the evening. What a pity he did not feel any of that bounty in himself now.

'I hope you don't mind my saying this, Din, but you look terrible of late. Is something wrong?' Bina's forehead and nose were freckled from the sun. She too was used to making hay. Cooking, thinning and making hay, women's work in summer. Now she wore a frown on those freckles, deepening her colour.

'What could be wrong?'

'I'm just worried about you, Din, that's all.'

'Worried? Sure, what's there to be worried about? I'm just busy, that's all.'

'Come on, Din, stop trying to cod me. You're walking around white as a sheet all day. I know Mother thinks you're going out at night. She says little, but I know what's on her mind.'

Dinny stared at his plate. A sop of hay blew across his hand and landed on his potatoes. He picked it out with the tips of his fingers and let it float away on the breeze.

'Out at night? Yerra, sure, I'd take an occasional traipse out alright, I suppose. A man can't stay inside all the time.'

'You know well what I'm talking about.'

Dinny said nothing but looked across the valley at the hill opposite. 'Tom Dinan should be cutting that field over,' he said, ''twas mad ready for mowing last week.'.

'Don't try to change the subject. You're going out at night with the IRA, aren't you?'

'So what if I am? Can't a man do something without being interfered with?'

'You're beginning to sound like your father. Stubborn as a bloody old mule.' She looked away. 'Anyway, I'm not interfering. I'm just worried.'

Dinny squinted into the sun. He couldn't tell Bina what was really going on, yet he couldn't afford to clam up and have her worrying even more.

'Do you remember four or five years ago when the Volunteers started up and we were all in it, even Bill, and you were in Cumann na mBan?' he asked. 'Do you remember the dances, the Irish classes, the concerts? Do you remember the day we all went to Cork to play in the band and I got the medal from Tomás MacCurtain? God what a day out we had.' Dinny tried to laugh. 'All I wanted to do then was save Ireland. To play my part. And I still do. And you marched along with the rest of us.'

'I did.'

'You even read the Jail Journal when I asked you to.'

'I did.'

'Those were innocent days, you'll have to agree.'

'They were. And then Bill and I got out because we had sense.' Bina said. 'When the murdering of the police started, up and down the country. And I thought you got out too, just like Bill and the rest of us.'

'Well, I did and I didn't.' He mulled over his food, staring into it, slow to give out information like a tight old shopkeeper counting his change.

'I tried to keep believing in what I believed in then. I stayed involved, half-in and half-out.' He tossed the potato skins into the stubble. 'I thought the conscription lads were just a bunch of cowards. They just joined up to save their skins. If you're going to die in Flanders, you might as well die in Ireland, that was their motto. I didn't want to be like that, Bina. I saw Bill join and then leave. Dozens of them left, the size of the Company dropped from 40 to nine or ten in a matter of a month. And I didn't want to be part of that cowardly crew. As far as I could see, we were still no better off, Ireland was still in chains.'

'Better in chains than dying on its feet.'

'Maybe. Then Dan Donohoe disgraced us, called us a bunch of no-good flag-waggers who were useless for anything but blowing and dancing and marching and wearing fancy style. I didn't like that. I was ashamed of our laziness. I could have walked away, I suppose, but I didn't. Maybe I was just naive. Maybe I stayed in it just for the excitement. I believe MacCurtain and MacSwiney were good men. Tadhg Manley is a good man. There are a lot of good people in this thing and I don't want to let them down. That's what it amounts to. Of course, that doesn't mean that there's not some dirty work being done.'

'Dirty work? What kind of dirty work?'

'I can't tell you.'

'Are you involved in it?'

'No, no. I'm talking about things that happened in the city.'

'Sure, the city is a thousand miles away from you, Din.'

'Hmm.'

'I think you should leave the IRA now, Din. Get out of it while you can. You know what's happening around the country since the police started recruiting those Black and Tans. Nobody's safe now. The Volunteers had it good for twelve months. Those days are over. Now those Tans are mad for blood. If you fall into their hands, you're finished. Fat lot of good Ireland will be to you then.'

'That's what Mother said. But you see, it's not that easy.'

'Why can't you?'

'I just can't.' He searched the width and breadth of the shimmering field for the right words. 'I know too much, I've seen things you wouldn't believe were even possible. If I try to get out now, they'd finish me off, or at least they'd make sure I got finished off.'

'They wouldn't do that. Dan Donohoe wouldn't do a thing like that.'

'Wouldn't he? I'm sorry to put it like this, Bina, but you don't know what you're talking about. They mightn't do it themselves. But they'd leave a few bullets lying around the yard. Then the police would get a tip off and the place would swarm with Black and Tans and we'd all be shot. We'd be useful too, as martyrs. Or they might take the easy route and shoot me as a spy.'

'But they couldn't do that. Sure you're one of them. I thought they only killed real spies.'

'They'll kill whoever suits them.'

'But you're one of them.'

'I am and I'm not. It's hard to explain. I've hardly ever even held a gun in my hand. Drilling with hurleys! What a laugh! You see, Bina, the men on the run are different to the rest of us. To them, we're just helpers. Then there's a really tough crowd in the city, who go around doing terrible things. Sometimes they're done around here too. And sometimes I'm called in to help.'

'But nothing bad has happened around here yet. This is a very quiet area.' She poured the tea from a bottle stoppered with a roll of the previous day's newspaper.

'You think so?'

'You mean it isn't?'

'I don't want to talk about it.' He blew on the surface of the tea, making small circular waves.

'You see, Dan Donohoe looks down on the people around here. He thinks we're an impure race because this is not West Cork or Kerry or West Clare where they all speak Irish and are steeped in the old culture. We're tainted by too much contact with the British, he says. British! Jesus, I never met an Englishman in my life! But that makes it easy for him to do pretty rough stuff, Bina. What we are to him are spear carriers. That's what we are. We're as disposable as that paper cork you just threw away. Now I don't have any problem digging trenches and cutting trees and the rest of it, if that holds up the enemy. I don't have any problem being a spear carrier, come to think of it. It's the other stuff I don't want to do.'

'What other stuff? For the love of God, Dinny, tell me.'

'Believe me, you don't want to hear it.'

'But surely you can get out of it?'

'Can't you see that it's not possible. And it's all because of where I'm living.'

'What do you mean "where you're living?" This is where we're all living. What's where you're living got to do with it?'

'I can't tell you that either, Bina. For the love of God, just leave me alone, will ye?'

Bina still believed in the decency of humanity and the decency of those who fronted the movement. 'de Valera wouldn't allow that 'other stuff' as you call it.'

'de Valera? These people don't give a damn about de Valera, or MacSwiney - they laugh at him behind his back. And I know for a fact that they had no time for MacCurtain before he was killed. He was too soft for them. Of course he's useful now, as a martyr.'

'I don't want you to be a martyr, Din.' There were tears in her eyes.

'Well, if I leave now that's what I'll be. A martyr or a spy. That's the choice I have.'

'This is an awful mess you got yourself into, Din, isn't it? A right mess.' Bina looked away and stared into the middle distance where, on a hillside beyond, a team of men were making up hay with pitchforks. 'What can we do?'

'Nothing. Except...'

'Except what?'

'There are rumours that there might be new structures coming in, in the Brigade. We'll see what happens then.' He finished his tea and threw the tea leaves into the grass. 'Maybe

Dan Donohoe might get picked up again and get a spell inside.'
He shrugged. 'Who knows? That would take the pressure off
us.'

'For the love of God be careful, Din. We don't want you
coming home in a box.'

'Maybe there are worse things than coming home in a box.'

'I don't know what to say to you, Din. I don't know what's
going to become of us at all.' She blessed herself and covered
her face with her hands.

'Listen, Bina. Not a word of this to anybody. Otherwise,
I'm goosed. Loose talk is dangerous now.' He stood up and
brushed himself down. 'Now I've got to get back on this
mowing. The fine weather won't last forever. The hay will still
have to be saved, even if Ireland isn't.

She turned to go.

'Be careful.'

'I will. Now you're beginning to sound like Mother.' They
both tried to laugh but couldn't and, as she headed back in the
direction of the house, he knew there was a distance between
them, a new gap in their understanding of the world. The things
he was witnessing most nights now separated him from ordinary
decent humanity. The experiences he was sharing with the men
of the night could not be shared with the people of the day.

12

Jimmy Hodnett lived in a low grey house under a sagging beech that leaned over the gable and half-covered the roof so that you could pass the house and hardly know that it was there at all. His wife had died in the 1918 'flu epidemic and he had four daughters, one of whom was married, another was away on service to a family in the city and the last two, Sarah and Lil, were still living with him.

He found it difficult trying to rear his daughters on his own. Young girls were surprisingly unpredictable and given to unexpected mood swings. While they were kind and generous to him, he felt he short-changed them in ways that he didn't entirely understand and he knew that he could never be a replacement for the mother they had lost.

Times were tough. Since he had been de-mobbed at the end of the War, he had no running water, his daughters had no shoes, he could hardly afford a drop of porter for himself nor tobacco for his pipe, so he had taken to mixing whatever tobacco he could scrape together with dried nettle leaves. One of the few pleasures he had left was to set this mixture alight and blow the oddly-scented smoke into the hob and watch it float up the chimney and into the high summer evening.

He had applied for dozens of jobs in Cork, Midleton and Fermoy but nobody wanted an ex-soldier whose only skill was the ability to march and shine his shoes and fire a rifle with a fair degree of accuracy. He could, of course, have signed up for the Black and Tans but he was glad he didn't, for the Black and Tans had turned out to be the worst parcel of ruffians that were ever foisted on the country. He'd help out a few farmers during the haymaking season and at harvest time and perhaps spend a few weeks picking potatoes in winter or thinning turnips in June. And that was about it, as far as paid employment went.

Of course, he had his meagre army pension that he collected every week. But that would hardly keep him in bread and tea. He was bitter with the Government for throwing him on the waste heap of poverty. This was the thanks he got after four years of fighting for King and Country, of trooping the colours, of every day risking life and limb, of taking the shell shock and the chlorine, of crouching, scuttering, waiting for the order to go 'over the top'. He suffered the rats and the mud and the deaths of most of his companions and the endless staring at the small slit of sky from the dug-outs and all for what?

Yes, Lloyd George and the Government didn't give a tinker's curse, that's what it amounted to; you did your duty, you fought for your country and then you starved. Thanks a lot, Colonel Pigeyes.

Not that Jimmy Hodnett spoke too much about the war. The whole business was too awful to be reincarnated in conversation. To speak of pain was to relive it. It was better, far better, to forget the horrors of one's life. After all he did come back from Flanders. That was amazing in itself. What right did he have to survive when so many others did not? Why was there no Hun bullet with his name written on it? Maybe there was a God after all, though Jimmy didn't believe in a God, not after what he had seen in Belgium and France.

He got drunk for a week in Amiens after Armistice Day and then caught trains across France and England and was demobbed. That was about it. He was back in civilian life again. His daughters hardly knew him, his wife fretted about this stranger in her bed. Now she too was gone, a victim of the plague that maybe he himself had brought with him, or someone like him, some wanderer in foreign parts, some bringer of contagion, a carrier of the fire of death.

He didn't even wish to contact his old comrades anymore. For Jimmy had seen too much death, too much terror, too much misery for misery to crave company. There was only so much failure you could take, the country was full of it, and too much despair. Nor did he join the Ex-Soldiers and Sailors Federation either. There was no point in reliving old glories that were never glories in the first place, there was no point in worrying about how the world seemed to have collapsed at war's end and how the 'flu came and then the pneumonia and took away nearly as many as the war itself.

But to despair is to sin and to sin seriously. Jimmy Hodnett was well aware of sin, so he did his best to hide his view of the world from his daughters with false bonhomie and silly jokes. They were young and innocent, there was no point in upsetting them with the knowledge of what he had seen and done and witnessed in the name of democracy and 'the freedom of small nations'.

He had, of course, considered joining up when the Government began recruiting for the police to put down the unrest that had been growing in Ireland. But he did not do so. For one thing, he would be turning against his own people, at least some of them. Besides, he had enough of killing, of the spurious camaraderie of the gun, of drilling and marching and hiding and fear. This was one war where he would not be a participant. They could get on with it without Jimmy Hodnett, thanks very much.

When he thought about it, he wasn't doing too badly, even if things were tight. For, despite his poverty, he didn't want for food. There wasn't much cash in his pocket, but he could just about eke out a living for himself and his daughters. He had an acre of good ground behind the cottage where he grew every vegetable under the sun, from potatoes to cabbages to carrots, from strawberries grown in barrels to save space, which he sold in Midleton, to parsnips and onions and scallions. He was a one-man greengrocer supplier.

And for meat, he snared rabbits all year round, he knew their runs and placed snares in little tracks and gaps in ditches all around the countryside. He walked out every morning into the dawn in search of his furry prey and gutted them and skinned them, rolling the hide off their backs like he was pulling off socks. And they went into the pot and he and his daughters ate well, though they hardly had clothes to stand up in or turf to light the fire.

What he didn't eat, he sold to a Mr Nicholson in Cork who exported game or, more often, he sold the rabbits to the mess in Victoria Barracks when he was collecting his pension.

And that was what doomed him. That and the fact that he had got his cottage and his acre as a form of pension for his time in the army and there were people around who didn't like that. So in a sense, he was doomed because of where he lived and because of another old skill he picked up in the army. (The army was good for developing arcane skills like whitewashing barrels and untangling barbed wire and sleeping under the stars when there was frost about.) For Jimmy had learned while in France to shave without the use of hot water or a looking glass. Every morning after breakfast he'd go to the stream that flowed past his house and there he'd shave, scraping off one segment of beard at a time and watch the soap suds float down the stream and the water clear and re-assert its mirror every minute with the smoothing of the ripples.

One morning he was doing this when he was surrounded by men in long coats and cloth caps who caught him under the arms and threw him half-shaven into a waiting car and carried him off without saying much or telling him where they were taking him. They didn't try him, they didn't beat him, they didn't threaten him, they just held a revolver to his side and told him to stay still for his own sake.

First, he thought they were Black and Tans. Then he realized from their accents that they were the IRA. He had been warned by a former comrade to get out of the country, as the IRA were rounding up ex-soldiers and taking them away. But Jimmy had ignored the warning because he could see no reason why they would want to harm him. He had broadly similar views on the Government to what he imagined they had, he wanted a free Ireland, he had little contact with the army and none with the police. There was no earthly way he could be accused of being an informer.

But this former comrade had left for England, for whatever reason, with his entire family. Jimmy Hodnett thought this was an overreaction and a complete misunderstanding of the ways of Irishmen. So he stayed where he was. He couldn't very well uproot himself. Where would he go? How would he feed his girls without his acre? There was no going anywhere for him, for he couldn't take his little patch of land with him.

Besides, in so far as he cared to do so, he could stand up in front of any Irishman with a clear conscience. And if the IRA were targeting ex-soldiers, they had an impossible task on their hands, for there were more than a hundred thousand ex-soldiers in the country. If they organized themselves they could wipe out the IRA in a month. There were many a household in the land that had ex-soldiers under their roofs - that is assuming that the ex-soldier wasn't already in an unmarked grave somewhere in France or Flanders.

From what he knew of the republican leaders they were not that foolish. Politics was numbers, after all. Turning against the old army men was likely to lead to political suicide. They would lose whatever gains they had made in the first place.

No. Even when they picked him up and took him flying through the country roads, cracking springs on the rutted lanes, lurching around bends in the back of the Ford, he believed he was safe. Even when they put him in this brick-lined vault that he knew was underground because it dripped so much and that looked like it had been used to house cattle, he did not think he was in too much danger. They never even blindfolded him. It was surely a case of mistaken identity. Time would prove him right and he would be released.

It was only a night or two later, when they took him to a lonely lane, somewhere on high ground, and told him to get on his knees and say his prayers that he knew they were going to kill him. He didn't protest too much. He knew it would make no difference. He had faced worse in Flanders. He pleaded for his children, asking what would they do if he was taken from them. He was told that the children of spies did not deserve to be raised and that the slur of the spy would stick to his family for generations. He protested, but there was no persuading them that, just because he was snaring rabbits for the barrack and collecting his pension, that he was not a spy.

They shot him in the Rea and dumped his body in the bogs and there was a simple reason for this and the reason was that he lived within a few miles of this place of secret executions, Elsewhere, he might have been left alone or warned and allowed flee to England, or else be shot and thrown on the side of the road. But due to the accident of his proximity to the Rea, he vanished off the earth forever. His cottage and acre were taken by the man who wanted it in the first place. His daughters were taken into care and his surname too vanished from the lists and parish registrars of East Cork. So Jimmy Hodnett became a non-person. It was as if he had never been there at all.

But one person knew he had been there and that person was Dinny Fitzgibbon and the difference between Jimmy Hodnett and the other prisoners that Dinny buried in the Rea was that Dinny actually knew him. The others were nameless men, city men, men in suits, men from other parts, some from west Cork and Tipperary, some were spies, some were hostages, some were nobodies about whom little was known. But Jimmy Hodnett was almost a neighbour and Dinny was inclined to believe him when he said that snaring rabbits and selling them to the barrack did not amount to a case of spying.

He also knew, of course, that this was just a matter of Dan Donohoe trying to make it look official, to make his men feel better about themselves. The real reason, and Dinny could only surmise this, was that he lived too near the Rea and Sing Sing - though he was two miles away from the former and three and a half from the latter - and that there was a possibility, just a slight possibility, that he might hear something or see something and report it. The other possibility, of course, was that Dan Donohoe was rounding up any ex-soldiers he could find and executing them. But that idea was absurd, almost too outrageous to contemplate.

13

It was late September, a blue cirrus morning, high in the hills among the late singing thrushes of the Rea. Dinny woke early and got the cows milked and the yard cleaned, while Bill took Doll with their one churn to the creamery. As usual, Dinny had a lot of work to do: dung to be forked out, outhouses to be cleaned, turnips to be cut.

After finishing the 'jobs', he came in to eat his breakfast, and his parents spoke of this and that: the weather, the hurling, the cost of everything, the price of land and the new priest who had come to the parish - anything, that is, except the Troubles. He listened to them as if they were a strange race and spoke a foreign language. He ate his breakfast in silence, as if he had become a mute in his own house, for he didn't want to speak about where he was going or what he was doing. An unspoken understanding, or lack of it, like a kind of truce, had descended on the house. Then his father left with his pitchfork and bicycle to help out the last of the threshings in the townland and Dinny began buttering bread and making sandwiches in the kitchen.

'Are you going threshing, a stóir?' his mother asked.

'No.'

'What are you doing, so?'

'Ploughing.'

'Ploughing? Where in God's name could you be ploughing at this time of year?'

Dinny paused, holding a butter-covered knife over a badly hacked hunk of bread and looked at his mother.

'Dan Donohoe's.'

'You're doing his ploughing for him?' His mother stared at him. 'Are you out of your mind? Have you nothing better to do? I'd have thought you'd have got enough of trying to set

Ireland free at this stage. You could be caught in a round-up down there.'

'I'm not saving Ireland. I'm just doing the ploughing for the man.'

She shook her head.

'You don't have to tell me what it's like for these people. They go off to save Ireland and they let the house fall down around them. They don't plough, they don't harrow; they leave the scufflers rusting on the headlands. This will all lead to rack and ruin, you mark my words. Sure, what kind of a farmer could be ploughing in the month of September?'

'How would I know? Maybe a farmer who wants to get in an early crop of winter wheat.'

'And that's all you're doing?'

'That's all I'm doing. As I say. Ploughing.'

He finished making his sandwiches and filled a bottle of milk in the scullery and got out of the house as fast as he could. He was now guilty, guilty of going against his mother's wishes, guilty because he knew that his parents' fears were well placed and better placed than they could have imagined.

Dan Donohoe was waiting for him in a grove of flat-topped pines behind his house. He had his hat pulled down to cover his ears. A potato digger was abandoned and stood leaning like a stork on the top headland. Donohoe's place was on the brow of a hill at the beginning of some of the most fertile land in East Cork. His father had bought the farm about ten years previously. It was a fine spread with gently sloping fields and a big house and several hundred acres and ten acres of trees around it and commanded a fine view of Cork Harbour and the land to the south.

Donohoe was shuffling urgently from side to side.

'Good man, you got here early.' He was a machine gun of words. 'I've winter oats going in in a fortnight. This is good ploughing weather. Hurry on, boy.'

Dinny wondered about the kind of men who ran the IRA. The brigade officers were mostly clean-living types, upright men, men of honour and fierce ascetics. Most were non-smokers and teetotallers. Dan Donohoe, though he was curt and impatient and was not an easy man to deal with, never let anything stronger than a glass of lemonade pass his lips.

They had no trouble killing for Ireland, and they would have no trouble in dying for her. But they refused a drink. They saw things simply. If somebody was not for them, he or she was against them and deserved to be treated as such. They looked to Pearse and MacDonagh, who walked to their deaths proudly, glad to be given the opportunity to make the ultimate sacrifice. Now with Terence MacSwiney, their new commander, by this time dying on hunger strike, the willingness to die for Ireland reached new heights and they knew no fear.

Dinny read somewhere that, over in England, there were twenty- five applicants every month for the post of Lord Chief Executioner. Such people emerged in times of crises. Had Dan Donohoe been English he would have been one of them. He had all the credentials for the job. He was Lord High Chief Executioner of the Rea. He was not the only executioner, of course, in the IRA ranks, for this was a war fought out in a whole range of small theatres with little connection between them. Every battalion had one or two who could kill and sleep easily in their beds afterwards. But Dan Donohoe was the most prolific killer in the Cork Number 1 Brigade and that made him the most prolific in the entire country. Dan Donohoe liked to chalk up killings and was enormously proud of them.

There were things, Dinny realized, that were way beyond his understanding, and Donohoe's hardy fanaticism and his almost gleeful capacity to kill without remorse was one of them.

They went into the yard and crept around by the back of the house to the stables. The house, though it had a good view of the surrounding countryside, was now regularly visited and searched by the British, with the result that Donohoe since his release had to be careful about being seen around his own place.

'It's the stubble field in front of the house. We only brought in the stooks last week. There's six acres in it. It'll take you a day or two. It should be easy to plough though. I had barley in it this year. So I didn't undersow it. There was no grass in it last year.'

Dinny thought it early for ploughing, even for winter oats, with the threshing still to be done, but he said nothing. Instead, he led two horses out of the stables and walked them around the rear of the barns and tackled them to a plough that had been left with the briars growing over it since the previous spring. Both horses were quiet; they would be easy to work with.

'She's a bit rusty,' Dan Donohoe said of the plough, 'but the board will shine up soon enough.'

'I'll be okay.'

'I'll be keeping myself as invisible as possible. If anybody asks who you are, just say you're working here. Don't give your own name, or mine, whatever you do. You should be alright. Call in on my mother at one o'clock. She'll give you a bite of grub. I'll leave oats and water in the stables for the horses.'

'No bother.'

Dinny walked the horses to the field and cut two furrows to mark out the headlands at the top and the bottom of the field. Then he began to plough from headland to headland, the horses walking gently, their view limited by blinkers, straining forward against their collars and dragging the ploughshare through the turning soil.

Dan Donohoe was right, Dinny thought. The ground was easy to turn. There had been a few days rain a week earlier and conditions were perfect for ploughing. The earth turned in shavings of dark brown. It was a good field, powdery loam, with very few stones. The fog cleared to a blue-swept day and a fresh wind came up from the harbour and kept the horses cool. Small clouds like rabbits' tails marched across the sky. It was fresh and cold, and, after a few rows, a flock of seagulls had materialized out of nowhere and were landing on the furrows behind him like loose newspapers. Some crows turned up as well, comical-looking fellows, with their little trousers rolled above their knees and their jittery walk as they searched the clods for worms.

After a few furrows Dinny began to warm up and took off his jacket and threw it into the headland. Stripped to his waistcoat, with the wind blowing through his shirt, he was beginning to enjoy himself and was whistling and talking to the horses when he heard a shout.

'Hey, you! Hey! Plough the other side first.'

It was Dan Donohoe. He had come back from the top fields and was standing by the gap into the yard and was shouting like a town crier using his cupped hands.

'Plough the other side first.' He gesticulated frantically with his arm, pointing towards the opposite side of the field.

'What difference does it make?' Dinny shouted back. 'This is going grand as it is.'

'What am I telling you? Plough the other side first and be said by me.'

'Oh, all right,' Dinny muttered to himself. 'It's your field.'

He lifted the plough and crossed to the right hand side of the field to open a new land. The horses shook their heads and flicked their tails and reluctantly clanked to create a new furrow, as if they were happier in the rut they had been used to.

It was when he was halfway down the field that he suddenly discovered why Donohoe had wanted him to plough that side first. For there, beside a clump of ash, a few feet in from the ditch, were two freshly dug graves.

Dinny pulled on the reins and stopped when the horses reached the spot. One of the graves seemed to have been dug the previous night for there was damp soil beside it, and the other was perhaps a few days older. He expected the horses to shy rather than walk over the soft soil but they did not. So Donohoe had wanted the ploughing done quickly to cover the evidence of his work for Ireland. Dinny looked back towards the headland but Donohoe had gone. Gingerly, he guided the plough over the graves with each row he ploughed. He was afraid the sock might snag on a piece of clothing or, worse, bring up some human remains. But nothing like that happened. The ground ploughed like any other ground and by dinnertime the first fifty feet by the ditch was finished and there was nothing to distinguish the graves from the rest of the field.

He met Dan Donohoe and his mother at dinnertime but said nothing about what he had seen. And Dan Donohoe said nothing either. Everything went on as normal; the talk was of the weather and the planting of oats and whether or not the days would hold good so as to shorten the winter.

14

'Do you have any idea what it's like to be invisible?'

Those were the words of a friend when he first learned that Ted Mills was leaving Dublin and going to live in Cork.

At nearly five foot eleven and broad shouldered from years of physical work, Mills could hardly be described as invisible.

'No.'

'Well, mark my words, you will.'

The words had been spoken in jest ten years earlier but they still shone bright with meaning. This friend, a fellow Dubliner, had himself lived in Cork for two years and worked as a pharmacist's assistant in Patrick Street and knew how the exclusion and stratification of Cork society operated.

'I just want to warn you,' he had said. 'Outsiders are not seen in Cork. They are not wanted. The world will go on all round you. You will watch it as if you were looking at a picture, but you will never be part of it.'

In 1910, that was a strong enough warning about the insular nature of Cork society, and Mills arrived at Glanmire Station well prepared. He had never failed to fit in anywhere he had worked before and was determined that Cork was not going to beat him.

He found it an odd place, though: a sort of Charlie Chaplin of a city, shambling along, making a fool of itself in outsiders' eyes but always managing to remain upright. A droll town. If Cork were a person, it would be a cheeky insolent little upstart. It was no wonder Cork was such a rich breeding ground for rebels. It was no surprise either that, when the rebellion came, it was mainly centred in Cork, that self-styled capital of the South, a breezy disrespectful little town.

While Dublin looked to Liverpool and Belfast looked to Glasgow, Cork looked mainly to itself. There were maritime connections to Cardiff and Bristol, of course, but when a

Corkman thought of the centre of the Empire, he thought, not of London, but of Cork. The Corkman, as some wit had put it, was homesick even when he was at home.

But then, that was not entirely true either, as Mills found out over time. There was a whole range of different Corks, depending on what segment of society you found yourself in. Cork county was wide and agricultural and looked upon itself almost as an independent entity in its own right. For Cork was as layered as a wedding cake and, as an outsider, he could see it all. You had the mercantile and professional classes, the old Cork families; some Protestant, some Catholic, some even Jewish, with quaint names like Pulvertaft, Rohu, Jagoe, Camier and Beamish. Then you had the working class Corkman, a contemptuous, rather impertinent individual, full of caustic wit, the kind of fellow who signed up in great numbers at the outbreak of the Great War, fodder for the Empire.

Lastly, there was the county man: the farmer, the rural shopkeeper, the labourer and what was called the gentry. These people were indistinguishable from their counterparts anywhere else, and their towns and villages were the same as towns and villages the length and breadth of Ireland.

Mills realized soon after he arrived that he was lucky that his main dealings were with the country folk. He set up horticulture classes in Kanturk, Fermoy and Midleton for the first half of the week, Bandon and Macroom on Wednesdays and Thursdays, before operating out of the Model Farm on Friday and Saturday mornings. His motorcar, one of only a few hundred in Cork, was his most important piece of equipment. He got to know the county intimately and could tell, within a few miles, where a person was from by his accent alone. He saw himself as a student of Corkness and, as his children were growing up, he became more and more involved in the social life of the city. He was an active member of the Masonic Order and the YMCA and committees associated with the Church.

It was his children who allowed him to overcome the barriers of class and the various manifestations of snobbery that made up Cork society. Children broke rules, they made friends, they were like emissaries forcing integration on people. Mills might be an outsider but his children were not, they had Cork accents and spoke with the quaint precision that was the distinguishing feature of the better off Corkman.

Mills often thought about the strangeness of his sons speaking differently to him. This lead to an abrupt cutting-off of his own youth, as if his pre-Cork existence was an appendage to his current life. He had a choice; he could either go with it or retreat into being an old fuddy-duddy, dreaming of London and Dublin and his past as a somehow better place. Mills decided to follow the lead of his children and, as a result, had what amounted almost to a second childhood during the years when his sons were having their own. He found himself involved in all their activities, for they weren't yet at the age where fathers were about as welcome as a toothache. Mills knew that, with his sons aged fourteen and fifteen respectively, he would get no more than a year or two more of this kind of enjoyment before they left for some far corner of the Empire or grew too rebellious to want to be seen too close to him.

These were the last of the best years of parenthood and he wanted to enjoy them, moulding, insofar as it was possible, the character of his sons in the process. For if he knew anything, it was that if you wanted to foster the development of Christian values, you had to lead by example and show the nature of good deeds by doing good deeds yourself. So Mills found himself in the middle of his web of committees, from horticulture to sporting, from Bible classes to summer camps, so that his brain sometimes felt like Piccadilly Circus. Though he had long since learned to organize himself, his pockets were still filled with notes at the end of every day, with lists of things to be done. Popularity brought its own drawbacks. He also had the not inconsequential matter of running his horticulture courses in the midst of the mounting disruption caused by trenched roads, blown up bridges and fallen trees, delayed mails and trains.

After the arson attack, when his nursery was burned down, as he raged against the crass stupidity and the kind of criminal mentality that could destroy something from which everyone benefited, he expected to get a lot of sympathy from his friends. And indeed he did get some kind words from his Church of Ireland acquaintances but they were muted and framed with caution. Protestants were afraid to speak out too loudly in case they should bring trouble on themselves. Voices carried a long way in the void of a chaotic country. His out-of-town friends, all of whom had a passion for gardening, the Annesleys, the Longfields, Col Grove-White, Mrs Bence-Jones were suitably appalled. But in the city it was different. The so-called loyalists, both Catholic and Protestant, were careful to keep their heads down. Better to say nothing. 'We don't want to draw their attention on us, you see.' Grove-White said. 'Our lives may very soon be in the hands of these people. Like it or not, the Sinn Feiner is the coming man. So the less said about these matters, the better.' And his Catholic friends were equally circumspect. Respectable people kept their heads down and lit their fires in the drawing rooms behind their orchards and their high walls and hoped the politicians would sort the country out. By and large, these people kept off the streets, cowed by the lawlessness of the country. They just hoped it would all go away.

So Mills found himself increasingly incensed at the cowardly reaction of respectable people in Cork at the growing power of the Republicans. The natural enemies of the revolution were like rabbits paralysed when they know that a dog is near. To his sensibility, this was capitulation before the forces of evil. If this kind of appeasement was to be the norm for a so-called civilized society, then he would be better off getting on the steam packet and sailing away from Cork forever. Because, what the so-called respectable people were doing was handing the country over to the murderers and then letting them do what they liked with it. The ruthless were set to win the day.

So, for the first time since coming to Cork, he felt that the prophecy of his invisibility was indeed being fulfilled. People avoided him, as if he was now a victim and they did not want to be associated with victims. In Blackrock, where quiet decency reigned, Mills, despite all his efforts, was an outsider once again. Enormous damage had been done to horticulture in Cork and nobody seemed to care; the people of the city were terrified. As one man said to him: 'there are more important things in life than red roses and good carrots.'

But Mills cared. If he was an outsider, then he had an outsider's naivety and fearlessness. He was not going to let a crowd of hoodlums in from the hills get away with destroying his life's work and the legacy he was trying to leave for the next generation.

So he did what very few in Cork were prepared to do at the time. He reported the arson attack to the police. In fact, he made two visits to Union Quay police barracks and gave the full details of the Sinn Feiners that presaged the attack, even to the extent of giving Mahony's name. As a result, Mahony was arrested the following day.

What he did not realize was that both his visits to the barracks were noted by IRA spies and that the very officer he gave his statement to was in regular contact with IRA intelligence. So Mills's statement was in IRA hands almost before it was filed in RIC records. By giving Mahony's name and describing the others he was now officially labelled a spy.

What he did not also realize was that the IRA increasingly needed new enemies to shoot, that is to say, enemies that were easy to shoot, in order to keep pressure on the British. (Soldiers and police were being confined to barracks, which meant that civilians believed to be loyal to the Crown such as ex-soldiers and loyalists, especially Protestants, were increasingly being targeted.) Mills was now an official 'informer'. He was also a Freemason and was equally unaware that since the start of the year the IRA had managed to compile lists of the leading Freemasons in the city with a view to holding them hostages, to be shot in reprisal for British executions and attacks. Mills felt safe enough, even after he had reported the burning, but this was an illusion.

15

'Why can't they get somebody else to do it?' I'm always the fool who's left to bury them.'

Dinny was in the forge with Ned Murphy, shifting nervously from foot to foot. He spoke in a rapid whisper for he knew the first farmers, who were still at the creamery, would begin to arrive at ten o'clock to get horses shod or gates made or axles turned or wheelbands put on carts. Then he would have to hold his tongue.

'I don't know, Dinny.' Ned Murphy was working the bellows and piling charcoal on the fire and stoking it into a red hot mound. His face and arms were black as the hob he was stoking and he wore a huge leather apron that made him look like a fat old woman baking cakes in a filthy kitchen.

'I tell ya something, Ned. I'm sick of being a bloody gravedigger. I'm fed up rooting in holes and throwing people into them and firing earth in on top of them. I'm the spademan of the republic and it's doing me no good, I can tell you.'

'You'll get used to it, or at least so I'm told,' Ned Murphy said.

'That's what Jim Blake said too. But I'm not getting used to it. In fact, it's getting worse. I've heard of Tommies getting to hate their officers in the trenches. I'm going that way now. I can't even stand the sight of Dan Donohoe at this stage. I don't know if I can face going up there again, Ned, if you want to know the truth.'

Ned looked at Dinny out of the corner of his eye, while sizing up a length of iron to fashion into a horseshoe.

'What are you saying, boy?'

'I can't do it anymore. I can't do it and that's all there is to it.'

'Is it the burials or the killings?'

'The burials and the killings. I have no idea in the world who these people are and what they've done. And I'll tell you something else: it's no easy job getting up in the morning and tackling a horse when the night before you saw some fella's brains being scattered all over the rushes. I'll have to live with that for the rest of my life.' Dinny fidgeted nervously. 'I'm no good at it now. That's what it comes down to. I can't sleep, I can hardly eat. The last time, I had to drink half a bottle of whiskey to do it. The stuff cut my stomach in two, but I slugged it back in spite of myself. My nerves are getting at me, Ned.'

'You only think that, boy.'

'I don't just think it. I know it.'

'What do you think you should do?'

'I need to get away from here, away from the Rea. I hear they're talking about setting up a flying column. I asked Donohoe about it and said I wanted to join, but he fobbed me off. He said that columns were a useless waste of time. He said O'Hegarty was off in Mid-Cork setting one up but that there would be no place for me in it. Anyway, he made it sound like a cod of a job. Then I asked about East Cork and he nearly laughed in my face.'

Ned Murphy picked up half a dozen iron bars and stuck them into the fire.

'Maybe it's not all that simple.' He turned the bellows again. The heat in the charcoal changed from red to orange to white and ate its way up into the iron bars.

'This is not what I had in mind when I set out to free Ireland,' Dinny said.

'Listen. There are dozens of lads around, especially in the city, who have no problem in blowing people's heads off and leaving bodies strewn all over the place. But that's not Dan Donohoe's orders. We have to do the Intelligence end of things. That's our job. We're under the direct control of the organization in the city. We have to deal with the spies, do the trials and interrogations and so on. You must remember these people are vermin.'

'Aw, come on, Ned. We're the brigade's dumping ground, that's what we are. Dan Donohoe is the brigade's executioner. If there are trials and interrogations going on, then why don't we see any of them around here?'

'But they are going on. They're going on elsewhere. We get the prisoners after they've already been tried and sentenced. You mightn't see that, but that's what's happening.'

'Hmm.' Dinny remained unconvinced.

'I'm afraid, getting rid of the bodies is part of our duty. The Republic will thank us.'

Ned Murphy took the first of the orange glowing bars from the fire and with a heavy hammer began to beat it like rubber over the anvil. Flakes of metal fell like shooting stars extinguished on the pile of grey filings beneath.

'Okay, let's look at this sensibly.' The iron bar was now horseshoe-shaped. Ned flattened it with several more blows of the hammer and got a punch and began punching holes in it. 'You want to know about flying columns. I'll tell you about flying columns.' He looked out the forge door in case anybody was eavesdropping.

'You didn't realize it, but you stumbled into a bit of a minefield when you asked Dan Donohoe about a column.'

'I did?'

'As far as I know it's like this.' Ned Murphy shaped the ends of the horseshoe and stuck it into a trough of dirty water to cool it. There was a hiss and a cloud of steam rose in the air. He left the shoe where it was and folded his arms and began to speak in earnest.

'You see, Dinny, the Brigade is setting up a column and Dan Donohoe was right when he told you it will operate west of the city. I think there's a belief that operations in West and Mid-Cork are safer than they'd be here. Also, the people are believed to be more, how shall I put it, favourable to the cause, if you follow me. Sinn Fein and the Gaelic League and so forth have always had more support in places like Ballyvourney, Inchigeela and Coolea than they have had around here. Now it's

107

my belief that there's just as much activity around here as goes on in the west. Reading the papers, I would say that Crown casualties are just as high here as they are in West Cork, probably higher. Of course, the enemy is much stronger here and that provides more targets.'

'Soft targets, anyway.'

'Except that Sean O'Hegarty doesn't think so. The Gaffer is in love with the crowd in mid-Cork. His people come from there. All the big skirmishes are being planned for there and all the arms and so on are being channelled west.'

'But that will leave us very exposed.'

'Exactly. There's been absolute ructions over it. O'Hegarty and the boys from Midleton have been coming to blows over this. The Gaffer and Diarmuid Hurley hate each other as much at this stage as either of them hate the British. The boys down east feel they've been betrayed by O'Hegarty.'

'That sounds bad.'

'It gets worse. Didn't Hurley hold him captive in Midleton for three days and three nights.'

'Jesus!'

'Could you credit that; Hurley captures the commanding officer of the entire Cork Brigade and holds him to threaten him that he wants sanction for his own brigade. The Irish, you see, were always better at fighting between themselves than they ever were at fighting the British. Eventually the Gaffer is released. But he can't do a thing about Hurley. They're as stubborn as a pair of oul mules. He's up in Cork and heading west and Hurley is down in Midleton. Hurley's lads will stand by him no matter what O'Hegarty says. So the Gaffer has to cool his heels.

'To cut a long story short, Hurley's battalion has been more or less ignored by Brigade HQ. They're operating independently, with no support from anyone. He's been left to his own devices but he has no weapons to speak of. Because they've all gone west. They're hopping in Midleton over it. After all, it was they who took them off the British themselves in the first place. And Tadhg Manley is in jail. They've fought a war for the past twelve months, before anyone else even started, and this is the thanks they get.'

'Where's Hurley now?'

'Laying low somewhere around Midleton, I'd imagine. I think O'Hegarty sees him as a bit of a loose cannon. Well, if he is, he's a decent and upright one. And he's had a lot of success with little help from anyone. He's attacked and destroyed half a dozen barracks, from Carrigtwohill to Castlemartyr with absolutely no support from outside.'

Dinny was appalled to hear that senior officers of the Brigade could fight so much between themselves. But he wasn't surprised. What he was hearing now about Sean O'Hegarty only confirmed what he had always heard about him: that he was a hard officious sort of fellow who jealously guarded his own patch with something approaching complete paranoia.

'What about Dan Donohoe?'

'We're in a funny position here because Dan Donohoe has always been O'Hegarty's man. It's the Cobh versus Midleton rivalry, you know yourself, parish pump stuff. So we're kind of a half way house. The rift is wide and we're slap bang in the middle of it. I'll give you two words of advice when it comes to Dan Donohoe: don't run O'Hegarty down to his face and don't praise Hurley. Keep your mouth shut and you'll be all right. But asking Dan Donohoe how to get into Hurley's column is like asking the devil how to get into heaven. You'll get no answer, or if you do, it'll be the wrong one.'

Dinny heard the sound of tackle and the grind of wheel bands on the road outside. 'Someone's coming.'

'I'll tell you what we'll do,' Ned Murphy whispered, 'if you want to get out of this business, I'll keep my ear to the ground. If I hear anything, I'll put in a spake for you. I'm sure with a push we can find someone else to do the burying. What's more, the way things are going, there'll be less of a need for getting rid of bodies now, most companies are more than happy to leave them lying where they're shot.'

'At least they'll get a Christian burial that way.' Dinny looked towards the door.

'I don't think the Christian side of it would worry Dan Donohoe too much.'

There was a long shadow in the light of the doorway. It was Tom Forde, a local farmer with an old wheel rake to be repaired. He came from a mountainy townland, not too far from Dinny's, his legs were long and thin like a cowboy's.

'Am I interrupting something?' he asked.

'Not at all, Tom, come on in,' Ned laughed. 'We were just talking about this and that, you know, passing the time.'

16

It was the beginning of winter and Dinny was working in the outhouse in a cloak of inky dark, cutting turnips for the cows and yearlings. It was half-past seven but he liked to work outside as late as possible. He was finding it difficult being in the presence of his family; their questioning silence and careful conversation were making him sullen and withdrawn. He fed the cows with sliced turnips, climbed a bench of hay and sharpened a hay knife and, with long thrusts, began to cut enough for the following day. He had carved out ten feet when his father came from the house to call him.

'There are visitors inside for you, boy.'

'Visitors?'

'John McCarthy and a few others. They want to talk to you.' His father scratched his head under his hat. 'They won't tell me what it's all about. It seems I'm of no use to them. You're the only one they want to talk to. That's what they say, anyway. Looks like you're an important man now, hah?' his father said more in resignation than bitterness.

Dinny stuck the knife into the bench.

'We'll see.'

There were six visitors waiting for him when he went inside: three men, including Jim Barry, another neighbour, and Tom Forde, the farmer he had met at the forge the morning he had his discussion with Ned Murphy, and three women in shawls and bonnets. It appeared to be some kind of delegation of locals, with John McCarthy, their next-door neighbour, acting as spokesman.

His mother was making tea and looking anxious, preparing sandwiches for the visitors. It felt like confession on Good Friday. The men were tense. The women were quiet but fidgety.

'No thanks, Mary,' John McCarthy said, 'a cup in the hand will do us fine.'

'You know everyone here,' his father said as they came through the door. 'They want to talk to you about something. The best thing for you to do is go down to the Room. You'll have privacy there. I'll go out and get a few sods of turf and light the fire. Then you can go ahead with your discussion.'

'Thanks, Denis,' John McCarthy said.

Now Dinny felt nervous. He looked from one to another of his neighbours but none of them would look him in the eye. Whatever was going on, it seemed to be pretty serious, for the neighbours, in particular the women, huddled close to one another as if they had just seen a ghost. It struck him that he might well be the ghost himself. His mother led them into the Room, which contained all the best furniture and the best cutlery and delph. The Room was musty; it was rarely used. It was kept especially for visitors, though visitors rarely went in there, except for the Station Mass or the occasional visit of the priest. The only time it was fully used was for dinner on Christmas Day.

'Take a seat there, all of you and make yerselves at home. If ye want more tea, I'll be in the kitchen,' she said.

His father too had become uneasy and didn't know what to say. He busied himself by lighting the fire. He rolled a few pieces of newspaper and some kippins and within minutes he had a good blaze going. Then he gave John McCarthy a bucket of turf.

'Throw that on as soon as it needs it. There's a good draught in that chimney.'

'There's a good draught in it all right,' John McCarthy said, trying to keep up the small talk.

'I can't interest anyone in a drop, I suppose?' the father said. 'Or a drop of sherry for the ladies?'

The visitors shook their heads.

'Good enough, then. Stay for as long as ye like. Ye know yeer always welcome in this house.'

112

'We know that, Denis.'

Then father and mother departed and Dinny was left alone with the neighbours. They looked at him and looked at each other and each was reluctant to speak, as if whatever they had to say was too big for any one mouth to deliver. When nothing was forthcoming but a deluge of unease, Dinny took the initiative. He was, after all, a soldier of the Republic and soldiers of the Republic have to be decisive.

'Well, what can I do for you?'

'You talk to him, John,' one of the women whispered and nudged John McCarthy forward.

'Yes, well, em, I've been nominated to talk to you, Dinny. We know you're a nice boy, so you may listen to us when others will not.' John McCarthy hung out his words delicately as if they were sodden clothes put out to dry in the tense air. He rolled his cap in his hand.

'You see, Dinny, we can't do the threshing.'

'You can't do the threshing? Why?'

'Well, we can't stand in the yard below with the smell.'

'The smell?'

''Tis overpowering, Dinny. Nobody could stand it. There's bodies buried in the quarry below. I don't know, the gravel must have shifted or something. I wouldn't go in there. You see, things have been happening, Dinny, people have been seeing things and...well, let's just say it's...it's very bad. So we all decided to get together and tell you ourselves. There's talk of ghosts and things and...well...' he turned to the women behind him. 'I think I should let these three ladies tell you themselves.'

Han Murphy, Mary Shea and Babe Roche stood behind John McCarthy and the other men. They were threading Rosary beads through their hands and their faces were white as fresh snow and they were clearly petrified as if they had seen a legion of the dead five minutes before they walked into the house.

'Tell him what you saw, Babe.' John McCarthy said.

Babe Roche looked up from her beads. She seemed the most forthcoming of the three.

'There were rumours, you see,' she said.

'But we didn't believe them at first,' Mary Shea said.

'We don't listen to rumours,' Han Murphy said. 'If you were to believe everything you hear ...'

'You see, we were at the dinner over at home today,' Babe Roche went on. Dinny noticed that none of the women were able to speak his name, though they knew him nearly as well as they knew their own families. 'When Han turned up. She was in the most desperate state, weren't you, Han?'

'I was indeed,' said Han.

'Their dog Shep, Murphy's dog, that is, brought something into the yard. Han's brother Pad went out, didn't he, Han?'

'He did.'

'The dog had,' Babe said finally, 'the dog had, the dog had ... a human hand in his mouth and he was ... he was eating it.'

'Han came over to us straight away,' Mary Shea said. 'Didn't you, Han? We heard the rumours that someone had been shot in the sandpit above in Murphy's land.'

'That's on our land, alright,' Han Murphy said. 'A disused sandpit.'

'So to cut a long story short, we all went up together to the sandpit. And it was terrible, there were two of them and one of them was there a lot longer than the other one. And the smell! We had to cancel the potato picking in the next field.'

'People have been seeing ghosts too,' John McCarthy said, 'and strange lights up in the Rea at night. And there's all these rumours and now it seems they're true.'

'Rumours?'

'Rumours that the IRA people are carrying out executions up in the Rea almost every night of the week.'

Dinny said nothing.

'This can't go on. People are in dread of their lives; people are afraid to go out at night for fear of what they'll see. People are afraid to walk certain roads even in the middle of the day in case they'll be shot; now they're afraid to go into their own fields in case they'd turn up something terrible.'

114

John McCarthy was gesticulating with his hands as if he was de Valera himself delivering a speech at a political rally.

'When these ladies came to see me today, I decided to ask around, to see if other people knew anything. I can't say I was too surprised at what I found. So, to cut a long story short, we decided to organize a delegation to see you. We know you're a Volunteer.'

Then Tom Forde stepped forward and said: 'Jim came across another body in his own land above by the Rea last month. Isn't that right, Jim?'

Jim Barry, the other farmer, then spoke. 'I thought it was someone trying to carry out pishogues by burying a calf,' he said slowly. 'Then when I sank the shovel into the earth I saw that it was a dead man, so I covered him up and said nothing to anybody until today. I wanted to call the priest but I was afraid I'd get into trouble.'

'When was that?'

'Over a month ago.'

'And then Jer Long was out with the beagles last Sunday week and he came across a body in a fox covert over by Ballybrickeen Bridge.'

'God knows how many of these there are,' John McCarthy said. 'And then people are seeing lights and hearing shots and cars are passing in the middle of the night. There's black work going on, Dinny, right in our midst, and we can't help knowing about it.'

Dinny bit his lip. On the one hand, he could deny everything about the killings. On the other hand, he felt he had a responsibility as an soldier of the Republic to listen to what the people had to say and to do his best to assuage their fears. He decided to take the line Dan Donohoe would take, even though he wasn't too happy about it.

'This is war,' he said. 'They were British soldiers.'

'Except that they didn't have any uniforms on,' Jim Barry said.

'Except for one,' Han said.

'They're enemies, though.' Dinny was under pressure and was surprised at himself for trying to justify the killings.

'What about this?' John McCarthy stretched his hand out to Jim Barry who handed him something. It was a brown Rosary beads with a weathered silver cross.

'This came off the body above in my land.' Jim Barry said. 'I wanted to leave it with him but it just kept coming to the surface so I said it was safer to take it. I hid it under a stone for the last few weeks.'

'That unfortunate man was a Catholic Irishman,' John McCarthy said.

'I don't know anything about that. I don't know everything that's going on around here. People from different areas are coming and dumping bodies around here. These are terrible times. He was probably an informer. There are a lot of dangerous characters about.'

'People are afraid, some even suggested we go to the police.'

'And draw the peelers down on top of us?' I hope you didn't do anything like that. That would be a very bad idea.'

'We didn't, because, again, we were too afraid.'

'There is a new authority in the country now,' Dinny said, falling back on Republican rhetoric to try to defuse the situation. 'And I agree, this is a matter of the gravest urgency. It is a matter to be brought before the Sinn Fein courts.'

'You must try to stop it, Dinny. We don't care how you do it. It's very hard to keep on living here with this sort of thing going on all around us.'

'I'll see what I can do.'

'Talk to Dan Donohoe, Dinny. He has a lot of influence with the IRA, so we're told.'

'He may have influence or he may not. All I know is that I don't have any influence. But as I say, he's just the local man. There may be outsiders involved too.'

'Just promise us you'll do your best to put a stop to it, Dinny, will you?'

'That I will promise. You have my word on it. But whatever you do, don't dream of going to the police. The people who do these things are not to be messed with. I'm saying that for your own good.'

'We know that. Thanks, Dinny.'

'It's just that I'm not sure my intervention will make any difference.'

'We'll go now, Dinny. You can only do your best, boy.'

John McCarthy stood up and the women smiled at Dinny, relieved to be unburdened of their grim knowledge. It was almost as if he and they had become normal neighbours once again.

'One more thing,' Dinny said, 'before you go. I want you to take me to these bodies, if you think ye can manage it. I'll have to organize a burial for them. We can't have corpses lying about the place like that.'

'Oh, thanks Dinny. We knew you wouldn't let us down. We knew you'd see the sense of what we're saying.'

He felt sympathy for these decent people and shame that they should have to come to him on a matter like this. They were simple people; inarticulate in matters of complexity and decorum; they were blameless in the situation they found themselves in. He felt warmth towards them and pity for them and pity for himself, and he didn't know which was worse.

The visitors headed out into the darkness with their storm lamps. Dinny followed them. John McCarthy and the three women walked with him as far as the sandpit. He was surprised at their courage, which contrasted with that of Tom Forde and Jim Barry, who scampered home as quickly as they could on one excuse or another.

When they reached the sandpit, a thick mist was roiling in over the high sand banks. The wind whistled in the tufty grass along the ridges. Dinny felt vaguely nauseous.

'There they are, over there,' Babe Roche said, pointing.

Suddenly an overpowering stench hit him. It seemed that rotting flesh was everywhere. There was rustling in the bushes as a rat sprinted up the bank.

'I can't go in there,' Han Murphy said. 'I can't bear to see them again.'

'I'm not going in either,' Mary Shea said.

'Well in that case, keep one storm lamp and wait here.' John McCarthy said. 'Will you show us, Babe?'

'I don't want to go,' Babe Roche said. 'But I suppose I'll have to.'

The three of them, Babe Roche, John McCarthy and Dinny went into the back of the sandpit and there, growing into the circle of light made by the storm lamp, were two bodies, one sitting on a mound; the other thrown on his face about five feet away. The one on the mound was partially decomposed, the sockets of his skull staring into space, perched like a decayed monarch on a throne of sand.

'He's been there a good while, from the look of him,' John McCarthy said.

'Oh, my good God,' Babe Roche said, putting her hand up to her mouth. 'Would you look at that. I don't believe it.'

The other corpse was that of a man in his thirties. He had obviously just recently been dumped there, for there were spots of fresh blood on the sand around him and a neat hole was drilled in the back of his skull. A stained red handkerchief was tied around his head.

'Would you look at that,' Babe Roche said again. 'He had boots on this morning. Now they're gone. And, God between us and all harm, he had a pocket watch too. I remember it as sure as day. It was hanging out of his waistcoat there, just there. Now that's gone too. Somebody must have come and taken the boots and the pocket watch since we were here this morning.' Babe blessed herself in the light of the lamp. 'What kind of person would do a thing like that?'

'Are you sure about that, Babe?' Dinny asked.

'Sure? I'm as sure as I am that I got up this morning. It was just there. And he had those grand boots, fine new boots. The poor fella. God between us and all harm.' Babe blessed herself again and took out her beads and began to pray.

Dinny was puzzled. This did not seem to be Dan Donohoe's handiwork. Donohoe would be too careful to leave bodies lying around in a place where they could have a bad effect on local morale. One or two bodies were enough to frighten people into silence. Any more and they might start asking awkward questions, like they were doing now.

While Babe Roche prayed, Dinny, with great reluctance, shone a lamp in the direction of the other corpse. This one was dressed in a policeman's uniform. The flesh was partly rotted off his face, his hair a sort of tangled mat on his skull. Marauding animals had eaten almost up to his elbows and he looked like a handless regent surveying a kingdom of darkness.

Dinny took out his handkerchief and put it over his mouth to lessen the stench. It was then that he noticed the sugáns tied around the shrunken knees of the dead man and he felt the gall rise inside of him. He bent over double and vomited all over the sandy ground.

'The poor old Sergeant,' he said when he finally finished throwing up. 'He might have been a policeman but he wasn't a bad auld devil.'

'What's that?' John McCarthy asked, surprised.

Dinny felt tears coming into his eyes.

'And I thought he was going to be released' was all he could say. 'What a fool I was.'

When Babe Roche saw how upset Dinny was, she put her arm around him and brought him out onto the road. Then the women stood around him in a circle and tried to console him by telling him there were no victors, only victims, in this war, as in all wars, and that they were all victims and that things would improve when this was all over. They promised to pray and do Novenas and get Masses said for the dead men. Finally, he told them to go home and thanked them for their concern.

'Will you be okay?' Babe Roche asked.

'I'll be okay.'

They went to John McCarthy's house for a spade and returned to the sandpit and, with John holding the lamp, Dinny climbed to the top of the sand face above the two corpses. He furiously attacked the dune grass that grew there and cut a deep trench. Using the spade as a lever, he set off a landslide of sand and gravel to cover the corpses from the elements and the marauding predators of the night, both human and animal.

Then he and John said a decade of the Rosary. When they had finished, he headed for Corrigans, where he knew some of the IRA men were drinking, to discuss the concerns of the locals with Dan Donohoe. When he couldn't find him there, he went home again where he lay in bed for another sleepless night.

If he hadn't been so distracted when he called to the pub, he would have noticed that Con Foley was wearing new boots and he was flashing a new pocket watch around the place. He didn't notice it then, nor did he notice it later, and it was probably just as well.

17

It was a bleak morning in late-November. Dan Donohoe was in Cork, walking along Lavett's Quay, watching the gulls squabbling over bits of sewage in the river. The Lee was as green as pea soup or fresh lettuce. A cold breeze whistled down the chimney pots from Blarney Street and people going to work huddled from the wind. Donohoe could never get used to this city; it was full of loyalists and spies and go-by-the-walls. Sly cornerboys hung around every street corner, barefoot urchins played in the dirt, runny-nosed women in shawls sold stiff fish and pale chickens from prams on the Coal Quay.

These were dringeán people. He might not be very tall himself, but he knew the strength he had in his shoulders from years of work. But these were a weedy race, these dwarfs of the tenements, stunted pygmies living in the dingy clothes-drying squalor of the backstreets. Poverty made spies out of everyone. The IRA men in the city, by contrast, were brave and few in number; he could count them on the fingers of two hands. And they were braver still because they had to live in this pit of beggary. They had to be able to see above the poverty, rise above the slums, they had to be able to envisage an Ireland free and do something about it. These were the active squad. There were less than a dozen of them but they did more damage than legions of troops.

In his own situation, of course, in the countryside, it was easy enough, the rebels had the support of the people, by and large. And if they didn't, that was easily enough sorted out. In the city, people were already having enough of a struggle, trying to put a bite in their mouths, without having to worry about the future of Ireland. Where life is cheap, principles are even cheaper.

Dan Donohoe thought of the women on the quays having to sell their bodies to feed their children. That was the state of affairs with Ireland; we sell our bodies and sell our souls to the enemy to stay barely alive. It was a situation that could not be allowed to continue.

He walked to Patrick's Bridge where a soldier looked him over, but let him pass. Donohoe had his revolver strapped inside his boot. He would have been shot on the spot if it was found on him. What he was doing was dangerous, but the best form of defence was to be out there, right among them, laughing and joking. Then they'd never suspect you. The Irish could always laugh in the face of their oppression.

He remembered five years earlier walking along Patrick Street. He was younger then, naive, a mere country gorsoon, and was nearly tricked into joining the British Army by a crafty recruiting sergeant. The recruiting sergeant, a man called Mohally, who was now high on the IRA's hit list, tried to slip a shilling into his pocket. That was in 1914. If he had been found with the shilling he would have been obliged to join up. That had happened to Andy Dunlea, a neighbour of his, a man with a young family. He had been tricked into joining the British Forces and was never seen again; he was killed in action in Gallipoli.

That was Dan Donohoe's first exposure to the duplicity of the British. And then there was the biggest betrayal of all: in 1916, when the Cork Volunteers were tricked into handing their arms over to the Lord Mayor by the Bishop, the wily bastard Danny Boy, on the promise that they would not be passed on to the authorities. Of course, they were. Another promise broken. You couldn't trust John Bull's men or their agents. You couldn't even trust a bishop. There would be no peace in Ireland until every last one of the buggers was cleared out or put down.

As he walked, the city was waking up, the people were beginning to go about their business, the shutters of shops were coming off, the pavements swept, the horse dung cleaned up, the awnings clattered into place. Oh, city of dreams, of sadness and poverty, of beggary and banks, of the needy indigent people, a sub-race of the noble rural Irish. They should really be left to stew in their own alien malice, these people who lived off the British shilling in the vicinity of barracks, Dan Donohoe thought. With their sly ways and their back-street cunning they should be left to rot. However, when we save Ireland, we will save you too and even you will benefit from the glory that is to come, even if you don't deserve it.

Dan Donohoe looked in the shop windows. The Cork Holly Bough was already for sale, a Christmas newspaper with a dark red cover that was bought by everyone though the title was owned by loyalists. Decorations were going up in shops. Santas were beginning to appear, Christmas fripperies, when important business had to be done. Cork's commercial life; owned by the lackeys of the Crown, and they weren't all Protestants either, not by a long chalk. Witness the crowd who were running the spy ring out of the GPO, before they were sorted out by the men of the Brigade, bastards and Catholics to a man. The thing is, the loyalists kept down the poor. They would have to go too, go or be pushed, those lickspittles of the Empire. The poor would still be there when all this was over. It would take more than a revolution to get rid of the poor.

He made his way through the narrow streets, through the legions of the mendicant poor with their baskets and boxes looking for donations, to the garage run by Jim Blake and his brother Miah.

When he went into the garage, he found Jim in a back room at work on a Crossley Tender he had taken from two Black and Tans at Johnson and Perrots. (The two Black and Tans were long since stretched in the Rea.) He was trying to repair the chassis and turn it into an armoured car. Fanbelts, fuel pipes, spanners and gear wheels hung from the walls. The floor was covered with engine oil. Jim Blake ignored him and continued to tinker with the car.

In ones and twos the men turned up, furtive in their long coats, guarding against the wind, hiding their weapons. After they were seated, Dan Donohoe asked rhetorically: 'Where's Sean O'Hegarty tonight?' Sean O'Hegarty was a gentleman, a good gaffer; he sent down the spies; loyalists, lackeys, soldiers and Tans, and asked no awkward questions. 'Where's Florrie?'

The reality, of course, was that Dan Donohoe didn't give a damn where Sean O'Hegarty was, or Florrie O'Donohoe or any of the legion of pen-pushers from Dublin to Bantry. He was warlord of his own patch. Didn't Sean O'Hegarty himself put it in a nutshell to him when he said, 'The English are the boss now. But if we win, then you'll get East Cork. You'll be the boss then.'

'Sean O'Hegarty is back in Ballyvourney, organizing the column. That's where he is. And Florrie's in England. On a secret mission.'

Of course, some day politics would return. And, when it did, a political future could best be made in terms of the number of Crown forces put out of action. Status in Dan Donohoe's view was best achieved by chalking up as many enemy killings as possible. In the absence of ambushes or spectacular escapades, direct action with the enemy was hard to come by. And while Sing Sing provided a number of low and middle ranking policemen and soldiers, the number was not significant.

It had to be augmented to gain the respect of his leaders and the people. Dan Donohoe had to produce more dead British soldiers and Tans than were available to him through the channels of the city IRA. And the easiest way to do that was to assign a soldier's rank and regiment to every spy who was sent to him. That way, he could outgun even Tom Barry by some margin. Throw in a few ex-servicemen who were, in his phrase, 'lower than a snake's balls' and a handful of loyalists and tramps, and you had your soldiers, your army and your enemy.

'Could I call the meeting to order?' Mick Twomey, the local battalion commander, said. 'Are we agreed that we have the fighters but we don't have the hardware?'

The men nodded their assent.

'And we're agreed that Dublin doesn't give a shit about us?'

Again they all agreed.

'So we'll have to take matters into our own hands. With a bit of luck, Mick Leahy's visit to Italy will help and your bomb factory should make a useful contribution too.' (Dan Donohoe was supposed to be building a bomb factory underground to make grenade casings but they were having difficulty in getting the foundry temperatures high enough to make the iron hot enough to pour.)

'There's no good in raiding barracks anymore. The ones that aren't burnt out are too heavily guarded. But we should still do our best to snipe at all armed posts as often as possible. To remind the enemy that we're here and give his morale a bit of a rattle.'

'But the Special Operations Unit is going to be even more important now, as we'll see in a minute. And I'm not talking about the bomb factory.'

Jim Blake tapped his box of Player's Number 1 on the palm of his hand to get out a cigarette. 'What are we going to do about this?' He shoved a slip of paper across the table to Twomey.

'I was about to come to that, Jim,' Mick Twomey said, picking up the sheet of paper and brandishing it in the air. 'You all know what this is, don't you? But just in case any of you are living in cloud cuckoo land, this is the famous dispatch from His Majesty's Government to the effect that, within the Martial Law area, anybody found carrying arms is liable to be shot on sight. We all know the implication of this dispatch.'

'Sure, they're doing it already.'

'They are, but this gives it official sanction. We have to make an adequate response.'

'That's easy. We'll increase the pressure on them.' Pete Cronin said. 'Any Crown personnel, either armed or unarmed, is a legitimate target. We do what they do; shoot 'em on sight.'

'Sure, aren't we doing that already.' Jim Blake said. Sometimes Dan Donohoe thought Jim Blake was a bit on the thick side.

'You're doing it, Jim.' They all laughed.

'There's an old proverb; you poison the chicken to kill the fox. That summarizes what we do more than anything else.'

'Through the chair. I feel Sean O'Hegarty is making a mistake spending so much time and energy organizing columns.' Dan Donohoe said. 'We'll have too many men in the one place and they'll be too exposed.'

'But look at Tom Barry, look at Kilmichael,' Pete Cronin said.

'Kilmichael's all right. But the enemy wasn't expecting it then. Besides, what was Tom Barry doing there? He was outside his own brigade area. He was in our area, trying to make a big splash, that's what he was. The Gaffer didn't take too kindly to that.'

Dan Donohoe had met Tom Barry only once. He didn't have too much time for him. He had this fancy accent that he had picked up in the British Army and he had a greatly inflated opinion of himself. He was Field-Marshal Barry, the Kitchener of West Cork, though it didn't do to say so, now that he was a hero after blowing away fifteen or sixteen Auxies.

'I don't care what Tom Barry has done. Tom Barry's been lucky so far. Keep it as small as possible, that's the only way to beat the enemy, in my view.'

'I think what Dan is saying,' Mick Twomey said, 'and I have to say I agree with him, is that, in the long run, the grenade and the mine are far more effective weapons than the flying columns. The bomb is the man for the future. You plant it, you set it and you make yourself scarce.'

Mick Twomey tapped the desk with his pipe for emphasis. 'Now there's something else we need to discuss. Can I bring the discussion back to this other document here,' he said, reaching into his pocket for another sheet of paper. This was one of the Brigade lists: a list of spies, informers and Crown personnel who were to be considered for assassination or execution. It could vary in content from actual spies like the bastard Quinlisk, who was trying to track down Michael Collins, right down to the most lowly ex-soldier who might have said the wrong thing to the wrong person in the wrong public place at the wrong time.

'What happened last July?'

Mick smoked steadily. He was a big man, six and a half feet tall and broad as a gate. He had a square handsome face and was a noted hurler. He had shot Quinlisk himself – turned the bastard around and gave him a few more in the face – and many others, including Monkey Mac and the syphilis-ridden Walsh outside the South Infirmary. The pipe gave him an avuncular easy-going appearance, though he was far from easy-going.

'So what happened last July, lads?'

They all looked at him blankly.

'What happened in July was that the Orange bastards in Belfast started murdering our people and driving them out of their homes. A hundred people were murdered in cold blood. Are you with me?'

'I know all about those lads.' Dan Donohoe, said. 'From my time in Crumlin Road Gaol. I have first-hand experience of the sound of loyalist mobs and they baying for blood.'

'Ten thousand had to flee their homes.'

'Sean O'Hegarty said to leave the Protestants in Cork alone,' Pete Cronin said.

'And why? Not through any great love for them but because, he says, we'll have to live with them when this is all over. I'm quoting his very words. And he's right, he's absolutely right. We're soldiers, and soldiers obey orders. And I'll be the first to admit that GHQ in Dublin agree with this, they want us to keep away from the Protestants per se. Dick Mulcahy says we're not to be seen as sectarian, if you know what I mean. Our quarrel is with the British Government, not with the Protestants, and that's true enough.'

'No person shall be regarded as enemies of Ireland, whether they be described as Unionist, Orangemen, etc, unless they are actively anti-Irish in their actions. Those are GHQ's official orders and Sean O'Hegarty subscribes to them,' Mick Twomey said. 'We are not sectarian.' He paused. The men listened.

'Now of course, if we were to wait on GHQ for everything, we'd still be farting around on our backsides like we were in 1916 and '17 and '18. Wait for Dublin to make a decision and you can throw your hat at it. Now I happen to agree that we'll have to live with the Protestants if we get the British out. But that doesn't mean we have to treat them like schoolchildren in the meantime. Do ye follow me?

There were no dissensions.

'Now there are people who will tell you that the Protestants don't do any spying for the British for the very simple reason that they don't have any information to give. That, down here, they're shitless about us. And that's a good argument. In fact, I'm of the opinion that our own Catholic neighbours and indeed some of our own members may well turn out to be the worst informers on the cause. Up until now we've killed whoever had to be killed, plugged whoever had to be plugged and we did it without reference to their religion.'

'Except that Sean O'Hegarty is away and I'm in charge. And I have here, in the heel of my fist, actual concrete proof of certain groups who have been actively spying for the Crown.'
'We hardly have the door closed on the GPO crowd when now this turns up. You've heard of the Young Men's Christian Association, the YMCA? Well, I have it here that these so-called Christians, the Junior Section, I may add, are being paid a basic rate of ten pounds a week for spying and that there's a reward of forty pounds for information leading to the capture of prominent IRA personnel, that's us, boys, and what's more, there's a further fifty for information leading to the capture of Sean O'Hegarty. Now what I'm suggesting is that this constitutes anti-Irish activity of the worst and most serious kind. I think we can safely assume that Sean O'Hegarty and GHQ would be behind us if we decided to shut down this hotbed of spies. Does anybody disagree with this assessment?'

'I say we go get them as soon as possible.'

'I say we burn down the place.'

'I'll go in there with a machine gun,' Jim Blake said, 'and I tell you that by the time I'm finished, there won't be a spy left standing in any YMCA.'

'I say we keep our powder dry, we say nothing, we pick them up in ones or twos and get whatever information we can from them and then, one by one, they all disappear.' Mick Twomey clicked his fingers. 'Sean O'Hegarty himself gave me the go-ahead to pursue this course of action.'

'And there's another thing. Listen carefully. We'll have to do this as quietly as possible, because if we machine-gun the YMCA or burn it down, the bloody Examiner and the Constitution and the press in England will make a meal out of it.'

'I say we machine gun the Examiner office and the Constitution, as well, while we're at it,' Jim Blake said.

'No. I was going to come to that, Bob,' he addressed Bob Lankford, one of the city men, 'you get some men together and sort out the presses of both the Examiner and the Constitution. A few sledgehammers applied to the right places could be a lot more effective than shooting. Can I trust you to do that?'

'No better man.'

'This YMCA is like a wasps' nest. If you get one, he'll lead you to all the rest. We keep cool and they'll all end up in the bogs and not a word will ever be known about what happened to them.'

'That's grand by us, Mick,' Dan Donohoe said. 'We'll look after our end of it.'

'Are we all agreed on that?'

'We're all agreed.'

'Okay, let's go get those Orange bastards.'

The meeting ended with decisions made, strategies worked out. Then the men moved quickly on account of the curfew and some of them spent the night in the back rooms of a brothel on Cornmarket Street. Because of the new regulations of martial law, nobody could move till dawn. The beds changed owners in the morning and the girls who normally slept in them, on returning to their own beds from the boats where they entertained foreign sailors, prayed that the gunmen had not brought in fleas with them.

18

Dinny walked like a man who is asleep into the dim echoing silence of the church and genuflected before the tabernacle. The sound of his hobnailed boots on the tiles seemed loud as a thunderclap, scrape, scrape, then thump on timber. There was no light on, only the sanctuary lamp, the still, hanging eye of God. He got into a pew, knelt down and put his face in his hands. The silence was high and beautiful, the church always reminded Dinny of childhood, of Christmas morning going to the crib, of prayers, hymns and wonder. If God was in the church, then He was a very quiet person, Dinny thought, and yet He was there, in all His towers of silence.

He blessed himself and tried to pray but failed. At the side of the pew was a glass box with half a dozen pennies at the bottom of it. For the Black Babies. He would pray for the Black Babies, except that he didn't think he had the right to pray for anybody. Heaven was cut off from him because of the things he had seen in the Rea. The poor Black Babies. The poor were often here in the church - the poorest were always the holiest - but they were not as poor as he was.

He was woken from his reveries by a low creak as the door at the back of the church opened and two old women in shawls shuffled in. They nodded to him as they passed and made their way towards the front pews and, with arthritic genuflection, knelt down and took out their Rosary beads and began to pray.

'Incline unto my aid, O God. O Lord make haste to help us,' Dinny could hear their whispers in the silence of the church. And he could hear his own heart beating. He tried to pray but his soul was a well with a broken rope. There was nothing in it. He searched the depths to pull up prayers but no prayers came.

He looked up from the cradle of his hands. At Easter when he was a child the sunlight came through the nailed feet of the crucified Christ in the stained glass window. Then he felt hope. But there was no hope now, just an emptying out, a hollow cavern in the space where his soul should have been. And there was no charity, for he wasn't allowed charity. To be charitable would mean he would put his own life in danger and the lives of others. As for love? Well, there was no love, nor could there be, for who could love the burier of still-warm dead men?

There was a second creak. The door opened again and let in another shaft of light. It was the new curate. Dinny felt a surge of relief, for he knew that whatever hope he had of absolution it would have to come from the curate. Bishop Cohalan had finally been as good as his word, and had issued an edict to the effect that anybody involved in political murder or kidnapping would be automatically excommunicated. The parish priest, an intimidating man with a whiskey face and thick glasses, had said that anyone helping the rebels in any way was guilty of grievous mortal sin.

The curate, however, was said to be more sympathetic; IRA men from all over were coming to him to hear their Confession. He was a young man of upright bearing and a strained nobility that was frightening in its pallor and he wore a long cassock that brushed the floor with sweeping drama.

The priest genuflected and knelt on the last pew by the door. He opened a prayer book, took a purple stole from between the pages, kissed it and put it around his neck. The two old ladies looked up from their beads and, seeing who was there, made their way with some difficulty to the seats nearest the confessional. Then they put their heads in their hands and fingered their beads again and began to pray even more fervently than before. Dinny didn't move. He went on staring at the altar. He didn't want to go into the confessional until the old women had gone.

After a few minutes the priest took his watch from his breast pocket and opened it and looked at it and, satisfied that the time was right, stood up, genuflected and entered the confessional by the middle door.

132

Dinny waited. After another few minutes the first of the old women went into one of the cubicles. He could hear the rattle of the shutter being drawn and the mumbling of two voices inside. Then the second woman went in. More rattling, more mumbling and the first woman came out. Finally the second woman came out and all was silence but for the cooing of wood pigeons on the trees outside.

Still Dinny waited. After five minutes, the priest looked out and, seeing that there was nobody else for confession, came out himself, went back to his pew, took out his breviary and began to read again.

Eventually, after what seemed an eternity, the two old women blessed themselves and got up to leave. When they had gone, the priest stood up and came over to where Dinny was kneeling.

'Do you want me to hear your Confession, my son?' he asked quietly.

'Yes, Father,' Dinny whispered.

'We can do it here if you like, or in the confessional.'

'In the confessional, Father, if you don't mind.'

'You are afraid?'

'Yes, Father.'

'God is good. Just remember that.'

The priest gathered up his stole again and put it on and went back into the confession box. Slowly Dinny got up. He felt old and made his way as stiffly as the old women into the cubicle.

The shutter shot open and he could see the priest's profile through the grill, his face leaning into the shadows, his hand up to his forehead. He began to mutter the prayers in Latin. Then he said in English:

'How long has it been since your last confession, my son?'

'Seven, eight months, Father.'

'Seven, eight months! That's a long time. Is there a reason for this?'

'I've been on the run, Father, for a time. And then when I came back, well, I couldn't get myself to go.'

'Was this because of the Bishop's edict?'

'Partly yes and partly no.'

'So you're a Volunteer?'

'Yes, Father.' Dinny knew, because the priest referred to him as a Volunteer, that he would not be too harsh on him. If it had been the parish priest he would sneeringly be referred to as a rebel or a bandit or worse. Words were weapons, as much as any gun. He said he was on the run because it would be easier to explain what he had been doing. While he had not technically been on the run, the priest would understand his position precisely. Besides, it was true in spirit and would save him from having to do too much unnecessary explaining.

'I've done terrible things, Father. Terrible things altogether.'

'Go on, my son.'

'We've been killing them, a lot of them, as many as two or three of them a week over the recent past.'

'Them?'

'Spies, informers, stool pigeons, some policemen and soldiers too, and Tans.'

'Did you know them?'

'I recognized only one. An ex-army man. You might have heard of his disappearance.'

'Was he from this parish?'

'Yes.'

'Hodnett?'

'That's him, Father.'

'And the others, you didn't know any of them?'

'No, Father. That's the problem. They're brought out to us from other places, from the city and God knows where else. We don't know who they are. We keep them in Sing Sing and then we wait for further orders.'

'Sing Sing? What is this?'

'That's what we call it, Father, where we keep them. I'm not at liberty to tell you where it is.' Dinny whispered. 'I'm under a vow of secrecy.'

'That's all right, my son. I don't need to know. What happens then?'

'We wait for orders. Sometimes we are told there are courtmartials. Other times I think the Captain, my commanding officer, just makes up the orders as he goes along. Maybe the Brigade commander gives the orders, I'm not sure.'

'And then?'

'Then we take them up to a place; a bog, Father, and sometimes get them to dig their own graves and shoot them into them or, more likely, I end up having to dig the graves myself.'

'Those are terrible deeds you are doing, my son. They go against all Christian teaching.'

'I know, Father.'

'Do you do the shooting?'

'I don't. At least, I haven't yet. Usually the Captain does it. He's less squeamish about that sort of thing.'

'Would you say he's sparing you?'

'You could say that. Maybe it's that he doesn't trust us to do the job properly. I think he sees us as only cábógs, Father.'

'How many people do you think you have executed in this way?'

'I don't know, Father, fifteen, sixteen. It could be as many as twenty at this stage.'

'Do you interrogate them or torture them?'

'No, Father. They're just sent to us from Cork and it is up to us to do away with them. We are just carrying out orders.'

'What would happen if you refused to carry out these orders?'

'I'd say the Captain would shoot us just as easily as he'd shoot the spies.'

'I've no doubt he would. Are these mostly army people, military officers, you're killing?'

'Mostly spies, Father.'

'Spies? How do you know they're spies?'

'Well, that's what we're told.'

'But you're not sure what spying they've done?'

'I can't say I'd be sure, Father.'

'But they're civilians?'

'They are, Father.' Dinny could hear his own voice whispering in the dry hollow cube of the confessional and it seemed to him to be the voice of a stranger.

'As you know, this is a very grievous matter, particularly in view of what the bishop has said. However, would you say that what you're doing is retaliation?'

'Retaliation?'

'For what the Crown Forces do?'

'It's not necessarily retaliation, Father. It just goes on, like. It was going on since before the Tans came, though of course it was much less frequent then.'

'I'm afraid there's blame on both sides in this conflict. The Crown Forces have been responsible for some terrible atrocities, often against innocent people. Civilians are taking the brunt of this, on both sides.'

'I know, Father.'

'The Church believes there is such a thing as a just war in certain circumstances. In this instance, though, Rome is divided. The Dáil and the British Government have both made representations to His Holiness to take sides. So far, nothing's come of either move. It is my opinion, one I may add I don't share with the Bishop, that this is a just war. Now whether what you are doing is just or not is another matter. In my view, the Lord might not regard it as just, but it is no worse than what the other side is doing.'

'Maybe not, Father. But they are not shooting people they know nothing about in the back of the head and rolling them into holes in the ground, like we do.'

'They're shooting people at random in the streets. They've begun to execute young men in barracks. They've begun drumhead courtmartials. It's the same thing. Maybe you need a rest. You should take a break from this kind of activity.'

'There's no chance of a break and no rest so far as I can see. What I'm afraid of is that I'm committing a mortal sin every time I go out with the boys doing those jobs. Now that we've been excommunicated, how can I ever get back from all those sins? Will there be no forgiveness ever, for any of us? Will I, will we all, burn in hell for all eternity?'

'I'm your confessor. It is up to me to forgive your sins or not forgive them. The Lord has given me the power to forgive any sin. That's at the core of my ministry. Now I'm forgiving yours, do I make myself clear?

'You're giving me absolution?'

'As I see it, you are a soldier. You are following the orders of your commanding officer and he is following the orders of his commanding officer and so on. If they give an order, then it is your duty to obey it. If you are just carrying out orders, orders that you have no choice but to carry out, then I don't see it as a sin as such, however hideous and unchristian the whole business may seem. Your choice is to kill or be killed, if you want to look at it simply. Chaplains of all denominations in the trenches in the Great War had to do this all the time. If you are only following orders, your conscience is clear.' The priest coughed and turned to face Dinny in the confessional so that Dinny could smell food, onions or something, on his breath.

'If, on the other hand, it is your decision to act as judge and jury and if you execute somebody without evidence or without due knowledge of what they had done, then it is on your conscience and it is and will be' - the priest emphasized these words - 'a mortal sin and your soul will be in mortal peril and eternal danger. That is a very different matter. Do I make myself clear on this?'

'Yes, Father.'

'I want you to be sure you know exactly what I'm saying. If you are the one to make the actual decision that somebody is to die, then that person is on your conscience. And in that case we all know what eternal punishment is like, don't we?'

'Yes, Father.'

'Now for your penance, I want you to say a decade of the Rosary for the souls of the men you have helped to execute and

I want you, as soon as these troubled times are over, to do a Novena to the Sacred Heart for the souls of all those unfortunate misguided men that you take out of this life. I want you to pray that their souls, as well as your own, will find their way to the Lord. *Ego te absolvo, in Nomine Patris et...*'

Dinny was surprised by the priest's leniency. He was hoping he would help him find a way out of the predicament he was in. But, instead of guidance, he was getting a carte blanche to keep on playing his role in the killings.

'Human life is sacred in the eyes of the Lord. You should do everything in your power to avoid taking it. However, I can see that there may be times when taking life is unavoidable. So long as you're only carrying out orders and not making them, your behaviour is only the same as that of any soldier in any war. There is culpability on all sides but the principal responsibility lies with your leadership. You are just a footsoldier. Now I know that the Bishop would say that this is not a war, that what you are doing is merely murder, but I am your confessor, and what I say in this confession box is what counts. However, you will face the fires of hell if you sit in judgement on somebody and if you are the one to take the life of an innocent man. Is that clear?'

'Clear enough, Father.'

'You may go now, my son. I absolve you of your sins in the name of the Father and of the Son and of the Holy Ghost.' He blessed him from behind the grill and repeated the prayer of absolution in Latin. As he got up to leave the confessional, the priest whispered aloud. 'God save Ireland.'

'Yes, Father. God save Ireland.'

As Dinny saw it, God was the only one who could save Ireland but even He would have His work cut out for him to make anything of the mess the place was in now. As he emerged into the dim light of the church, his mind was still not at ease. He had hoped that Confession would lift the weight off his mind but instead it just made him even more confused. Only a handful of priests would have had enough republican sympathy to grant him absolution and he had managed to find one. A situation where one priest would absolve him, while another would run him out of the church couldn't be right, either. In fact, it made no sense at all. When is a sin not a sin? He said his penance and left the churchyard. He was no happier than he had been when he went in.

19

The same evening, Dan Donohoe slipped in home for a cup of tea. While he was 'on the run', he was really only half 'on the run': so long as he didn't sleep at home, his chances of being captured were slim. There was no sign of his mother, so he made himself a cup of tea and settled down to catch up on the news in the Cork Examiner that the Bishop of Cork had decreed that all IRA activists who took part in killings, ambushes and kidnappings were to consider themselves excommunicated. Part of the city had been burnt down a few days previously by Black and Tans in retaliation for an ambush at Dillon's Cross. The excommunication was also in retaliation for ambushes.

'Cohalan, you melted hoor,' he said, 'you're showing your true colours now. I'm sorry now we didn't plug you when we said we would.' Of course, Bishop Cohalan had been threatening since 1916 to do something like this; he was just nailing his colours to the Imperial mast. But it didn't make the slightest difference to Dan Donohoe. He had long since decided that those who believed in religion were deluded fools, strangled by a noose of vague superstitions and mumbo-jumbo-speaking men who wore frocks and spoke in Latin. It might affect some of his men who were not so free-thinking, but not him.

It was not a good day: word had come to Donohoe that morning that Dinny Fitzgibbon would not be joining the Company for the next few days, because he was in bed with the 'flu. Some 'flu, Donohoe thought: the 'flu of fear. Young Fitzgibbon was soft. He wasn't exactly cowardly, but he had no real guts for the fight in hand. The best volunteers came from mountainy parishes, places rich in rushes, snipe and furze, but poor in greed and the grasping of big farmers. They had the ability to suffer and make sacrifices. In general, you could equate good land with bad people and bad land with good people. That was the problem with East Cork; too much of the land was rich; the people, who had done well out of the Great War and the Land Acts were complacent and wanted only to make money. The men from the hills, on the other hand, were a fine upright breed, they were the fellows who believed in freedom. Whatever idealism there was in the population and whatever hope there was for the country was to be found in the hardy men from the high country.

All in all, Dan Donohoe felt he had done a good job in marrying the different traditions he had to contend with. He had working class lads from Queenstown or Cobh, as he now preferred to call it, he had stonemasons, shoemakers, foundry workers, mechanics, carpenters from the city and he had the sons of labourers and small farmers, men from every walk of life, working together, fighting together in a spirit of comradeship for the glory of Ireland. He had something Pearse would have been proud of, a unit that was getting results.

It was strange the way things had developed. First you had the Presidents of the Sinn Fein clubs; wishy-washy types, the lovers of pomp and ceremony who were more interested in songs and banners and flags and were filled with self-importance. Those boys were quick to scatter when the going got tough and with them the priests who sometimes attended such meetings in the early days.

Dan Donohoe had always believed that the best activists in the fight for freedom were atheists, more or less. They were free of the chains of religion, set loose from the shackles of tired superstition and its backward-looking rules. There was no point in the existence of God when He let the British rule Ireland and grind her into the ground. What God would allow a dozen rebellions to fail and leave the oppressor in charge as he'd always been? It was the same old story. The god who ran Ireland was the god of the merchants and the shoneen towns, the respectable god of property, the god of banks and businesses and small shifty shopkeepers, the god of money and commerce and backward-looking boot-licking conservatism. But he would show them all that the only god worth talking about was the fellow who roared out of the barrel of a gun.

And now the bloody bishop had the nerve to call decent men murderers. And what about the murder campaign waged by the British? What about the Black and Tans cutting the tongues out of people or nailing their hands to doors or slicing open their bellies with bayonets and burning their homes to the ground and factories and creameries, the very buildings that people needed for their livelihoods?

That was all right by the bloody bishop. John Bull could have his terror campaign, but Ireland couldn't. Jim Blake had the right idea when he took young lads joining the active squads out into the countryside and got them to look up at the stars and say 'fuck you, God'. Fuck you, is right.

Of course, Dan Donohoe had to tread carefully on the matter of religion among the country boys. Those fellas liked their God, they liked their prayers, they liked to trot off to Confession like so many branded cattle. So he kept quiet about his own opinions and made sure that Jim Blake and the others from town didn't go about the countryside declaiming their own particular religious views, or lack of them. Some of his own local Company would be shocked if they had even the slightest inkling of what he or Blake thought on the matter of religion. These pious lads were pawns to be used in this game with the British.

It was simple enough: the IRA was cleaning up the country when no-one else would: arresting, trying and expelling the lower orders. Carrigtwohill had been cleared of the tramp and tinker class, Midleton had been cleared of all undesirables such as ex-soldiers, thieves, wife-beaters, shawlies, separation women and all the drunken rabble of the lanes. The clean-living, hard-working, sober IRA was against squalor, drunkenness, prostitution and idleness.

Donohoe's thoughts shifted back to Dinny Fitzgibbon, a boy from the hills, as good as gold but with no fight in him, with bags of good intentions and ideals but somehow brittle and untempered like bad cast iron. Lads like Dinny were not battle-hardened and would never be. They would crack under pressure. Still they had their uses.

Donohoe was at a loss as to what to do with Dinny. Maybe he should give him a break. On the other hand, he was still needed for jobs up around the Rea. And war is war. Dinny hadn't been in jail, listening to Orange mobs roaring for his blood; he hadn't been on hunger strike or seen his beloved leader starve himself to death and fade away till nothing was left but a bag of ribs and cheekbones so high they seemed to scream out of the coffin for revenge. Dinny hadn't suffered for Ireland, and that was the difference between them.

Dan Donohoe closed the newspaper and spat. That shrivelled fool of a Bishop Cohalan made him sick. And the bloody Redmondite newspaper was about to get it too and not a day too soon. He went out into the yard and was about to head up to Corrigans to try to find some of his men when he heard Jim Blake's car come up the hill from the main Midleton road. This usually meant an execution was in the offing. Donohoe went behind the hayshed where he found an oilcloth full of .45 bullets in a rabbit burrow under a privet hedge. He counted out six bullets and put the rest back in the burrow. He already had his revolver loaded. The six spares were in case of emergencies.

The wine-coloured Buick, low on its springs and groaning from a heavy load, pulled into the yard where it shook to a halt like a Fordson tractor, steam issuing from radiators into the frosty air. Out of the car hopped Jim and Miah Blake and Pete Cronin. They had with them a prisoner with his hands tied behind his back and a jute bag over his head.

'We got one of the YMCA bastards,' Pete Cronin whispered in Dan Donohoe's ear, 'one of the infestation of spies that operate inside in Marlborough Street. His name is Pearson. We laid a trap outside the YMCA. He walked right into it. First he blabbed away. He thought he was safe as houses, he admitted straight off that he was watching Mick Twomey's house. Mick got some more information off him before he all gummed up.

Now he's saying nothing. We've got to get the rest of the names off him before we do the job.'

'Well, we'll see what we can do about that,' Dan Donohoe said. 'Right. We'd better get to work. Jim, take off the bag. I want to see his face.'

Jim Blake untied the bag from around the man's neck and lifted it off. The face underneath was that of a boy of about fourteen or fifteen. He had a shock of straight blond hair and a bewildered look on his face. He blinked and looked around at his new surroundings, shivering.

'This fella thinks he's the Prince a fuckin' Wales,' Jim Blake said.

'Listen, Pearson. Don't think we don't know all about you and your little circle of informers,' Pete Cronin growled. 'You were caught spying on the house of an officer of the Irish Republican Army.'

Pearson said nothing.

'Don't think we're going to stand by and let our people be killed because of a nest of rats that passes itself off as a youth club to people of your persuasion.' Dan Donohoe said. 'What do you do in this YMCA place anyway?'

The boy swallowed.

'Come on. Cough it up, boy. What do you do in your little secret society?'

'It's not secret. Anyone can join.'

'Can they now? To do what?'

The boy hesitated. 'Good deeds.'

'Good deeds! By Jaysus, yeer deeds look pretty good, right enough.'

'We're a youth club. We raise funds for the missions and hold Bible Classes and excursions to Crosshaven and...'

'Excursions to Crosshaven?' Dan Donohoe growled. He moved fast as a cobra across ten feet of cobbled yard and caught Pearson around the neck and began to throttle him.

'That's all, is it, boy? Bible classes, excursions to Crosshaven? Raising funds, that's all, is it?' he roared, 'you little fucker.'

The boy began the choke.

'Check his pockets.'

Miah Blake went through the boy's pockets and found a wallet, which he opened and found a ten shilling note and some change inside.

'Ten shillings.'

'Ten shillings, just as I suspected; cash that you got from Captain Kelley above in the barracks so you could spy on us. Isn't that right, boy?'

Dan Donohoe let go of the boy's neck and the boy swayed on his feet and stared at him as if he couldn't believe this was happening.

'I don't know what ... what you're talking about.' he sobbed and suddenly, as if he just realized the danger he was in, the tears rolled down his face and he began to shake.

Dan Donohoe stood back and looked at him as if trying to decide what to do next.

'Okay, let's think about this for a minute,' he said calmly. 'We know that you and your friends are being paid ten pounds a week to pass information to your buddies in the RIC.' He measured his words carefully. 'We know that you get forty pounds for information that leads to the arrest of prominent members of the legitimate army of the Republic. We even hear you'll really be in the pink if one of our leaders is caught. '

The boy stared at the ground and said no more but kept on crying and the men began to get embarrassed looking at him.

'Look at me, ya fucker,' Dan Donohoe roared. 'Cut out your weeping and look at me.'

The boy looked up. Dan Donohoe tapped his fingers together. Then he took out his revolver.

'See this? This is a Webley .45. This was taken off one of your army friends a year ago. He didn't live to see the following day, or any day since.' The boy looked glassily at Miah Blake who smirked back at him.

'I'll show you something else.' Donohoe went into a nearby barn and came out holding a hammer and a six-inch iron bolt. 'Now do you see this? Do you know what this is? This is what we use around here when we need to put a bullock down. This is what we call a humane killer. Hold his head.'

Miah Blake caught a fistful of the boy's hair. Dan Donohoe stood in front of him and put the bolt to his forehead and held the hammer back in his other hand.

'This is what we do. We hold the bolt like this and, bang, one flake of the hammer and the biggest bullock goes down. There's no pain. This is humane. Do you see what I'm getting at?'

The boy said nothing but began to choke on his own breathing.

'On spies like you and other bad bastards, we usually use this,' he cocked the revolver and placed it against the boy's temple. 'This is our humane killer.'

'Now I'm going to tell you something and I want you to think about it. And take your time thinking about it. You're not going to get out of this place alive, one way or another, but there are a number of ways an execution can be performed. That is one way. This is another.'

Then he said to Miah Blake: 'Go up into the loft there, Miah. There's a length of reins hanging on a hook on the far wall. Bring it down here to me.' Blake went up into the loft and emerged half a minute later with the rope.

'Now, you're coming with me, sonny boy.' Donohoe caught Pearson by the lapels of his jacket and dragged him up the stone steps to the loft.

'Now Miah. See that pulley up there,' he pointed to a pulley hanging over the loft door that was used for hoisting bags of grain into the loft. 'See if you can get the rope through it. That should be strong enough to take the weight of this little boyo here.'

'Don't do this ... please!' the boy cried.

Miah Blake climbed up on the iron railing and slipped the rope through the pulley. Then he got down and began making a noose at one end of it.

Pete Cronin looked at Dan Donohoe and furiously shook his head.

'You can't do this, Dan,' he whispered. 'Mick Twomey gave us specific instructions to get as much information out of him as we could first.'

'I know what I'm doing.'

'Now, Mr Pearson,' he addressed the boy, who was being held shaking over the ledge by Jim Blake. 'If you're not going to give us the information we need, we're going to execute you by hanging. If, on the other hand, you give us that information, you will be executed by a firing party. This is the humane way and we are humane people. You will feel nothing.'

'I don't know what you're talking about.'

'Right, so.'

Dan Donohoe took the noose and slipped it over Pearson's head. Then he got the others to pull the rope until it was taut. The boy's head was yanked to one side.

'Now we're going to pull you up slowly so that you're going to choke to death. That'll take five, possibly ten minutes. I'm told it's a very painful way to die - you turn black and blue, and you'll have a huge mickey standing out at the end of it. You have a straight choice, we can kill you like a man or hang you like a dog. It's up to you.'

The boy shivered but said nothing. The thought occurred to Pete Cronin that the boy was so well spoken and well reared that it was a shame to kill him.

'You'll talk, boy. By the time we're finished with you, you'll talk. He took the penknife and cut the cords tying Pearson's arms. Pearson rubbed his wrists and brought his hands to his face and covered it.

'The boys here will string you up for a bit and, as they're pulling, you'll start to choke. If you want to give us the names of the other people in your YMCA secret service outfit who are doing 'good deeds' by giving information to the enemy, you raise your hand. If not, we'll hang you and put you where no one will ever find you. Boys.' He indicated to the others to pull on the rope as he put the sack back over Pearson's head.

The rope had barely tightened on Pearson's neck when his bowels loosened and he soiled his trousers.

'The cowardly bastard can't even control himself,' somebody said.

The men pulled the rope tighter. Pearson's body began to lift. Then just as his feet began to leave the ground, he raised one hand.

'Let it go, lads.'

Pete Cronin and Miah Blake dropped the rope. Pearson's body fell back to the ground. Donohoe loosened it from around Pearson's neck.

'Don't do this to me. Please, don't do this to me. I'll tell you anything you want to know.' Pearson croaked and gasped as the noose was slackened.

'Right so, boy. Say what you have to say.'

'What you say is true. There is a reward ... for information on the Sinn Fein people.' He had difficulty in speaking. 'Forty pounds. But that's well known. And there is a reward of fifty pounds for information that might lead to the arrest of John Hegarty. That's offered to everyone, not just us in the YMCA...'

'John Hegarty? The man's name is not John Hegarty.' Dan Donohoe gave Pearson a fierce clatter across the face with his closed fist. 'And he's a bigger gentleman than you'll ever be.'

'Hold it.' Pete Cronin stayed Dan Donohoe's hand. 'Go on, tell us more,' he said quietly.

'My people are decent upright people but they don't know anything about Sinn Fein. If I thought...'

'Thought made a right fool of you, Pearson, didn't it? Now we want names or you'll swing.'

So Pearson began to call out a list of names, six names that he simply took off the top of his head in order to avoid the humiliation of being presented naked, erect and soiled to his family. They then took him out into the yard where Pete Cronin, Jim Blake and Dan Donohoe formed a firing party. He was told to get on his knees and say his prayers. He was executed by revolver while Miah Blake went on lookout.

After the shot was fired - only Dan Donohoe had a live round, to save bullets and qualms of conscience - Miah Blake ran into the yard saying that he had spotted a motorcar approaching along the main road from Cork.

'We'll have to get rid of him fast,' Pete Cronin said.

'Pick him up,' roared Dan Donohoe. 'Clean up the blood and the shit. There, Miah, for Christ's sake use a bit of straw. Follow me. Quickly.'

Miah Blake did his best to clean up the blood and brain matter from the cobbled yard. The others picked up Pearson's sagging body between them and followed Donohoe into his mother's sitting room. There they tore up four floorboards and placed Pearson beneath them as if he were an incubus in some devilish womb. Then Donohoe knocked the boards back into place with a few taps of a hammer and covered the whole thing up with a rug.

Meanwhile, the car turned off the main road and began to climb the hill towards the house. The men hid but emerged again when they recognized the car. It was a Ford; steam issued from its overheating radiator. When it came to a halt, Mick Twomey and two of his men stepped out. Dan Donohoe emerged from the privet hedge to greet them. Mick Twomey was heavily armed, with a Parabellum and a Peter the Painter hanging out from under his jacket.

'We've just come from Ballyvourney,' he said, 'I thought the bloody car would never get us here. Where's Pearson?'

'Executed.'

'Jesus, ye were in a hurry, weren't ye. Did ye get any information out of him?'

'A few names.' Dan Donohoe listed the names Pearson had given them.

'That might be them all right. There's only one way to find out.'

Mick Twomey told them how he himself had questioned Pearson on the night he was picked up and how Pearson, sure he was in no danger, calmly admitted to have been watching Mick's house.

'You won't believe what he said next though. He said to me, cool as a cucumber, that he had also been watching Tomás MacCurtain's house on the night he was murdered.'

'He what?'

'He said he trotted off down to King Street and told Swanzy that MacCurtain was in. "What did you get for that", I asked him. "A glass of port," he said. "You were well paid," I said. How about that now? A glass of port for selling Tomás MacCurtain.'

'I'm sorry now I didn't cut the balls off the little fucker and hang him up below at Dunkettle bridge.'

'No, no. Not a good idea. The press would make a meal of it. He has to vanish, and the rest of them will have to vanish too. We have to avoid bad publicity. That's why I had to go see O'Hegarty. The Gaffer says we got to get 'em all, but with as little fuss as possible. As we planned, we'll have to put the newspapers out of business as well. As you know, Lankford has been delegated to sort out the Examiner and the Constitution. Let's hope he doesn't make a pig's mickey of it.'

'Where do we pick the rest of 'em up?' Pete Cronin asked.

'There's a place near Blackrock where all the little Orange pricks meet to smoke cigarettes and play tennis and act grown up. We swoop, we pick them up, sooner rather than later. Otherwise, they'll get wind of what we're at and maybe flee the country.' Mick Twomey lit a cigarette. Blue smoke wafted into the cold morning air. In the weeks leading up to Christmas the Cork No 1 Brigade succeeded in rounding up the suspects named by Pearson. They were executed and buried on Donohoe's farm and the two Cork newspapers were put out of business to prevent unwelcome publicity. As a result, in the language of the Brigade, a major and extremely dangerous enemy spy circle had been successfully eliminated.

20

It was the week the lights went out in late November that Ted Mills began to get worried that the republicans might finally come to get him. The Corporation, controlled by Sinn Féin, decided not to switch on the streetlights in protest at the imposition of martial law. The winter was coming in, making for an even deeper darkness, a city without lamplight, a warren of gloom and uneasy shadow, with the odd car screeching by with some victim to be killed by any one of several factions. Men, some on the Government side, kicked down doors and pulled out fathers and shot them on the footpaths. The benighted city had never seen the likes of it. It was the safest time in the history of Ireland for murderers of all kinds to carry out their business.

Still, the citizens of Cork went to work, ducking their heads from the winds of death, just as they had done when Mills's nursery was burnt six months earlier. There was even the usual Cork black humour in it. 'You couldn't fart in Cork,' a gardener in the Model Farm used to say, 'but the Volunteers would smell it before you would.' His friend Lionel Fleming, who was working for the Irish Times in Cork, was accosted one evening while walking along Patrick Street by a young man in a cloth cap with what looked like a revolver in his pocket. 'Put your hands up!' the young man whispered in his ear and indicated to Fleming that he was to walk ahead of him down a side street. Fleming, convinced he was about to be murdered or kidnapped, did as he was told. Then the young man said:

'Keep your hands up. Now, tell me one thing and tell me no more. What day of the week have we?' Then he burst out laughing and ran off. Fleming was one of the lucky ones.

Up to that point, Mills felt secure in the knowledge that the more salubrious suburbs, such as Blackrock where he lived, were somehow immune from the killings that went on in the inner city. He had his friends and his neighbours, good neighbours, on either side of him. He played golf and watched his sons play rugby and cricket; he ran summer camps in Crossshaven; he was a member of Douglas Golf Club and the Royal Cork Yacht Club.

What could be safer than large houses on gentle slopes, high walls against the rapacious poor? Big gardens, tropical shrubs, variegated ivy and scarlet Virginia creeper, Caruso and John McCormack playing on gramophone records in the fireside drawing-rooms. Evenings in by the piano. The newly rich: Catholics and Protestants with money in their pockets; heaven to a horticulturist.

Then it all went wrong. In March, MacCurtain was assassinated and it looked like RIC officers were the killers. MacCurtain was an honourable man. Mills himself was of the view that MacCurtain was assassinated by a direct order of Dublin Castle. The killing had all the hallmarks of being planned well in advance. Rumour had it that the officers who did it were all from out of town.

In early November he got a threat in the post. It was written in letters laboriously cut out of newspapers and pasted onto a sheet of paper.

'Spy Mills,' it read, 'you're next. Harbouring spies under your roof. Leave Cork immediately if you know what's good for you.'

Mills was puzzled. How could he be harbouring spies under his roof? He did not know any spies. He assumed the threat was from some disgruntled former student of his, somebody like Mahony who never turned up in time for class a day in his life and failed exams a ten-year-old would have passed. So he ignored the threatening letter. He did not suspect in a month of Sundays that the spies in question might be his own sons. Still, he began to get worried about having reported Mahony, and the responsibility began to weigh on him. At the start of 1920 it was obvious on which side righteousness lay, because everyone knew who the murderers were. By the end of March that was no longer the case; the RIC and the Black and Tans were now as big a gang of murderers as the IRA. Mill began to make plans to get out of Cork.

But he was still in Cork by the time winter came. By now the city had descended into its hell of apparently random killings. People were murdered, cut down in their prime, respectable citizens like Beal, the manager of Woodford Bourne and Alfred Reilly, manager of Thompsons. Others began to disappear like McManus of the War Pensions Office and a prison warder, Griffin, and Downing of the Discharged Soldiers and Sailors Federation. It looked as if there was a campaign to exterminate anybody with any connection to the Crown. Nobody was safe. Others were shot by men with English accents. Scores were shot at in the street by faceless gunmen, others went out to work and didn't come home and were never heard from again.

Then young Pearson vanished. He lived up the street. His father was an electrician in the Cork Electrical Company. Pearson was in the YMCA and was friendly enough with his sons. It was far from clear what had happened to him. Anybody could have taken him, if indeed he had been taken. He could have had some terrible accident; he could have fallen into the river. There was any number of possibilities. He could have been picked up by the police or army in any one of its many round-ups and was being held in some internment camp somewhere.

When the boy failed to turn up for his tea and was not heard from for three or four nights, his distraught mother called into Mills to see if he knew anything about him from his contacts in the YMCA. He said he didn't; that it was always possible it was just a random abduction of a Protestant boy. He told her to wait for a ransom note. He told her there were people well capable of kidnapping somebody from what they believed was a well-off family and looking for a thousand pounds ransom to hand him back, though he had never heard of anything like that actually happening. However, if he had been taken by the IRA the threatening note suddenly began to make sense. If Pearson could vanish then so too could has own kids. Mills now visited the auctioneer to put his house up for sale and began to have sleepless nights as he waited for the midnight knock on the door.

21

The mistake he made, he now realized, was that he did not leave the country immediately after the burning and take his family with him. It might take a while, but he would eventually find a job as a horticulturalist in England. He was inclined to blame it all on Churchill. Churchill knew only one way to operate; fight fire with fire. But throwing oil on a smouldering powder keg was no way to put a fire out. He had no imagination. He made a mess of the Boers, he made a mess of Gallipoli, now he was making a mess of Ireland. It was all right to give carte blanche to the Black and Tans to carry out a campaign of murdering and looting when you were safe over in London. But for a decent citizen trying to live daily life in Cork, it was an entirely different matter.

Besides, the republicans were far too subtle for that. They had their organized riots and their hunger strikes and their prayers and rows of women lined up outside the prison walls, wailing and screeching and clutching their Rosary beads. The performance was enough to melt a stone. Public opinion, even in England, which had been appalled a year earlier by the IRA's murder campaign, evaporated overnight from the Government side once the Tans were sent in. And the hunger strikes placed enormous pressure on the Government. This was exactly what Sinn Fein wanted. Even the Pope and President Wilson got in on the act of criticising the Government.

He should have left for England while the going was good. Now he just hoped it was not too late. Regret was a high storm that blew through his mind night and day and whistled around the edges of all his thoughts. Then he counter-argued that, if he had gone, he would have lost everything, his Blackrock home, his beloved gardens, his friends in horticulture up and down the county, his family and his wife's family. Some local cattle jobber type would get his house at a fraction of its value and set up a statue of the Virgin on the landing and destroy his orchard for no other reason than that it was worthless to him.

Then there was the matter of fitting in. He was an Irishman, first and foremost. Though he had gone to the Royal Agricultural College in Chichester and studied at Kew, he knew virtually nobody in England. He had been an outsider in the South with his Dublin accent but he felt at home. The problem with being an Irish Protestant was that he was regarded as English in Ireland and Irish in England. He and his family would always be outsiders, no matter which way they turned. Besides, his boys were at Cork Grammar School and he didn't want to move them. They were happy, they loved Cork, they had been born and reared there. They had their picnics and their sport; they had their friends. It made no sense to move out just because he reported Mahony who deserved anything that was coming to him.

Then another loyalist disappeared and fear began to grip the families of the loyalist community like a raging virus. The houses of Protestants in Blackrock mysteriously began to go up in flames. The violence seemed completely random. Many in the area began to contemplate leaving Ireland and a significant number did so. Pearson's family of course were in great distress. They had no idea whether their boy was dead or alive. Nobody knew anything, nobody saw him being picked up, nobody saw what kind of car took him away, if indeed he was taken away in a motorcar.

For the curious thing about Cork was that nobody ever saw the gunmen, from whatever side, actually do anything. For all their reputation as talkers, Cork people's silence was as deep as the sea. The police were worthless, the Army worse. The Masonic Hall ceased to hold meetings, deeming it too dangerous. The American teas that the ladies committee of the YMCA had planned for the spring had to be deferred indefinitely.

Mills did an inventory of his possessions and with the help of his sons piled them into cardboard boxes. He contacted Nat Ross to arrange the transport of his furniture. Packing up his possessions and clearing out his house was one of the most distressing tasks he had ever done. He felt like he was dismantling his entire being in the process and upsetting his family. His wife, Matilda, a brave Cork girl, was on the verge of tears because she knew she would be leaving her own family too. He gathered familiar objects and packed them away, wondering in what kind of circumstances he would see them again. He contacted his sister in London; he would stay with her until he had sorted out his life. Moving was the last thing in the world he wanted to do, but he just had to do it.

22

It was noon on a December day. Dinny was snagging turnips in the field behind the house. The air was carved out of frost and icicles hung like runny noses from the corrugated roofs of the outhouses.

He was listening nervously for the sound of the Angelus bell. That would be his signal to go to the Rea. He was back to his old job again after a gap of six weeks.

The previous night, word had come that he was to dig a deep grave in the Rea, big enough to hold several bodies, in preparation for more executions. It was less than a month since the delegation of locals had called on him to get him to try to stop the killings.

Dinny decided he would follow his conscience and have nothing further to do with the goings on in the Rea. If he had to stop a bullet or be shot as a spy along with whatever prisoners were there, he was prepared to do so. He knew just one thing; his conscience could take no more of putting strangers into holes in the ground. There were things that were worse than death, and living the way he was living was one of them.

He heard the Angelus bell, blessed himself, faced towards the distant spire and said the Angelus. Then he removed the sacks from around his knees and headed for home.

Half an hour later, he and John McCarthy waited at the top of An Bóthar Uaigneach for the firing party to arrive. They might think twice before executing someone in front of John McCarthy, a respectable man and a Sinn Fein judge, somewhat of an elder in the community. Out of habit, Dinny brought his shovel and pick, just in case. They could bury them themselves if they wanted to.

Ten minutes later, Dan Donohoe and Daithi O'Brien arrived with two prisoners. They were on foot as it was by now unsafe to travel by car in the martial law area. Daithi O'Brien had captured the two men outside Cobh and, after being held overnight in Sing Sing, they had now been 'sentenced' to be executed.

Dinny watched the four come up the lane. It was broad daylight, the shadows full of unmelted frost. The men walked as if treading on air. The silence of the Rea was high, blue, clear and cold and was broken only by the call of a woodcock. The church bell rang again; there must be a funeral taking place, Dinny thought, clarion of a lost decency. A dog barked somewhere in the distance.

Executions by day marked a change in Company policy. But it was safer now to travel by day than to risk movement during curfew hours. Yet despite the general deterioration of law and order, the area was still more or less free of enemy activity. The absence of overt actions such as ambushes meant that neither the British Army nor the Black and Tans were tempted to come snooping around.

Dinny shaded his eyes to look into the low winter sun. He thought captors and captives made for an odd-looking crew, traipsing along An Bóthar Uaigneach like men going to a fair. Dan Donohoe, small and broad in his cocked hat and rapid walk; the more loping stride of Daithi O'Brien and the two spies, tall men, stumbling along reluctantly with their hands tied behind them, going to their deaths with their heads bowed.

Why didn't they try to make a run for it? Dinny wondered. They could have escaped, if they had a plan and had coordinated their movements. They could have distracted their captors, at least long enough for one of them to get away. A man could run a long distance, even with his hands tied. But none of them ever did that. Maybe they were too badly rattled from the terror of staying in the living grave in the cemetery. Frightened people were strangely docile. He had seen sheepdogs go like that before they were shot. It was as if they had known their fate all along.

And there could be no doubt that Sing Sing did have a terrible effect on those who stayed there. The colour and flesh drained from men's cheeks and they emerged into the light, thin-faced and haggard like dogs after days in a kennel, stark, staring, raving, haunted, mad. One man was said to have developed webbed fingers, like a goose's foot, another thought he was getting the stigmata. And they always knew, though they were never told, that they were already down among the dead. Sing Sing sapped a man's spirit and his will to live; it broke his soul and made him want to join the other corpses in the graveyard. The spies knew what was coming; ghosts had walked into their eyes.

The soldiers were braver; they rarely begged; many of them went down honourably and defiantly, swearing allegiance to King and country. As a result, they were, ironically, held in high regard by their executioners. There is a code of honour among the soldiers that is upheld even in the face of death.

'Well, are you ready?' Daithi O'Brien said to Dinny when they got within earshot.

'I'm as ready as I'm going to be,' Dinny muttered, casually folding his arms across his chest. But he didn't look like he was going to spring into action to help anybody.

The four men stopped and stared at him. The spies were gagged and looked puzzled.

'And what the hell does that mean?' Dan Donohoe asked.

'It means this. I'm a local here and the locals have formed a committee to try to stop this killing in their backyard. They don't like it. They want it to stop. This ... this is all right for people like you,' he faltered. 'But you don't have to live here.'

Dinny was surprised to hear himself speak like this. It was as if he had become two people: one Dinny was talking bravely, while another Dinny was swaying against his shovel nervously.

'We are after discussing all the people who are being buried here and we have come to the decision that we don't want any more executions in this place.' John McCarthy said officiously.

'You have, have you? Well, that's news to us. Why didn't you tell us that before now and it would have saved us the walk,' Dan Donohoe said with a little laugh. 'That's great patriotism, that is. These are the kind of people we're saving Ireland for, Dave.'

'There are enough ghosts up here already.' John McCarthy said. 'People are finding corpses; dogs are dragging human remains into farmyards. This can't go on.'

'It can't go on? I suppose you're right, it can't go on.' Daithi O'Brien sighed.

'I would rather you would take away those two prisoners and do your work somewhere else, not under the noses of the good people who live in this locality,' John McCarthy said, holding his hat in his hand and fiddling with the hatband, as he nervously shuffled from one foot to another.

'Well, Donohoe, they're not going to be shot at all so,' Daithi O'Brien went on. 'And they're not going to die. That's good news lads, isn't it?' he said to the prisoners. 'What do you think, Donohoe?'

'You've got me bate there, D,' Dan Donohoe said.

'I don't know what we're going to do with them so,' Daithi O'Brien went on loudly, 'unless you want to make bacon with them. I don't know at all, at all.'

Then he spun around and drew his revolver and, firing rapidly, emptied its contents into the head and chests of the prisoners. As they went down, their eyes wide open with surprise, he said:

'Come on now, Donohoe. Let's skeet. Now boys', he said to Dinny and John McCarthy, 'ye can bury those two or ye can turn yeer arse to them and face the consequences.'

With that, the two IRA men turned and walked calmly away, muttering to each other, as if they had done nothing more dramatic than gather a few sheep for dipping.

John McCarthy, who had never seen anything to prepare him for this, stumbled and leaned against a hawthorn tree. His mouth opened and shut; his jaw dropped and he looked like he was chewing something too big for his mouth as he stared incredulously at the backs of the departing men. 'Jesus, Mary and Joseph,' he muttered, blessing himself. His hat fell from his grasp and he bent and staggered to pick it up.

'What in God's name will we do, Dinny?' he stammered.

'Get the shovel' Dinny said grimly. 'We'll have to do as they say.'

Soon there was no sound except the scraping of shovels and the whistling of the wind through the furze bushes and the gurgling of drains deep under the yellowed grass and there was nothing else moving except roots coming up out of the clay and the low cold clouds coming in over the distant hills.

23

Mills had just booked a passage on the mail boat for England and was on his way along the South Mall to the auctioneer's office to make the final preparations for putting his house up for sale. It was a dull day, damp with late November rain.

After Pearson had vanished a few weeks earlier, he had put a plan in place with his wife that if anything were to happen to him that she was to take the boys immediately to the docks and get them all on the mail boat for England. He had a good idea what his fate would be and had decided that he was prepared to sacrifice his own life if he could be sure his wife and sons were safe.

As he passed Suttons, two men with revolvers and long coats jumped out of a doorway and bundled him into a car that was parked nearby. They held guns to his ribs as they made their way across the city, out through Blackpool and into the steep hills of the Northside. Soon he had no idea where he was. At best he guessed he was somewhere around Carrignavar, between north and east, between Blarney and Glanmire and that was an awful lot of countryside. He knew what to expect. He didn't think that the Army or the police would ever be able to find him, even if they tried.

The men who captured him said little, they just held the guns to his side as the car careered around the country roads. They smelled of sweat and damp clothes. They were thin faced, intense men who looked like they had spent too long out in the wind and rain.

The IRA intelligence was good; they had people at every street corner monitoring the movement of loyalists and visitors.

All respectable people with English accents were assumed to be spies. Every new arrival in the city was noted by the IRA and followed. Everybody coming or going from barracks was spotted and, when they returned to where they came from or where they were staying, they were identified and their names added to secret IRA lists.

As for himself, there were only two ways he would get out of this predicament. He could try to escape or face a bullet. And if he did try to escape, he would find himself deep in enemy territory. With his accent, the locals would almost certainly turn him over to the rebels. He might be fortunate enough to meet up with someone he knew from his horticultural work or even a patrol of RIC or Army, but it was unlikely. He didn't rate his chances highly but resolved to make a run for it if he got the chance.

It was now almost dark and they had travelled about half an hour when they ordered him to get out of the car. He was sure they were going to kill him on the spot, as they marched him across some fields in the near darkness to a farmhouse. He started praying for his wife and sons, praying for their safety and hoping they had made the mailboat. But instead of being shot, he was interrogated by a man who looked very like MacSwiney, the dead Lord Mayor. They asked him about the 'Junior Secret Service' which, as they put it, operated out of the YMCA. They kept going on about this 'Junior Secret Service' and a 'Senior Secret Service' and seemed quite obsessed that there was a big Protestant conspiracy afoot which was gathering intelligence on their men. He did not know what they were talking about and told him so. Then one of them brought up the subject of Mahony and the arson attack on the Model Farm. He admitted he had reported on Mahony because he could see nothing to be gained by denying it. Besides, he felt he might increase the chances of his wife and boys getting away to England if he was seen to give them something.

They kept him in the house for two days and told him he was now a hostage against the execution of IRA men held by the British. He was surprised they didn't torture him. In fact, they treated him rather well, bringing him food and old newspapers when they could get hold of them. Some of the gunmen seemed decent enough. Others, and he thought in particular about the men who captured him in the first place, were clearly fanatical in nature. He could see it in their eyes. One of them, the driver of the car, had a twisted face and a stony stare and sucked on cigarettes when he was not trying to hide them in the heel of his fist. Men like that, and there were a lot of them in the Tans and, he imagined, in the IRA, could follow a leader and carry out orders to the letter, no matter what those orders were.

They held him for over a week and he got the impression that they were waiting for developments in Cork barracks, either execution or some reprisal against their own side. They moved him from one hideout to the next: a gate lodge under trees, an outhouse in the middle of nowhere, an old stable with a horse collar on the wall, several farmhouses. Once he was even held among beer barrels in the stale cellar of a public house.

Then one night, the men guarding him said they were going to a wake and had to bring him with them, because they were under instructions not to take their eyes off him. When they arrived at the farmhouse where the wake was being held they locked him in the henhouse and went inside and had their fill of drink. From time to time, comically and graciously, they passed pints of porter to him through the slot in the door where the hens came and went. The porter was too sweet for his taste: it was flat as dyke water but he drank it, though the black and white hen shit did nothing to enhance his thirst.

That night he tried to escape when they opened the henhouse, hoping that they would be too drunk to catch him or shoot straight. But they caught him at the end of the lane and tied his hands and legs together with binder twine. They dragged him back to the henhouse and threw him face down on the filthy straw and kicked him a few times, muttering and cursing to themselves.

He tried to keep track of the days and dates. He knew he had been picked up on November 29th. The weather was cold, his nose ran, his feet were frozen. Frost made odd lacy shapes on the insides of the windows of the various places where he was being held. There were at least two men guarding him at any one time and they were always armed. He tried to engage them in conversation but, though they were civil and courteous, they were highly suspicious of him. They were convinced he was a very dangerous spy. They told him as much. Still, they gave him an old coat and a jute bag that he put over his shoulders to keep out the cold. One of them even gave him the Cork Holly Bough to read.

He tried to console himself that, with each passing day, there was a growing chance that his wife would have enough sense to bundle herself and their boys onto the steamer for England.

After six nights they took him into a warm farmhouse where a big fire was lighting. There, in the kitchen, under a picture of the Sacred Heart and a red perpetual lamp, they cross-examined him again. Three of their officers sat around the table, a middle aged man with grey hair and week-old stubble that made him look like an ageing monk and a huge frightful looking fellow who looked like a bear. With them was a smaller tough-looking man with a moustache and strange shrivelled ears, who seemed to be the next in command after the older man. The younger boys, his guards, stood around the doors, self-consciously handling their revolvers. In this mockery of a trial, they found him guilty of spying for the Crown. He was sentenced to be shot. Finally, playing for time, in the hope of sending them off on another wild goose chase, he admitted to spying on some houses in Cork. He gave them a list of fictitious names and the names of those who had already been kidnapped.

As they led him away, they asked him if he had anything to say for himself. He asked that a minister be brought to him. They told him that while they would like to facilitate him, it was out of the question in the middle of the war they were fighting.

Then they led him into a graveyard, where he was sure he was going to be executed immediately. He would die under a full moon, he thought, in a graveyard rather than a garden, which had always been his wish. He waited for them to blindfold him and make him kneel down in front of a grave. Instead, they took him behind a briar-covered tomb and, to his surprise, let him down several steps to a sort of underground passage. There, the big bear-like man who had been guarding him reached inside his coat, took out a bottle of whiskey and handed it to him.

'Here,' he said. 'You might need this.'

Then he took a key out of his pocket, lit a candle and opened a padlock. A heavy iron door swung open and Mills heard the last word in the world he wanted to hear.

'Daddy!'

In the candlelight he could see them, Freddy and Stephen, sitting there in the dirt, in a sort of filthy tunnel, their eyes huge with tears and terror, shaking and clinging to each other. Their shoes had been taken from them and they stood barefoot, shivering in the mud. He put his arms around them and tried to reassure them that everything would be alright. But he knew they did not believe him. The door clanged shut behind him. There was nothing now but darkness and dripping water and cold mud under their feet.

For the rest of the night they huddled together and did their best to console each other and the boys tried to be brave for each other and for their father. 'The Lord is my shepherd; I shall not want,' they prayed. The boys pulled their collars tightly and tried not to cry, their teeth chattering from cold and the dripping stones overhead. 'Yea, though I walk through the valley of the shadow of death, I will fear no evil; for Thou art with me.' Mills tried to believe in the power of the prayer. He hoped even more fervently that his sons believed in it. He had failed them, failed everything he himself had believed in, failed his religion, failed his community, failed his wife, failed his family. He had tried his best to do his duty and this was where he had ended up.

He faltered as he tried to continue the prayer but Freddy took up the end of the last verse. 'Surely goodness and mercy shall follow me all the days of my life and I shall dwell in the house of the Lord forever.' His sons were braver than he was.

Then they stood as upright as they could in the confined space, and put their arms around each other and quietly began to sing Abide With Me as they waited through the longest night of their lives for the door to open.

Dan Donohoe and his men shot all three of them in a narrow ditch at first light. They were allowed recite The Lord's Prayer before they were shot. Freddy and Stephen went first. They were crying and in a terrible state, calling for their mother. Mills, who by this time was blind with tears and half-drunk from the whiskey, watched his sons twitching and moaning in the dirt and tried to crawl on his hands and knees to them. They pushed him in on top of them and shot him. And so father and sons lay there, with the rain falling on them, in a last grotesque family embrace.

The IRA men scampered to their hideouts and their homes and left the bodies where they lay. On their way they called to Dinny Fitzgibbon, who was still asleep in bed, and told him there was another job for him to do. Reluctantly, he got his horse and cart and loaded the bodies and headed off up the narrow laneway to the mountain. There in the December drizzle, wondering who the man and the two boys were and what they might have done to deserve this fate, he buried the last bodies he would ever bury in the Rea.

24

Dinny, at his swearing-in to the IRA, had vowed to defend the Republic and obey orders, regardless of what those orders were. It was the duty of a soldier not to question the commands of a superior. The Bishop could pray for Irish freedom and officiate at Tomás MacCurtain's funeral and praise the man's decency and condemn the police and the government for their part in his murder. Nine months later he would excommunicate the IRA for carrying out similar murders. The Bishop was consistent; he could draw a moral line in the sand; murder was wrong, no matter who did it. The priest had walked all over that line. Dinny was inclined to side with the Bishop.

In the weeks before Christmas, Dinny found he was burying boys, with no idea who they were or what they had done or why they had to end up in a boghole in the middle of nowhere. He couldn't help wondering why the IRA had suddenly started killing youngsters. For revolutionaries to go to the trouble of rounding-up and executing fifteen-year-olds, the kids must have been doing something truly terrible. Yet nobody ever told him what it was. It seemed to Dinny that, no matter what they had done, that a good hammering would be punishment enough.

A week later, word came from Cork that some very important prisoners were to be housed in the graveyard. Dinny was given the job of cleaning out the vault. This he did, emptying the latrine bucket and cleaning out the straw. He found a six penny bit on the floor under one of the makeshift beds and put it in his pocket. As he was finishing up his work, Ned Murphy came up the lane to the graveyard and made his way between the leaning headstones to where Dinny was securing the padlock on the door to the prison.

'You don't like what's going on, do you?' Ned said.

'No.'

'Well, none of us do. But it has to be done.'

'I suppose so.'

'We've a new job for you tomorrow morning.'

'What?'

'This will be the last one. I promise. You know that four of our boys are on death row and that they will be executed on Saturday?'

'I know that. I can read the papers.'

'Well, Brigade command has decided to take hostages in the city to hold against the executions. These will be loyal loyalists, the worst type of spies. These are the kind of people who are honoured, even grateful, for any help they can give the Crown. In fact, it's like an obsession with them. It is proposed that we capture at least four of these people and that we hold them here and let the British know that we plan to shoot one of them for every one of our boys shot.'

'I don't know if I... '

'I know what you're going to say.' Murphy put up his hands. 'I know you're feeling the strain. Dan has decided you won't be involved, either in holding these prisoners or in executing them, if it comes to that – which I'm sure it won't. Surely be to God, the British will see sense on this.'

Dinny did not believe that. The only sense the British ever saw was to make things worse by even more murder and arson than the IRA. The proof of the pudding was the stinking ruin that was now Cork city.

'This is a top secret job'

'Then why tell me?'

'Because tomorrow morning you'll have to go down to Little Island with a horse and trap and pick up the first of these prisoners.'

'I thought you just said...'

'I did. I'd have sent Foley but he's gone down to Midleton with a dispatch. And Mike Canavan got delayed last night. There was a roadblock inside in Tivoli. He had to take to the hills. God knows when he'll be back. But don't worry. I'll be with you.'

Dinny sighed.

'All right. I'll tackle the pony after the cows.'

'Never mind the cows. Your father and Bill can milk the cows. This is more important. Make up some kind of excuse. The drop-off is at half-eight to suit the tide and to get in just after the end of curfew. We have to be there at exactly half eight – at that little inlet just beyond the Island Gate. Meet me at the forge at half seven and we'll go on down.'

Dinny said nothing but when he came up the four steps from the vault he felt suddenly dizzy as if the was drunk but he knew he wasn't. When he stepped out onto the green sward of the better-tended part of the graveyard, Ned Murphy put his arm around his shoulder. 'You're a good lad,' he said.

The following morning they were sitting in the trap by a small inlet on the eastern side of Little Island where the fields ran down to the sea and it looked at high tide as if the whole harbour was a flooded field and the ragged winter grass was sliding into the sea. The contours of the shoreline were a complex web of inlets between Fota and Little Island. A fog was clamped on the land; the sea was smooth as a grey plate with the odd oily slick passing down from the city to the west. There was no wind and no sign of anything moving in the shapeless mist.

The thought occurred to Dinny that for someone to navigate the harbour in such conditions they would have to have a very good knowledge of the area. Big ships came down from the quays at regular intervals, leviathans out of the fog; collisions in the harbour were a regular occurrence. To cross from the south side of the river with the sky down on the ground and find an inlet like the one he was sitting in you would have to know the harbour well and be an experienced sailor.

There was no sound, a cormorant stood on a rock observing the scene; two gulls glided overhead, even the waves made minimal slosh on the grassy verge. He looked at his watch; it was twenty to nine. Nothing could come out of this, he thought. Whoever might venture into this miasma would get lost, carried by the currents down to Passage and beyond. Then, just as he was wondering if perhaps he should turn around and go home, he heard the splash of oars and the creak of oarlock on wooden stanchions. As he stared into the nothingness a rowboat like a lost and mythical leviathan gradually emerged from the fog. It was a large rowboat of the kind that plied the lower harbour and was capable of carrying a dozen people or a half dozen people and two cattle or a quarter of a ton of coal. This time however it contained just five people and was piloted by a broad-shouldered man in his thirties who sat on the prow and ordered two other men on the oars to pull on their timbers to beach the boat smoothly on a patch of sand at the edge of the descending field.

The oarsmen Dinny vaguely knew to be members on the Blackrock Company but he did not know their names. The other man he knew because he had brought several fellows down to Dan Donohoe to be held in Sing Sing for execution and he occasionally called around when big shots like Seán O'Hegarty were in the area. He had on him a good suit and hat and sat in the stern of the boat. He looked like an accountant on his way to a meeting were it not for the fact that he had a Webley in his hand which he vaguely waved in the direction of two prisoners who were sitting blindfolded in front of him. It was the prisoners who interested Dinny. They looked to be young lads, probably no more than seventeen, and though they had strips of sheeting tied around their heads and sat slumped on the wooden benches and their hands were tied, they were clean and tidy with their hair well combed and they were dressed completely in white as if they were coming from some kind of ceremony.

When the boat beached the man on the prow rose and jumped nimbly onto the shore. He got a rope and tied the boat to the trunk of a hawthorn tree. He moved quickly as if he was well used to this kind of thing and pulled on the rope.

'Come on. Get a move on,' he said to the men on the boat.

The oarsmen stood up and the boat rocked under them. The man who was in charge turned to Dinny and Ned Murphy who was holding the pony by the reins.

'Here are your instructions. They are not to see a thing,' he said, nodding in the direction of the young men, 'they are to remain blindfolded at all times. If they're released they could find their way back here and bring the enemy with them. They can't be walked out, even at night. You understand what I mean by that?'

Dinny nodded. He knew the procedure: that they could not be exercised meant that there was a reasonable possibility that the prisoners might be released.

'Don't worry,' Ned Murphy said, 'we are well used to this kind of work.'

'Pass me that.' The man pointed to a jute sack that was under the seat at the stern of the boat. One of the Blackrock men pulled out the sack – it was a Goodbody grain sack with large G printed on the side – and passed it to the man on the shore who in turn tossed it up into the trap to Dinny.

'Mind that. It contains the possessions we found on these two when they were captured. It is important that it not be tampered with and be kept in a safe place. If these are to be released we want to give them back their bits and pieces. We can't be seen to be barbarians.' The man smiled. Dinny tucked the sack in under the seat of the trap.

The oarsmen got out of the boat and waded into the sea and held the boat while man in charge helped the two prisoners stand up and guided them out of the boat and onto the shore.

One of them had difficulty in finding his feet and had to be held upright.

'Don't worry,' the man said to them, 'you'll only be here for a day or two. Then you'll be free to go. If you cooperate with our people you'll be fine, you understand?'

The young men nodded dumbly.

Dinny and Ned Murphy helped the two prisoners climb onto the trap. The boss man clicked his finger and pointed. One of the oarsmen picked up two other empty sacks and tossed them to him. When the prisoners were seated, he handed the sacks up to Dinny. 'You know what to do with these?'

Dinny nodded. He pulled the sacks over the heads of the two men.

'This is just for security,' Dinny said, 'so that you will not know where you're going.'

Both prisoners nodded. Then one of them spoke:

'Can you let our mothers know that we're being well looked after?' He was well-spoken but his voice sounded muffled as if he was speaking in some kind of puppet manner.

'Don't worry,' the man said. 'We're going back to the city now. We'll get word to them that you're being perfectly well cared for.'

'Thanks,' the boy said.

With that the man in charge got back into the boat and the two Blackrock men pushed off and, half-soaked, clambered in after him. With a couple of long pulls on the oars and the three heads staring into space like marionettes the boat turned and slid off into the mist that seemed for some reason to be its proper home.

Ned Murphy climbed up onto the driver's seat and gave the pony a slight whack of the reins. 'Hup, Doll,' he said and the trap lurched and they made their way up through the winding roads towards Knockraha.

Murphy was to be as good as his word and Dinny had no further part in the holding of the hostages. Two more were lifted on the Lower Road by the city men and brought down to Sing

Sing to be held against the shooting of IRA prisoners. The following Saturday, when the executions in Cork jail were due, Seán O'Hegarty arrived to oversee either the release or execution of the prisoners. The men awaited the arrival of the Cork Examiner which would tell them whether the Volunteers in Cork had been executed or not. But they did not need the Examiner because Con Foley had been in town and arrived off the early train from the Island Gate with the news that the four IRA prisoners in Cork Military Detention Prison had been executed. 'Ye know what to do', was all Seán O'Hegarty said. And indeed they did. On the Saturday night the group took the four prisoners – the other two were ex-soldiers – and shot them and buried them in the Rea.

The following morning Dinny went up into the loft and took down the jute bag containing the possessions of the two youths which he had hidden up in the rafters. He opened the bag with a feeling more of transgression than curiosity, knowing that nobody would ever see the contents of the bag again. It contained two towels, a pair of glasses and a fistful of change at the bottom. It also contained two pieces of equipment he had not handled before, though he knew what they were from photos from the newspapers. They were tennis racquets. One was almost new with barely a scratch on the rim. The other was older and had a name etched along the shaft. It read: Ken Hosford, Citadella, Blackrock Road, Cork. These two had obviously been playing tennis when they were picked up. Dinny tried to imagine what it must have been like to be all dressed in white, playing tennis one minute, and being whisked off to a hole in the ground the next. He took the change and put it in his pocket. Then he took the contents of the sack and went across the fields and went down into the glen at the far side of the farm and dug a small hole and buried the racquets, the glasses and the towels. On the way back he did a detour to the village where he went into the chapel and dropped the change, along with the sixpence he had found earlier in Sing Sing, into the poor box. Then he went home to another sleepless night.

It was while excavating the dug-out for the bomb factory and drawing away the soil and shale with his horse and cart that Dinny began to have the first of his visions.

It began over a period of weeks, when he had had a vague feeling that he was never alone, that lurking somewhere, just beyond the edge of his vision was somebody always walking alongside him. He had no idea who that somebody was. So far, the figure had never looked back and beckoned on him to follow. But sooner or later he knew it would.

He thought of Sergeant Lehane having visions of the Blessed Virgin while lying in the vault but he knew his own visitations were something entirely more sinister. This double was himself, yet not himself, for it was also the shadow of the men and boys he had witnessed being executed. This double was the shadow moving around the dark side of a stack of barley or the invisible part of a new moon, a pale negative waiting for him to step into it.

He would give anything to be able to feel ordinary again, to be part of the lives of ordinary people; a labourer scouring hedges, a carpenter making window frames, a farmer bucketing milk to new born calves, life in all its tedious normality.

The day before Christmas Eve he was in the pit excavating for an arms dump along with Ned Murphy, slinging earth out of a hole, when he saw a face coming towards him out of the wall of earth he was working on. The face, which had a hole in the middle of its forehead, was that of Thomas Deveney; he was still pleading as he had pleaded on the night he died six months earlier.

Ned Murphy put down his shovel and stared at Dinny, who by now was mumbling unintelligibly and punching the air with his fists.

Dinny raised his shovel to protect himself and shouted at the spectre to go away. He staggered, his eyes glazed and his arms reached upwards as if he was shielding himself from a great light. There was a look of appalled horror on his face.

'Are you all right there, son?' Ned asked.

'They're...they're coming for me. That's all I know.'

'Who's coming for you?'

'You don't know who they are. But I know who they are and I know they're coming for me.'

'What are you talking about?'

'It keeps happening over and over again, the same things, the same sights, the same sounds; the earth, the digging, the bodies. I'm here and there at the same time.'

'The Tans won't get you, Dinny.'

'It's not the Tans, it's the dead people, all the dead people.'

Ned Murphy put his arm around Dinny's shoulder.

'Hey, it's all right, son, nobody's going to get you. There's enough of us here to mind you. We'll look after you.'

Ned Murphy wiped his brow. Ever since they started building the bomb factory, he had noticed that Dinny seemed very jittery. He had difficulty in concentrating on anything for very long. A rat in the hedge, the sound of a crow banger, the call of a quail over the bogs was enough to frighten the daylights out of him. On one occasion he was even spooked by the sudden swerve of a flock of starlings flying west.

Ned Murphy had heard about similar behaviour from lads who had been in the trenches: soldiers, shellshocked out of their minds, panicking at the sound of a shot going off, smelling imaginary gas, seeing rats where there were no rats, crying at the slightest thing and calling out the names of dead comrades over and over again. Dinny had become like one of those war crazed soldiers: moody, irritable, angry and suspicious, which was a complete contrast to his normally genial nature.

'You'll be all right, son,' Ned Murphy said. 'Here, take Doll's reins. The cart is nearly full. There's only an hour of light left in the day.'

Dinny shivered and climbed up out of the pit to where Doll patiently waited for him. At least this time, it was earth in the cart, not dead youngsters.

He led the horse away to a glen at the far side of the field where he untackled the shafts and lifted them high to tip the soil into a gully. By the time he got back to Ned Murphy he had recovered some of his composure.

'I don't know what happened to me there,' he said, trying to make light of what he had seen, afraid that Ned Murphy might think he was mad. 'Maybe I'm coming down with something, maybe that 'flu is on the way back.'

'Don't worry, son. We'll make some great stuff here yet.'

'Stuff?'

'Grenades, bombs, mines.'

'Oh, yes, of course,' he said, as if he had forgotten why they were there in the first place. Ned Murphy shook his head. You think you know somebody, he said to himself, and then they turn out to be completely different to what you had expected.

But Dinny knew exactly what was happening to him; his visions were clear as pebbles on the bottom of a spring. The boys and men in the graves were coming back to haunt him. The killings were appearing in flashes before his eyes, dissociated flashes, bits of visions coming and going with no apparent connection between them. These shards of the events of the Rea stuck into him like pieces of a broken window. But the pieces never combined to make the full pane, they were just jagged shards of the past that rendered him numb and made him think he might really be going out of his mind.

And sometimes he saw coffins and dead bodies parade along the road before him, other times it would be the more recently killed nameless boys and the loss to their families who would never find out what happened to them. The burden was simply too great for Dinny to bear.

In several dreams he saw himself lying on his own deathbed with nobody around him. Then, from every corner of the room, would come the sound of hissing and spitting. He could hear it in the flickering candlelight and the dim shadows; the long low lament of the lost souls, the spirits of the murdered men and they all rustling and hawking at him. These faceless ones would keep gagging and spluttering until eventually he would wake up, sweating. He would sit up terrified for the rest of the night, afraid to fall asleep again, in case the demons would come back to haunt him.

Now it was apparent that the days would bring no respite from these hallucinations either. He lived in fear of going completely mad. As a result, he had become quite a whiskey drinker, for a young fellow not long shaving, regularly calling on Moss Corrigan for naggins of the stuff. He could now only sleep when anaesthetized by a cup or two of raw malt or poteen. His bedroom stank of alcohol every morning.

25

It was late in the evening of St Stephen's Day and he was working on his own in the stall, flinging out dung and scattering straw to make bedding for the cows. His parents and sister were away visiting cousins, as they always did on St Stephen's Day. In the weeks after the burial of Ted Mills and his sons, despite not being asked to help with any further executions in the Rea, Dinny found that the nightmares and ghoulish daytime visions continued. He had just locked the cows in for the night when he heard the dog barking, followed by the rattle of tackle and the creak of cartwheels.

A pony and trap arrived into the yard with two strangers in it. The sheepdog scooted out in full flight, his tail flailing behind him, barking at the wheelbands of the trap.

'Lie down, Carlo,' Dinny shouted at the dog. 'Go to bed.'

He took the pony by the bridle and held it as the two men got down. They were about his own age; young lads in caps and light overcoats; pale and serious, they were shivering with the cold. The taller one, a good-looking fellow, spoke.

'Are you Denis Fitzgibbon?'

'Junior or Senior?'

The strangers looked at each other.

'We don't know. We were just told to ask for Denis Fitzgibbon of E Company, 4th Battalion, Cork No 1 Brigade.' The men had city accents; they pronounced Denis as Dunnis. Dinny was wary of strangers - the British were known to be sending intelligence officers dressed as tramps into active areas. But these fellows' accents were so perfectly Cork that they were unlikely to be some sort of British undercover operatives - two of whom he had buried the previous month.

'I'm that man,' he said eventually.

'The Brigade command is sending you two prisoners that we apprehended last night,' the tall one said officiously. 'These two are part of the Crown's forces and they have already been sentenced to be executed. We believe this is the detention area for that kind of operation.'

'Go on, Jackie, get on with it,' the smaller fellow who wore glasses and looked thinner and more frightened, said. 'Let's get out of here. It'll be pitch dark in an hour. This place gives me the creeps.'

'Don't mind him, Mr Fitzgibbon. He's just a city lad, and city lads aren't used to the countryside. They think it's all darkness and boogie men. I spent a lot of my own youth in Newcastlewest, if you know that part of the world.'

'I've heard of it.'

'We have two boyos here in the trap,' the first one said. The smaller fellow opened the back of the trap, lifted a tarpaulin and there, huddled underneath, lay two lads of around his own age in good suits, bound with twine and gagged with handkerchief; they fitted each other on the floor like twins in a timber womb. They peeped up over their gags, eyes bulging in the half-light like frightened cattle going to a fair. Their expressions reminded him of the big questioning eyes of Charlie Chaplin.

'I don't do this type of thing anymore,' Dinny said.

'But this is the Company of Captain Dan Donohoe, isn't it? I mean he's the officer in charge?'

Dan Donohoe was away at a brigade meeting and Ned Murphy was gone to Cork. That meant that, technically at least, Dinny was in charge.

'It is.'

'Well, we were told to hand these two over to the custody of Captain Donohoe's Company. And seeing as you're in charge, we've our part of the business done. We can't spend the rest of the evening around looking for Captain Donohoe. Can we, Michael?'

'We certainly can't,' Michael replied. 'Your instructions - and this has been confirmed by HQ - is to sort out these two.'

'Come on, Jackie, let's dump 'em and hoof it back.'

Dinny stuck his pitchfork into a pile of straw. The cows stood outside in a line with sad faces, longing to be let in.

'I'll make sure they get properly looked after,' Dinny said, eventually.

'Good man yerself.'

'Let's get them on the ground so,' Michael said. With what seemed like a sigh of relief he climbed on the trap and pulled the first of the two men to the edge of the floorboard and rolled him on the ground. Then he did the same to the second. The men fell on one another and squirmed like worms, ruining their good suits on the súalach running from the base of the dunghills.

'Where de ya want 'em, boy?' Michael asked.

Dinny hesitated and stroked his chin. 'The best thing to do, I'd say, is to tie them to the pillars of the hayshed. I can sort them out later.'

'Right so, boy. Lead us to this hayshed.'

They picked up the two men and dragged them across the haggard to the hayshed. Then they tied them onto the uprights of the hayshed so that they stood up, wrapped around two H irons as if embracing them.

'They won't go too far now,' Michael said.

'They won't have to,' Jackie replied. 'Dan Donohoe is a great man for this kind of work, so we're told.'

'He's the best there is,' Dinny said.

'We're leaving 'em in good hands, so. Dowtcha, boy.'

The two Volunteers climbed back on the trap, smiles now broad as daisies on their faces. They couldn't hide their delight at having washed their hands of the prisoners.

This, Dinny thought, is how the responsibility for dirty deeds is passed on; everyone does his bit and hands the problem over to someone else. The lads who ran around the streets of Cork gathering information did not know that the end result would be a body or two dumped in a bog. The pale city boys who picked up such prisoners and bundled them into cars barely knew those who would put bullets through their brains. And the country boys for the most part believed the prisoners to have been tried and sentenced and worthy of death for a whispered crime of some vague but entirely sinister nature. They were regarded by all as 'bad people': spies, informers, loyalists or criminals.

The one called Jackie turned the pony around and cracked the reins and, in a clatter of hooves on the cobbles with the dog barking after them, they disappeared into the night. Dinny whistled to Carlo to stop barking and come back to him. When they were gone, he locked the sheepdog in a barn and wandered around the yard, kicking a stone ahead of him. Ireland had brought a few more of its uninvited guests to him. Now Dinny had to figure out what to do with them.

To buy time, he went back into the cow stall, scattered cut turnips along the troughs and opened the door for the cows to come in. The cows, smelling the feed, rushed past him one into each bail. He closed them all in, pulling the iron rings down over the tops of the bails. The cows snorted with contentment and shook their heavy heads and blew strings of cow snot against the opposite wall.

When he was finished he sat at the entrance to the stalls, staring out into the darkness for a long time. The sky had still a rim of slate blue to the west, the half-hearted shreddings of a short day. A gale was rising in the north, bringing with it showers that were half rain, half sleet, driving drizzle hard as gravel into the hills. A few farms across the valley had lights on as people worked outside, small lights, like half-blind eyes in the huge and empty countryside.

He heard a door slamming and saw Bill make his way to the outhouse to get his bicycle. Then a bicycle lamp went on and

Bill, easygoing and careless about curfews, pedalled off down the lane, singing loudly to himself.

Dinny went inside to the kitchen, filled the kettle and swung it over the fire. He banked the turf high and started to turn the bellows wheel. When the fire was roaring, he went to the bread bin and cut himself a few slices of Thompson's Best. He found bacon in the scullery, buttered the bread and lathered slices of bacon with mustard. He then made himself a large pot of tea and sat down to eat his supper.

When he was finished, he buttered still more bread, placed slices of bacon on top and made fresh tea. He strained the tea into two bottles, added milk, and plugged both bottles with rolled up newspaper. Then he put the lot into a basket, lit a storm lamp and went outside to the hayshed.

He found the two men slumped against the pillars looking very frightened. Lifting the storm lamp nearer their faces, he realized that they were both probably younger than himself; at a guess, they were no more than seventeen or eighteen, two more candidates for the bogs of the Rea. He shook his head and hung the storm lamp from one of the up-turned shafts of a butt.

'Okay,' he said, 'I'm going to take off those gags and I want no shouting or screaming, do you hear me? I want you to tell me calmly and quietly who you are, what you were doing and why you were picked up by our lads. And no funny stuff. D'you understand?'

The two men looked at Dinny, then down at the basket of food and then back at each other and nodded. Dinny opened the knot tying the handkerchief around back of the first man's neck. Then he did the same to the second.

'Okay, names first.'

The fair-haired one spoke.

'His name is Poynton and I'm Watchorn, we're with the 2nd Battalion, Royal 'ampshire Regiment.'

Ah, so these were actual soldiers! Well, that would make a change from recent events for Dan Donohoe and the Rea.

'But we're supposed to be with the Manchesters,' Poynton interrupted. 'You see, we wanted to join the Manchesters, but they put us into the 'ampshires instead.'

'Even though we're from near Bristol. We had friends in the Manchesters, you see. And we wanted to go to India.'

The story they told him was that they had enlisted in the British Army in Bristol only a few weeks earlier. Thinking they were going to India, they found themselves holed up in Cork, waiting for a destroyer that would take them to India. On the afternoon of St Stephen's Day, or Boxing Day as they called it, they were walking out with two girls in Tivoli when they were picked up by the IRA.

'They pulled the girls away from us. The girls were screaming.'

'They were very frightened.'

'We thought we were going to be shot on the spot.'

'Then one of them said; this officious little fellow who looked like one of their officers. 'e said....'

'...'e had a different accen' to the others. 'e said it would have to go through official channels, that we would first have to be tried and charged. I can tell you, from the faces of some of the chaps with him we were very lucky 'e was there. Otherwise, we would have been shot out of 'and. We know how the Shinner operates; 'e shoots first and asks questions afterwards.'

'You were lucky, I'd say.'

'What's your name?' Watchorn asked. 'Or are you not allowed to tell us?' He had an ironic expression on his face, as if he was amazed to have wound up in the position in which he now found himself.

Dinny considered for a minute. He was not supposed to give his name to prisoners.

'Dinny.'

'You're not going to shoot us, are you, Dinny?'

Dinny looked at them for a while, at the sad state of their best suits ruined by súalach, at the stench and wet smelly dampness they were standing in, at their attempts to be light-hearted in the face of fear.

'No. I'm not going to shoot you,' he said finally. 'And I'm going to do my best to make sure nobody else shoots you either. Which is why we have to be very careful and why you have to listen to what I say and do exactly as I tell you. Is that understood?'

'We'll do anything you tell us, mate. We don't mind.'

'Right. First, you have to understand, your life isn't worth a curse in this parish nor in several parishes around here.'

'We understand that.'

'Secondly, if word got out to my unit that I'm doing this, I'd be shot out of hand myself as a spy. So what I'm about to do is very dangerous for me personally. Now I'm doing it for my own reasons, mainly because I believe there's a God up there and He's looking down on me and I don't want to face the Day of Judgement with the two of you on my conscience. There are people who wouldn't have any such qualms. And if it was any other night of the year and you arrived here, I can assure you, you wouldn't get out of here alive.' When fellows like that turned up they were shot out of hand, Dinny knew. They would not even see the inside of Sing Sing. He did his best to sound as measured and reasonable as possible but his heart was thumping.

'Now there's a couple of things I want you both to be clear on. If you try to escape around here you'll be rounded up and shot - as sure as night follows day. The people will turn you into the IRA. And with what's going on in the country now, with your friends, the Tans, burning down the centre of Cork city, I don't think you'd blame them.'

'Those Tans, they're not our friends.'

'Either way, you're finished if you run.

'I intend to take you back to Cork, but I'll have to blindfold you so that you don't know where you're going and you won't be in a position to lead the enemy back to us.'

'Don't worry. We won't tell a soul about any of this.'

'Maybe you won't. But I'm taking no chances.' Dinny had heard a story that Sean Moylan in North Cork had released two British soldiers, who immediately led the military back to where his his column was billeted. The column was lucky to escape.

'The next thing is that if I'm stopped by the police or the army, I'm breaking the curfew. You'll have to stand up for me then and dig me out - make excuses for me. Work out some story. Do you understand?'

'Don't worry. We'll make sure our boys won't get their 'ands on you.'

'The other problem is if we're stopped by the IRA, I'll have to tell them I'm taking you to be executed and, if they tag along, the chances are that you will be executed. The only thing we have going for us here is that our boys tend to keep away from the roads at night because it's so risky. But it's something that might happen. I hope you're prepared for that.'

'We're in your 'ands, mate.'

'Okay, I'm going to release you now. I have some food here. I want you to eat it as fast as you can. Then I want you to get into my trap and lie down on the floor. I'll cover you with a couple of potato sacks. Just remember; if you run, you haven't a snowball's chance in hell.'

'We won't run, don't worry.'

He untied their hands and feet and they fell on the bread as if they hadn't eaten in weeks.

'This is very good of you, mate,' Poynton said, between chews of bacon sandwich and slugs of tea.

'We're deeply indebted to your kindness, sir,' Watchorn said.

'Don't thank me yet. Let's just hope we all get out of this alive,' Dinny muttered.

While they were eating, Dinny went to the stables and tackled his fastest pony and pulled the trap out of the barn. He got a few sacks and forkfuls of straw and threw them onto the floor of the trap. He went to the house and got his warmest coat and cap and found a pair of Wren Boy masks that he and Bill had since they were children.

'Okay, the plan is for you to hide in the back of the trap under these sacks. The bags and the hay will keep you warm, well, warm enough, anyway. You're to stay down unless I tell you otherwise. If we're stopped by the military, sit up straight and tell them that you were lost and that I found you out in the countryside and that I'm returning you to Victoria Barracks. If we meet the IRA, shove the masks on you and keep you're mouths shut and I'll tell them we're Wren Boys out collecting door to door.'

'What are Wren Boys?'

'If I had time now, I'd tell you.'

'It's Boxing Day, Poynton, you idiot. Mummers.'

The men climbed into the trap and huddled down among the sacks and the hay. Dinny climbed onto the driver's seat and buttoned his coat high to his chin and wrapped another sack over his knees and pulled his cap low over his ears. He tapped the pony lightly with the reins and went off down the lane under the low bare trees.

They went by the back roads in the direction of the city. The wind moaned steady and cold and the rain stung his face as if he was being constantly slapped with a wet rag. Showers loomed like grey battleships and spilled their contents and sleet ran down the back of his neck.

They reached Mayfield on the edge of the city by ten o'clock. They had not been stopped by anyone. On the high ground above Lota, Dinny pulled the pony in under a tree.

'Now lads,' he lifted the bags, ''tis shanks mare from here on in. You're on you're own now. Take off the blindfolds. Talk to no one, no one at all; your accents will give you away, as easy as that.' He clicked his fingers. 'Follow this road and it'll bring you straight to the Barracks gate.'

'But that will bring us through Dillon's Cross where a Shinner ambush took place just a week or two ago.'

'There are Shinners, as you call them, everywhere. It's not safe but it's a damn sight safer than where you came from. Anyway, I can't take you any further. So long as you keep your mouths shut you'll be all right. On the other hand, you might be lucky and meet a patrol of your own crowd.'

'Listen, Paddy - Dinny - we don't know how to thank you. If you ever get pulled in, we'll make sure you get treated fairly.'

'Thanks, but I don't think life works out as neatly as that.'

'Well, thanks all the same, mate. We were finished only for you. And don't worry, we won't tell anybody.'

Stiffly the two soldiers stood up in the trap and got out. Sheepishly they looked up and down the lane and looked at each other, undecided what to do next.

'That way,' Dinny pointed. 'Let on you know what you're doing and where you're going. Talk to no one. Just keep walking straight on to the top of the hill. Now, move.'

He turned the pony and trap around and headed back towards Glanmire. From the high ground of Mayfield he could see across into the harbour, where a huge moon was rising over the Great Island, casting fistfuls of broken light upon the water. Dinny stared at it and uttered a small prayer for the return of peace and normality to the land as he moved the trap through the familiar darkness of the lanes.

26

As he headed towards Dunkettle, he was afraid there might be a patrol on the bridge but he saw nothing. As the moon rose, the night got brighter and he felt he was moving through a shadow version of the day. He didn't want to drive the pony too fast; he wasn't sure how well Bill had fed her that evening. He let the reins go slack, sparks came from her shoes like flintlights from the stones below. All the warring parties seemed to be asleep.

He avoided detection until after he passed the Island Gate. Then, while he was going under a clump of spindly birch, he saw the shadow of a huge figure standing on the ditch, his back against the moonlight. The man jumped down off the ditch and shone a light in Dinny's face. The pony shied and whinnied as the trap lurched to one side. Dinny froze in his seat. All the possible factions that might be on the road in the middle of the night flashed through his mind and none of them were benign. He was sure he was about to be murdered.

'Where are you going, young fella,' a deep voice said, 'out on a pony and trap at this hour of night?'

'I'm going home.'

Dinny heard a revolver being cocked.

'Well, you're going to make a little detour first. You're going to get me to Midleton before daybreak.'

'I'm not sure if the pony will make that kind of distance. She's already got eight or nine miles in her legs.'

'Don't worry about the pony. There are a few places down the road where we can change that pony for a new one. That'll not be a problem.'

The man climbed up on the seat beside Dinny. Dinny could see him quite well in the moonlight. He was six foot three or four and dressed in khaki breeches and a sort of combat jacket and he had a high broad forehead and his lank hair was combed back from his eyes.

'I suppose I won't need this,' he said. Dinny could see him grinning in the moonlight as he uncocked his revolver and put it into a holster underneath his jacket. He thought from the man's strange combination of uniform and half-uniform that he was a Black and Tan. There were a fair few Irishmen in the Black and Tans, Dinny knew. With his military bearing he could also be an undercover British Army officer masquerading as an IRA man. Undercover men in breeches murdered several Volunteers in Carrigtwohill at night. Dinny resolved to say as little as he could and to do exactly as he was told.

The man settled himself down and slouched comfortably on the seat and stretched his legs in front of him. 'Ah, that's a relief,' he said. 'It's great to take the weight off the legs. I thought I'd be stuck there for the rest of the night. This cursed curfew has the country all up in a heap.'

Dinny flicked the reins and they moved out from under the trees and into the pale ribbon of moonlight that was the main road to Midleton. They rode in silence for a while. Then the stranger asked: 'Do I know you from somewhere, boy?'

'I don't think so.'

'What are you doing out travelling this late of a Stephen's Night?' He stared across at Dinny. 'It's not exactly good for your health to be out and about at this hour, is it?'

'Everybody's afraid to move, right enough,' Dinny replied.

'But you're not?'

'I'm afraid of this and that. I'm running errands, that type of thing. Just helping neighbours out.'

'Hmm.'

The man said no more and began to doze off beside him. Soon, with the rhythmic shaking of the trap, he was asleep.

They passed through Carrigtwohill, the scene of much army and police terror and the killing of civilian spies and IRA men. The village was quiet as a funeral as they slipped between the houses.

An hour later, they were on the Midleton side of Carrigtwohill when suddenly an owl came out of nowhere and swooped low and skimmed their heads and vanished silently over them like a broad black kite. Dinny was startled. The owl didn't make a sound but it frightened the pony who pulled against the traces and jerked the trap sharply to one side.

Suddenly, Dinny's passenger shot bolt upright.

'Jesus! What was that?'

'An owl.'

'Christ, I must have dozed off.' He shook himself.

'Dozed off? You've been asleep for the best part of an hour.'

'An hour? Good God. And you didn't throw me on the roadway or try to make a grab for my gun?'

'Why should I?'

The man turned on his lamp and shone it in Dinny's face.

'I knew I'd seen you before,' he said, as if he'd just realized he remembered something. 'You're one of Donohoe's boys, aren't you?'

Dinny was surprised that the man recognized him yet he found it oddly gratifying.

'So, tell me, do you dig the holes, hold the lamps or fire the shots?'

'I dig the holes.'

'And anything else that needs to be done?'

'I suppose so.'

'Like running errands in the middle of the night?'

'Did you ever hear of Diarmuid Hurley?'

'You're Diarmuid Hurley?'

'Me, no. I'm with him though. I'm Josie Ahern.'

'Ah, Josie Ahern. You took over in Midleton from Tadhg Manley when he was gaoled.'

'You knew Tadhg Manley?'

'He was my schoolteacher for a while. He was the one who got me interested in this whole business. He gave me books; John Mitchel and the likes.'

'You're a Christian Brother's boy?'

'I was, for a year. Then they took me out to serve my apprenticeship.'

'When Tadhg Manley was jailed he was an awful loss to us. He planned the taking of Carrigtwohill Barracks down to the last detail.'

'No one was shot?'

'No one was shot. That was then. This is now. We were all innocent then.'

They pulled into a farmyard owned by a family called Higgins and swapped the pony for one of Higgins's and made sure Dinny's pony got fed and watered and went on their way again. The moon was now right overhead and their shadows fell directly on the ground and they were followed by the persistent image of themselves on the passing gravel. As they were approaching the outskirts of Midleton, Dinny got an idea:

'Listen, do you mind me asking you something?'

'Fire away.'

'What kind of qualities would a fella need to be part of a flying column?'

'Are you thinking of joining us?' Ahern looked across at him and grinned.

'Yes. I've thought about it for a fair while now, in fact.'

'What do you need?' Ahern thought for a moment, 'I suppose the ability to fight. You need to be fit enough to be able to walk long distances. It's a help to be able to run fast, to operate under pressure. You'd need be able to shoot, preferably straight. And you'd have to have the stomach for killing as well, though I don't suppose that would be a problem to someone who has worked with Dan Donohoe.'

Dinny said nothing.

'And you'd have to know a bit about ordnance.'

'What's ordnance?'

'Munitions, arms, guns, bullets. Weapons in other words.'

'I could learn.'

'We could teach you, of course, a strong boy willing to work, as they say. There's one problem. You'd have to be nominated by your commanding officer to join us.'

'That means Dan Donohoe would have to nominate me. Unlikely, seeing as how he doesn't believe in flying columns.'

'Doesn't he, indeed? That fits in with everything else he doesn't believe in.'

'If the request came from you, I'm sure he might give in though.'

'I'll tell you now what you'll do. You know a place called Blossomgrove?'

'I've heard of it.'

'There's a disused farmhouse up at the end of that lane. It's owned, I think, by a farmer called McGrath.'

'That's not too far from one of our bomb factories.'

'That's the one. That's where we're holed up at the moment. Call up there tomorrow or after. I'll see to it that Jack O'Connell looks after you. He's our Quartermaster.'

'What about Dan Donohoe?'

'Don't worry about Dan Donohoe. I'll sort him out. Any friend of Tadhg Manley's is a friend of mine.'

The Higgins pony was a lot slower than his own and the road seemed longer than it actually was, winding under the moon that had moved to their backs so that their shadows now preceded them on the ground. The cement-coloured tinge of the new dawn was beginning to rise as they arrived at the outskirts of Midleton. The houses of the town were small turrets squatting against the eastern sky.

'I'll get out here,' Josie Ahern said. 'It's not safe for you to come into the town. The peelers are jittery. You're better off turning around here now, boy. If you want to, you can stay at Higgins's, they're a safe house. Get a bit of sleep. Your pony will be revived by morning and you can take her home then.'

'I might do that.

Ahern jumped down, climbed over a wall and disappeared from view. Dinny was sleepy and yet exhilarated at the same time. Suddenly he felt full of energy. He turned Higgins's pony around on the road and headed back in the direction from which he came.

27

He slept in Higgins's hayloft for a few hours and for the first time in ages he didn't dream about the Rea or anything he had witnessed in Sing Sing. When he awoke, it was late morning and he could hear comings and goings in the yard below. He was chilled and shivering and covered in flea bites.

He sat up. Small winter sunlight came through a dusty window and stained the whitewashed wall beside him. He could hear male voices in the yard talking about the price of potatoes and female voices speaking of the terrible things that were going on in the country.

He watched one flea bravely setting off across the broad of his forearm, a latter day Vasco da Gama of the tribe of fleas. He picked it up and crushed it between two thumbnails. He didn't want to bother any of the Higgins's and didn't want to be seen by neighbours. So he crept quietly down the stairs, out into the haggard and around the walls to the stables. He found his pony; she was as fresh as if she had been standing in clover since the previous night. He tackled her to the trap, which he had hidden in an outhouse the night before, and he managed to leave without saying a word to anybody. What words he had now were for the pony's ears only. That was the way it would be on the run, he fancied; there would be no time for the niceties of life, common courtesies had to take the form of silence; silence and fleas, the staples in the life of the guerrilla fighter.

Which was what he was about to become. He almost had to pinch himself as he considered the implications of what had happened the night before. Any friend of Tadhg Manley's is a friend of mine. Though he would be on the run, he knew it would not be through bravery or recklessness or even a burning love for Ireland. He would be on the run because he wanted to run away, because he needed to run away.

He knew it was his only option. He was suffering from some sort of geographical phobia when it came to the Rea. Releasing the two soldiers was some slight recompense for the horrors he had been involved in earlier, but it was a bad precedent for an IRA man to be releasing prisoners. It would not happen again. It was no way to fight a war. All he had done was to reduce slightly the head count that Dan Donohoe would come up with when he boasted about what he had done for the Cause. There would be two bodies fewer in the Rea; that was all.

The column, on the other hand, would allow him to continue on his own side, to be seen to be above reproach, to be perceived as brave, heroic, idealistic and daring, to be on a higher plane in the scheme of things than even Dan Donohoe, who was, at the end of the day, a mere executioner.

When he got home, the first thing he did was to soak all his clothes in boiling water and douse himself in louse powder. His parents didn't ask him where he had been or ask any other awkward questions. He ate his dinner in silence. Then he went with Bill to the farthest field, where they spent the afternoon snagging turnips, while Doll stood and stared calmly at the horizon. Bill didn't ask him anything about where he had been or what he had been doing. Rather, he whistled tuneless tunes and sang snatches of songs and commented absently on the weather.

That night, while they were eating their tea, Dinny announced his intention of going on the run. He did not elaborate further.

'God between us and all harm,' his mother said as she blessed herself. His father tried to persuade him to reconsider; he had more than an inkling of what had been going on in the locality over the previous six months. Finally, Dinny's mother got all of them to kneel down and say the Rosary to keep him safe from harm. The following morning he made his way to

Blossomgrove. The frosty air was sharp as new razor blades. The world looked as if somebody had uprooted all the trees, dipped them into sugar glaze and planted them back without disturbing the ground.

The derelict house in Blossomgrove was a mile and a half in from the road. Well-hidden in a clump of trees, it was the most desolate place imaginable, facing northwards towards the brown receding brow of the Nagle Mountains. It smelt of a hundred years of mould.

He knocked at the door but there was no reply. He pushed it open. Inside, there was nothing but decay and fungi like ears listening from old boards. As he turned to go, his heart full of disappointment, he heard a shout.

'Hey, young fella. Are you young Fitz?' It was Jack O'Connell. Dinny knew him vaguely from some of the Volunteer marches of a year or two earlier.

'That's me.'

'Josie said to meet you here. I believe you're off with the boys?'

'That's the plan, anyway.'

'Well then, you missed them. They left just two hours ago. You'll need this.'

Out of his jacket pocket he pulled a black service revolver. 'It's a Smith and Wesson and it's reliable. I bought it myself from an ex-service man. It's as good as new. Look after it well for me, will ya,' he said with a smile.

'I will.'

'I thought first you'd be better off without it, in view of the penalty for being caught in possession of arms.' Anybody caught by the military carrying weapons could be shot on the spot. 'But Josie says every man has to be able to defend himself. The only bullets I can spare are the few in the chamber and these few here.' He handed Dinny half a dozen .45 bullets.

'Where are the column gone?'

'They're gone down to Mogeely. They're staying in a house there. I can give you directions.'

'I'll head off there now.'

'I wouldn't, if I were you.'

'But I'm all ready to go.'

'Don't!' Jack O'Connell was adamant. He folded his arms as if to block Dinny's way.

'Why not?'

'There's a big stunt planned for tomorrow night. They won't want to know you tonight or tomorrow, they'll all be too nervous. Wait till the day after. They'll be able to show you the ropes then, if all goes well. You know what they say; never bother a man when he's busy. Take this and go back home for yourself. Enjoy the rest while you can. Life is tough on the run. You'll be a guerrilla for long enough.'

'Thanks.' Dinny took the revolver. It was heavier than he had expected, like an iron weight used for weighing grain. He put it into his pocket nervously. He didn't like the idea of going around with this murderous piece of metal in his pocket.

'What about Dan Donohoe? What does he think about all this?'

'Donohoe doesn't want you going. He'd prefer you to stay at home working for him. But if Hurley or Josie say you go, Donohoe has to let you go, much and all as he mightn't like to.'

Dinny shoved the Smith and Wesson up under his shirt. It was cold against his skin. He put the bullets in his pocket. As he did so, the thought occurred to him that the world was gone mad from guns.

28

At nine o'clock the following evening, ten RIC men left their barracks in Midleton on their nightly patrol of the town. They were divided into two groups under the command of a Head Constable; the taller group, all over six foot in height, were old RIC men; constables from the days before the 'Troubles', when this area was one of the most peaceful in the country. The smaller men were new recruits, so-called Black And Tans, ex-soldiers with experience in the Great War but with no knowledge of police procedures; good at killing and causing ructions, but worthless at police or political work.

This was a routine patrol, their second after the Christmas break. They made their way along the footpaths on opposites sides of the main street like a sheriff and deputies patrolling some Wild West town, two groups of five, each man ten to twelve paces apart. The shops were closed, the shutters down, the odd horse and butt with an empty milk churn was trundling out into the darkness of the countryside.

Midleton was a quiet town in a prosperous area, so peaceful, in fact, that the curfew had been lifted the week before Christmas to allow people to do their Christmas shopping. The policemen knew they were lucky to be stationed there; their fellow officers in Bandon and Cork city were having it much tougher, being shot at and often being assassinated by the gunmen coming in from the hills.

However, even in Midleton, they were now beginning to feel isolated. The Sinn Feiners had turned the people against them and the excesses of the Black and Tans in Cork and other areas just made matters worse. Nobody would speak to them now. A man in the town whose two daughters had been going out with policemen had vanished without trace. His daughters were tarred and feathered before they fled to England. As the police approached, people like shadows vanished into doorways. The wind came down with strange broken silence: papers blew along the gutters, a gate creaked, a bin rolled, a door kept tapping against its frame, the street was filled with the smell of horse manure.

A phalanx of a by now risible and declining authority, they reached an intersecting lane at the lower end of Main Street in extended formation. Suddenly, five doorways on either side of the street each yielded two gunmen who opened fire at close range. An elderly constable called Mullen, was killed instantly. Two Black and Tans, Thorpe and Dray, dropped to the ground and were later to die of their wounds, three others were also wounded but the rest managed to escape and made their way back to the barracks. The gunmen collected the guns and bullets from the dying and wounded and vanished into the darkness of the alleys. Any townspeople who heard the commotion were too afraid to come to help, so the policemen were left writhing and moaning in pain, their blood running down the footpaths and out onto the street.

An hour later, reinforcements from Cork, including two ambulances, were ambushed on their way into Midleton. A sergeant and a constable were wounded during this exchange. It was the most daring operation yet carried out by the Midleton IRA. It yielded eight revolvers and six carbines and a hundred rounds of ammunition. The IRA men were excited that night and celebrated well into the small hours in their hideaway out in Mogeely.

The following day the British burned out the homes of seven supporters, so-called 'known sympathizers', in the first official reprisal of the Troubles, though none of the owners had taken any part in the ambush. It was two days short of the New Year, a new year that would see even more killing than the previous one.

202

29

Two days after he had met Jack O'Connell, Dinny woke early. It was still dark as he ate his breakfast. An hour later, as the dawn was rising over East Cork, he was walking as fast as he could, skirting the edge of the Rea. When he reached the southern and furthest end of it, he didn't look back, but headed south-east, onto the road, into the rising sun. He would have cycled, but by now the use of bicycles had also been banned across the martial law area. He was wearing new boots that his father had bought for Christmas but had given to Dinny as a parting gift.

He carried over his shoulder a canvas bag containing ham sandwiches, a bottle of tea and in the side pocket he had two slices of Christmas cake wrapped in grease-proof paper which his mother had given him. His only other possessions were an oilskin raincoat, the revolver strapped to his ankle, his father's pocket watch and a Miraculous Medal and brown scapular that he had got from Bina to protect him from harm. To calm their fears he told his family he would be home in a week or two but his plan was to stay away much longer. He did not want to see the Rea for as long as he could help it.

He walked with a loping stride and the further he got from the Rea, the better he felt. He was like a man walking out from under the shadow of himself, like a man who has been buried in a hole and has somehow clambered to the surface to breathe the air again. The country was suddenly bigger, more expansive than it had been for months. He was amazed at how wide the world was, how huge the fields, how fresh the air. When he got out of sight of the Rea, he suddenly wanted to run off like a calf left out on fresh grass, but resisted the temptation. He had twenty miles to travel - that is if he made no mistakes - and he knew that, even by conserving his energies, he would do very well to make it to Mogeely in a day.

By nine o'clock the sun was out, the sky a driven blue; the wind was gone north, hunting showers down from the middle of Tipperary. His plan was to skirt Midleton to avoid trouble, to keep to the high roads where the military rarely travelled. He could make better progress that way. If he had to strike across the fields, however, God only knows how long it would take him to catch up with the column.

By mid-morning, after walking for two hours, his progress slowed when he entered a series of narrow glens with high larches piled up on either side. No sooner was he out of one hollow than he seemed to walk into another and, after a while, he got completely lost. The roads seemed to tumble into valleys, with no signposting or no indication of where north, south, east or west might be.

He had to rely on his instincts, on a vague notion that the rivers in that part of the country ran from north to south and that he had to cross them all till the town was below him to his right. But the trees and the twisting roads and the deep ravines kept puzzling him and then the sky began to cloud over and, shortly after midday, it got milder and began to snow.

It started innocently enough: a few flakes like insects lost from summer that melted into the ground as if they could pass right through it and emerge unchanged on the other side of the world. For a while the road remained dark, the air turned into flour and the sky grew into the blue-grey of old slate. Then as the snowing increased, some of it began to build up on the road and he could see his footprints stretching away behind him as if he was a phantom emerging permanently out of a powdered fog.

If he was lost before, then he was doubly lost now. Big dry flakes began to come as if pumped from some vast snow factory in the sky. They started to build up on the gullies and in the fields, they turned the trees into tall bearded men. Drains, rivulets and streams became the only black things in this white world: strange remnants of a lost planet.

He put on his oilskin and took out the instructions that Jack O'Connell had given him. From where he stood now, amid the whirling, swirling insects of the snow, he couldn't make head nor tail of the instructions. He looked forward and he looked back. He held the sheet of paper this way and that. He thought for a minute he might return home but, from the time he had spent walking, he figured that he must be over half way to Mogeely. This was the worst possible position to be in, midway between a distant home and a vague destination. He decided to push on, to get out of the valleys if he could. There was only one consolation; it was unlikely that the police or the Black and Tans could be out under these conditions.

He ate his lunch under the shelter of a culvert that covered a small stream. When he emerged some fifteen minutes later, he was amazed that it had snowed so much more and the tracks he had made on the way in were already half-filled. It was as if a little man of snow was going around behind him, dusting out his existence. He went back on the road, heading in what he hoped was an easterly direction. He was overheating in the oilskin and had to open it every so often to let the air in. Eventually, after what seemed an eternity of climbing into and out of valleys, he got back on level ground.

Gradually, it stopped snowing. The sky cleared, the wind came up and drifts, sly as lizards, shifted their weight into the lee of ditches. The world became a plane of white, and a silence like the end of time came down upon the landscape and nothing moved and no one made footprints except for himself and a single fox, the one pair of creatures out when all other creatures stayed in their burrows.

Suddenly, at a bend of the road between white ditches that stood like stooks of snow he thought he saw somebody walking ahead of him. Yet when he got to the spot there was nobody there and there were no footprints on the snow, just a smooth unruffled perfection. He knew then that he was still seeing the phantoms that had pursued him since the killings began.

He trudged on and began to tire and then in mid-afternoon he began to feel depressed, to carry the grim weight of his thoughts again. It began to grow dark and he panicked and feared that he was no nearer Midleton than he had been at lunchtime. He walked for another hour and the purple evening rose in front of him and the goldfish clouds to the west lost their lustre and became mere grey blots in the new landscape of stars. The trees around him shook and dropped shovelfuls of snow on the ditches. And then, as if surprised out of their sleep, all the heavens seemed to be suddenly raging with stars, a million pinholes into an unimaginable eternity and he knew it was time to stop. He blew on his hands and looked around and shivered to the marrow of his bones.

Half a mile away to his left, on a ridge facing the sky, he could make out a thin line of trees and in the middle of the trees a farmhouse where a light was shining. He went through a gap into a field and headed towards the light across the white landscape. His boots creaked in the snow. He would be easily tracked now, he thought, even the dumb Tans would know a trail of footprints when they saw one. Occasionally he waded without warning into drifts that came up to his thighs, as if he was a small boat sinking in some uncharted ocean. Once or twice he was so tired he staggered into deep mounds and his feet were wedged and he flailed about with his arms and he thought of sheep that go belly up in snowdrifts and he figured that if he died himself in one of them that it would be no bad way to go.

And he could feel the temptation to lie down in a snowdrift and make a bed of it and close his eyes to the pain but the light kept calling him on, calling, calling with the vague insistence of hope and desperation. Eventually, after four long fields, with his feet heavy as dreadnoughts, he reached the farmyard and went through a gateway into a haggard.

He feared he would not be welcome in the farm, for he could be easily tracked and nobody now wanted to run the risk of harbouring a rebel with the Tans liable to make a visit. He wanted to fall into a stable or a haybarn and fall asleep and move on the following day without alerting the owners but he knew he was too wet from stumbling in the snow to rest and that he could catch pneumonia from such a chilling.

So he went to the house. It was a low farmhouse with an iron roof, much like his own: iron thrown down upon thatch, a quickfire short-term renovation. A little path led into a tiny walled garden that was now stuffed fat with snow. A trail of tracks of birds' feet ran like little barbed wire marks along the windowsill; a Christmas candle surrounded by holly flickered in the window. At least it was a Catholic home: Protestants did not go in for Christmas candles in the window, or so he was always led to believe. Hesitantly, he knocked on the door.

After a minute it opened.

'Hello, who's there?' asked a girl of about twenty with a straight fringe of black hair.

'I'm on the run. Can I come in?' Dinny held his cap in his hand like a tramp or a mendicant let loose from some workhouse.

'I only work here. I'll have to ask them inside. If you hang on there a second.'

The girl closed the door and went back inside. Half a minute later she opened it again.

'They said you can come in.'

He stamped heavily on the mat at the doorstep, his boots making casts of snow, small strange perfect formations. He took off his oilskin and shook it, leaving as much of the melting snow as possible outside. Then he stepped through the low doorway.

It was warm in the kitchen, several gas lamps were lighting, a large fire flickered in the hearth. The room was decorated with berry-less holly on a dozen wall hangings, determinedly Christmassy. This was not a house of people worrying about men on the run. Two little girls of three or four in flowery dresses inspected him, their faces big and blue-eyed, shy and peeping from behind furniture at this damp snow-covered spectre.

'Nuala and Eileen, get back in here this minute. It's time for bed for you two. Now, come on, get your night dresses.'

A dark-haired woman was feeding a toddler with a spoon at the kitchen table. The little girls ran away furtively and hid behind an armchair and occasionally stuck their foreheads around the corner for a look. There seemed to be no men about.

'I'm sorry to burst in on you like this,' Dinny said, 'but I'm completely whacked. And I'm lost.' Dinny was embarrassed, he didn't have the cockiness of those used to being 'on the run' for Ireland. 'I'm sorry,' he said, noticing that the children seemed to be afraid of him, 'I must look a fright.'

'That's all right, lad. 'Tis a bad night.'

''Tis a bad night all right,' he replied.

'Is it still snowing?' The woman looked exhausted. She was pale and had dark circles around her eyes and wisps of hair fell on her face as is she hadn't had time to tie them back.

'It's stopped.'

'It's been a terrible winter. Sometimes I think it will never end.'

'Terrible. '

'Are you drenched?' the woman asked as she carefully took a spoonful of food from the cup in her hand and raised it towards the baby's mouth. The baby, a little fellow with a head of surprisingly curly black hair and an upturned nose, turned his head to one side and shoved the spoon away with a determined sweep of his hand.

'Saturated.'

'That's not good for you.' And to the baby: 'Just one more spoon of yum yums for Mammy. There's a good boy.'

The baby appeared to examine her face carefully as if trying to decide whether or not to do what he was told and then swallowed one more spoonful. Then his mother wiped his mouth with his bib and got up from the table.

'You should change out of those wet clothes. You'll catch pneumonia. Mary, get some of himself's clothes for the young fella and get the clothes horse and hang his own up there at the fire. I'm sorry we can't be more hospitable but, as you can see, we're busy enough as it is.'

'That's all right.' Dinny felt the heat of the kitchen baste him all over. He began to sweat.

'Listen, do you know anything about horses?' the woman asked.

'A bit.'

'There's a stallion with a stone in his hoof. Himself is outside in the stables. He has a lot to do. The help isn't great around here.'

'I could get that out,' Dinny said, 'or at least I often did so before.'

'Would you? His supper is going cold in here. He'd appreciate it if you could give him a hand.'

'I'll have a shot at it, anyway.'

He put on his oilskin again and went back out in the snow. The sweat cooled suddenly like well water on his back. He went into the yard where he found the farmer in a barn with a storm lamp measuring out oats for a stable of horses and filling buckets of water from a barrel. The farmer, a big square-faced man, looked at him, puzzled to find a stranger in his own yard at six o'clock of a winter's evening. 'And you are?' He scratched his head under his hat.

'Dinny'

'Hmm.' He seemed too preoccupied to take any notice of a total stranger turning up in his yard of a dark winter's evening. 'I asked Perry to help me with this, but the lazy ludramán is next to useless. As for Mike, God between us and all harm, what a pair of óinseachs I have to put up with. There's no end to it.'

'Your missus said you have a horse with a stone.'

'I have and he's a right devil. He'd kick the stars. I haven't had time to get around to him.'

'I said to her I'd try to get it out.'

'You did?'

'I'll have a cut off it, anyway.'

'Begod, boy, you're welcome to try.'

'Have you a knife?'

'There's one over there, stuck above that rafter. Light that lamp.' He handed Dinny a second storm lamp and a box of matches. Dinny lit the lamp and reached up behind the beam and found a curved blade that, from the look of it, had taken many a stone from many a horse's hoof.

'He's in the first stable there. Mind him. He's a moody bastard and he's nervous of strangers. It's the left foreleg. You'll know it from the way he's standing.'

Dinny looked in and saw that the stallion's ears were laid back in fury, his eyes staring. But he had a way with horses. He talked quietly to him for a few minutes and soon calmed the stallion down. Then he opened the stable door, lifted the foreleg and had the stone out in an instant.

The farmer came over to join him. 'Isn't that a holy fright now,' he said, 'He was damned slow about letting me near him, and I know me horses. And you just walked right in there. I thought the hoor might rear up on you.'

'It's just a knack.'

'Knack or not, it's a good knack. You're not looking for a job, are you?'

'No.'

'Just as well. I'd like to be able to give you a job but I can't at the moment. 'Tis too much help I have. Not that any of it is any use.' He lifted two buckets, one of water and one of oats and opened a stable door with his shoulder.

'That's all right. As I say, I'm not looking for a job.'

'Then what are you looking for?'

'Someplace safe to spend the night.'

The stallion put his nose into the bucket of water and its contents vanished in an instant.

'So you're one of these IRA fellas? We don't have much truck with that kind of thing around here, you know. I blame you lot for starting this... this Black and Tannery. A couple of hot heads, a fellow once told me, can set the whole country at each other's throats.' The farmer cleared his throat. 'War is no good for anyone. I hope you don't turn out like Perry and Mike here. They were out in the Great War; Wipers or some place they called it, and they haven't done a day's work worth a hat of crabs since they came back. That's what happens to soldiers.'

'I'm just trying to get to Mogeely.'

'Mogeely? There's good land down there and sensible people.'

'Well...'

'You're alright, boy. I mightn't agree with a lot of what you fellas are doing up and down the country but I voted for Sinn Fein and the other bastards are worse. Those Tans are the best weapons you lot ever had; murdering people in the streets and burning creameries. A parcel of bleddy hoors. But don't worry, I'll get you near enough to Midleton in the morning and you can walk the rest of the way to Mogeely.'

'Thanks.'

'Don't thank me, boy. I'd do that much for anyone with a bit of decency in 'em.'

'What about these fellows you mentioned, Perry and Mike, they're soldiers, aren't they? They mightn't agree with me staying here.' Perry and Mike, whoever they were, Dinny thought, were lucky to be living out of the range of Dan Donohoe's particular brand of patriotism.

'Is it Perry and Mike? You're afraid they might turn you in? Just because they were off in the British Army? Christ! You needn't worry your head about that, boy. They wouldn't rise off their arses to do less. Ever since those two amadáns went off to war, they're not worth a curse. They sit around all week waiting to draw their pensions. Those two don't care

211

enough about anything to turn anybody in. You're safe around here - not that I want this place turning into a safe house - but you know what I mean.'

'I think so.'

'Now go on in and change out of those clothes. They'll feed you inside and Mary will find somewhere for you to sleep. I'll be in in half an hour.'

'Do you want a hand with those buckets?'

'Well, okay, if you know what you're doing?'

'I do.'

They fed the rest of the horses, watered them, closed the half doors on the stables and shut the horses in for the night. By the time they went inside for their tea they had the instinctive rapport of men have who regularly work together. Dinny just hoped that, when he met up with the column, things would go this smoothly.

30

The following morning, the farmer took Dinny on his horse and trap across the high land and down the long hill towards Midleton. There was still a lot of snow about, but it had frozen overnight into black rivulets and a crisp crust had formed on the ground underneath.

'This is a great day for your kind of job,' the farmer said, blowing his nose, 'being on the run, going from here to there.'

At the top of Ballyedmond Hill the whole of East Cork lay before them, a plain of white land and white trees stretching to the far ridge that bounded the inland valleys from the sea. Slowly the horse made his way down the hill and, picking his way carefully along the margins of the road, managed to stay upright.

'There isn't a lorry in the country that could come up that hill on a morning like this,' the farmer said. 'There are horses for courses, don't you think? No motorcar can do what he can do.'

Dinny was in luck, although he didn't realize it. For if the farmer had read the Cork Examiner of that or the previous day (the Cork Examiner was back in business within a few days of the IRA smashing up its presses), he would have been less than happy about transporting someone who might have been involved in the Midleton shootings. But news travels slowly in a snowbound land.

'Now, the place you're going to is over there, about three or four miles at the most. You'll get there in an hour and you'll be as safe as houses with all that ice.'

'Thanks very much for the hospitality, your wife was very kind to me,' Dinny said. 'I was spun to the ropes last evening. I don't know what I'd have done if it weren't for you and your family.'

'Don't mention it, boy.'

When they got to the bottom of the hill, Dinny climbed down off the trap and placed his boots gingerly on the ground. Hobnails were good for snow but were like skates on ice.

'A cat wouldn't walk on this,' he said.

'Stick to the verge and you'll be all right. Now, off you go, quick.'

The farmer flicked the reins and drove off along the road towards Midleton, the trap juddering like a boxcar on damaged rails as it slipped onto ruts in the frozen snow. Dinny took the road to the left and headed east to avoid the town. He was told to take the third right and then go on for three miles and take the third turn left. The house he was looking for would then be the second farmer's place on the right. He got there by noon.

He was welcomed by a grey-haired woman in a blue apron. The column was billeted with her, she told him and he was welcome to stay so long as he wasn't a spy. When Dinny told her Jack O'Connell had sent him, she seemed happy enough. An hour later twelve or fourteen heavily armed men trooped into the kitchen. Being on the run was obviously taking its toll on them. They all had bags under their eyes and were sallow faced and gaunt, staring into the middle distance like climbers who had been out too many nights on the ridge of a dangerous mountain. None of them said anything. Each found a chair or a stool or the corner of a bench, sat down wearily and lay their rifles on the floor beside them. They eyed him with suspicion although, as he would soon find out, they were used to young followers hanging around the margins of the column. Dinny recognized some of them from the early days of drilling, though they showed no signs of recognizing him. They were followed a few minutes later by three more men: Josie Ahern, who loomed over everyone like a leaning pine tree; a smaller pale-faced man with jet black hair and heavy eyebrows and, to Dinny's utter amazement, trotting behind them, like an ever-attentive terrier, was Con Foley.

'Fitzy boy,' Con Foley said in surprise, 'what in God's name are you doing here? Was Dan Donohoe not able to give you enough action that you had to come all the way here looking for more?' Con Foley laughed his high distinctive laugh balanced as usual somewhere between sarcasm and stupidity.

'Something like that.'

'So you two know each other?' Josie Ahern said. 'I thought you might. Lads, this is Denis Fitzgibbon. He's joining us from today. He's been with Dan Donohoe, so he has plenty of first-hand experience of the enemy.'

None of the men's faces changed expression at the mention of Donohoe's name. It was obvious he was not particularly important to them, if they thought about him at all.

'This is Commandant Diarmuid Hurley, Denis, your new commanding officer.'

Hurley, the dark haired man, who looked small and insignificant beside the taller Ahern, shook Dinny's hand. His handshake was surprisingly gentle.

'Good to have you with us, Denis. We've a lot of hard work to do, God willing, and we're up against a dangerous enemy.' He spoke quietly, with the worn-out dignity of a priest who was tired from caring too much.

'Dinny was one of Tadhg's pupils.' Josie Ahern said.

'Oh, were you indeed? That's good. That's great.'

If Josie Ahern looked like he was enjoying his role, Hurley looked like a fellow who had suffered for it. There was something painful about his exhaustion, something almost ethereal; a tightness around his mouth that suggested many fruitless years given to the cause of Ireland; a sadness in his eyes that could see only one outcome from a war with an enemy of vastly superior resources. Here was a man made for martyrdom, if ever there was one, Dinny thought. It was hard to believe that here he was, sitting with Tadhg Manley's comrade in arms, the first man in the entire country to capture an RIC barracks and, Dinny supposed, one of the bravest men in Ireland.

'Joe,' Josie Ahern called to one of his men. 'Look after this boy. Make sure he gets everything he needs.'

'Will do,' a wiry, dark-haired lad at the back of the kitchen replied. But it was Con Foley, not the dark haired lad, who came to his side. His eyes were bright with excitement. He sat down beside Dinny, treating him like a long lost friend.

'This is fuckin' great, Fitzy boy,' he whispered. 'You'll really enjoy yourself with us,' he laughed. 'You should have been there the other night. Christ, what a night! If you'd only seen the faces of those Black and Tan bastards as they went down.'

'Now, you lads, stop making yourselves too comfortable.' Josie Ahern ordered. 'Get out of here double-quick and let the good lady tidy up her house. You can't expect her to get anything done with a gang of lúdramáns lying around under her feet.'

Reluctantly the men stood up, gathered their rifles like old sheepdogs cleared from the warmth of the kitchen, and filed out of the house.

The wiry dark-haired lad caught up with him and stuck out his hand. 'Joe Morrissey,' he said.

'We'll soon sort you out, Denis. It won't be long before you'll be shooting as straight as the rest of us.'

They crossed the yard and went up the steps into the loft over the outhouse, which they had been using as a makeshift dormitory. Hurley went to the end of the room and pulled up a chair and stood on it.

'Now, boys, to attention.'

The men lined up and stood to attention, their rifles by their sides, and clicked their heels. In their braces and breeches they were a motley imitation of all things military, with their shirt-sleeves and filthy clothes, their gun belts hanging haphazardly around them. But they stood up straight as any Tommy and stuck out their chests. With just a few dozen bullets each and their out-of-date carbines, they might be no match for professional soldiers but they had a stubbornness that belied their exhaustion and were shabby as old nags from twelve months of engaging with the enemy. A defiance and a fierce recklessness marked their faces and they had the bravery of a communal will and a common purpose.

Hurley spoke slowly as if trying to climb a mountain of exhaustion. 'I want every man to fold up his stuff and be ready to leave first thing in the morning. We're too near Midleton here and the railway line is only a few hundred yards away. We're very exposed. After the other night, as soon as the snow melts, the authorities are bound to get very active.'

'We can be sure that despite all our efforts there are informers out there noting down our comings and goings. Our best plan is to keep on the move. Now I've found a place, which I believe to be very safe. It's in an area where there has been little or no activity to date.'

Dinny thought with dismay that they might be about to go back to the Rea - the safest place in the brigade area - but he was wrong.

'We need a place where we can operate safely for a month at least. A lot of training will be needed, because we're planning a much bigger operation than anything we've tried up to now. The place was suggested to me by Maurice Ahern. Some of you may know where it is. It's just at this side of the No. 2 Brigade area. It's near Clonmult and we should be safe there for a good while.' Hurley smiled wanly. He seemed glad to be able to deliver good news. He gave the impression, in contrast to Dan Donohoe, that he actually cared about the welfare of the men under his command.

'Will there be motor cars?' somebody asked.

'I'm afraid not. The roads are too dangerous now.'

'More plodding for poor old Shanks mare, so,' Joe Morrissey sighed.

'I'll outline the details of the training and our plans once we get there. In the meantime, Lieutenant Ahern or Captain Whelan will fill you in on your duties. At ease.'

Some of the men fell on their bunks and started to chat amongst themselves while others assembled the rolled-up bundles of their meagre possessions. Dinny sat in the corner of the room observing them all.

'This is the best day's work you've ever done in your life, Fitzy, to get in with this lot,' Con Foley said loudly, and the men looked at him and laughed, happy to be joined by another soldier of the Republic.

31

The following day it had become mild again and the snow was gone from all but the highest ground and a light drizzle was rolling down from low grey cloud. The IRA men were on the move.

They were marching single-file from Mogeely to their new quarters, heavily-laden spectres manacled to their guns, wearing overcoats that trailed like grey tails behind them. With their rifles slung haphazardly over their shoulders, the men looked like a fleet of ships with broken masts drifting in a sea of mist. The wind cut through their loose coats, their knuckles were raw, they blew on their hands for warmth. Pieces of melting snow were scattered everywhere, belly-up like dead fish.

An argument was going on between the men as to whether or not the Black and Tans were cowards. None of them had ever been close to a Black and Tan, other than to shoot at him from a distance of ten feet. The consensus was that the Black and Tans were indeed cowards, the dregs of English jails, mercenaries capable only of rape and pillage but not soldiers in the true sense of the word.

But Dinny didn't think the Black and Tans were cowards. He had seen them on several occasions go to their deaths bravely, all but one saying they were proud to die for England. The exception was a young fellow who had begged on his knees to be spared, saying what would his mother do without him. Dan Donohoe only replied that it was a pity he did not think of his mother before he joined up to fight for the British Empire.

And the junior English officers who were buried in the Rea were brave too. These were lieutenants, intelligent men trying to pass themselves off as Irishmen, acting as undercover agents, carrying out the most dangerous tasks in the British army. When they were caught, they knew they were finished. They kept their mouths shut. They went down without a sound, other than to ask the IRA men to pass on some memento, a ring or a wallet or a pair of cufflinks, to their wives or families. And sometimes, depending on who was in charge, the mementos were indeed passed on. Dinny and Ned Murphy on several occasions ignored Donohoe's instructions that nothing was to be returned to the families of spies and put personal items in envelopes and posted them to England.

But Dinny kept his mouth shut about that. He let the IRA men with their conviction that they dealt with a cowardly and incompetent enemy. Speaking of what he knew would only make them suspicious of him.

During the march Joe Morrissey took Dinny aside and told him about himself and tried to explain the wonders of fighting in the column. He told him that, though he worked as a mechanic in Midleton, he was originally from Athlone, from a traditional republican family, that the police kept raiding his parents' house so many times that he had to go on the run and ended up in Cork among the Aherns and the Desmonds and their group. He told Dinny about the exploits of the column over the previous year: about the taking of RIC barracks at Carrigtwohill, Cloyne and Castlemartyr, about the ambush in Midleton where the three Tans were killed and the hijacking of rifles off the Cameron Highlanders at Milebush.

'There are nights here and we're going through the countryside to some new safe house or to an ambush site and we're out under the moon and the stars and the frost might be gleaming off the grass and the hedges and I can't help thinking but that these are the greatest days of my life.'

As he was saying this, Dinny had visions of one of the Black and Tans, a big Englishman, up in the Rea one night opening his shirt and saying to Donohoe to 'shoot me here, I'm proud to die for England. I bet you can't do it, you cowardly

Paddy curs'. But they did it and the big Englishman went down with the others into the wet pit of the Rea. It struck Dinny that if Joe Morrissey was brave, then the big Englishman was brave too. They were both sides of the same coin, brave fools sent out to die for the benefit of politicians. But Joe Morrissey wasn't for stopping. 'Then when we're trained and in position and each of us knows what the other will do, when we've worked out all the details in advance, when we know we're working as a team, that's the best feeling of all. When one man is just part of an overall unit, when we are all just cogs in this machine that we call the column, you know what it is like to be truly alive.'

Joe Morrissey smiled in the misty gloom and moved his rifle from one shoulder to the other. They were moving in single file and in pairs, trailing each other like a herd of exhausted animals. Dinny was full of regrets and wished he had not seen what he had seen. Then he could have been as enthusiastic as Joe Morrissey.

'Do you think I'll ever get a rifle?' he asked after a while. He knew that a rifle meant acceptance by the column and that mere Volunteers and dispatch-carriers did not carry anything like the same level of respect.

'It all depends. You'll most likely end up with a shotgun for a while. I wouldn't knock that though. There's more damage done with shotguns and revolvers in this war than was ever done with rifles. Still, you're right; what all the boys want is a rifle. It's a badge of honour. You'll have to wait your turn, though. You'll get one in time.' Morrissey was unstoppable. 'Below in Cloyne, just before Christmas, we were in this house, Dinny, surrounded by the Cameron Highlanders. Josie ordered us to make no sound. The military came in downstairs, kicked the doors down. Still we didn't make a sound. Then as they came up the stairs, Josie springs out onto the landing and starts blazing at them. By Jesus, you should have seen them run. Then one of them tossed a live grenade into the hall as he went out. Cool as a cucumber, Josie hopped down the stairs and kicked that bloody grenade out into the street. Up she went. Then Jack

Ahern went out behind a wall and kept the troops busy while the rest of us escaped. The soldiers ordered him to cease firing. Jack laughed at them. "After you, Tommy," he shouted at them. "After you, Paddy," one of the soldiers shouted back. By Jesus, you should have heard the laugh we had about that afterwards.'

He told Dinny about the various members of the column, about the reckless bravery of Josie Ahern and Hurley, about James Glavin who was known as 'Fintan Lalor' because he was so fond of the writings of James Fintan Lalor, the Fenian, about Pat Sullivan who was a university student in Cork and John Joe Joyce who, though he was only a young fellow, wanted to study medicine.

Dinny felt suddenly gormless, a worthless amadán unworthy of the company of these educated townies who had given up everything for Ireland. He felt as if he had been admitted by some quirk of spurious scholarship into some secret university of the wilderness that hitherto he didn't even know was there. This was education.

'There's a lot of bright boys around here so.' he said.

'Brains aren't necessarily everything when it comes to this kind of business. The best fellows here have never seen the inside of a school. There's more to life than brains. Go back nine months to a year and you'll see who the hard core are; the Aherns, the Desmonds, Tadhg Manley, Paddy Higgins, Whelan and O'Connell. The rest of them are like yourself: recent recruits. Apart from the escapade in Cloyne, none of them saw any action until last week in Midleton.'

'Sounds like that has created quite a stir?' Dinny wanted to hear what it felt like to be involved in so recent and newsworthy a 'stunt'.

'Well, it was dark, the middle of the night and we were waiting in doorways, shivering in the alleys. There was a howling gale going down the street. The younger lads were mighty nervous. We knew the Tans would be heavily armed. We had to get them before they got us. As soon as they came into range, Hurley fired the first shots and we followed. We took one each. The Tans went down. We couldn't see their faces. We didn't know whether they were dead or injured. Two ran and the rest surrendered. We got their guns and we skedaddled as fast as we could.'

'Were they Tans or RIC?'

'Half and half, I'd say. Though it doesn't make much difference at this stage. The rest of boys then set up the ambush for the reinforcements out in Water Rock. That was straightforward, so far as I can gather. It being the middle of the night, the police had lights. The boys just blazed away at the lorries. None of our fellows were injured. Then of course, the military burned down half a dozen houses as a reprisal. That brought more lads trying to get into the column. You were lucky to get in. The Tans and their reprisals are the best recruiting sergeant we ever had. They're like a high gale in a forest fire, you light the spark and they'll do the rest. It was only from the papers the following day that we found out we killed two, or is it three at this stage? You see, once a man gets a rifle in his hand be becomes a powerful thing altogether, he becomes bigger than himself, though he may be about to die, he thinks he's invincible and he doesn't care what he has to do. Can you understand that?'

Dinny's experience of war was entirely different. 'I suppose I do,' he said. 'And I'll tell you another thing: If I had to die in the morning so that any one of the men in this column might live, I wouldn't have the slightest hesitation in doing so. And I know the rest of them would do the same. I'm sometimes amazed at how these men have put selfishness aside. Maybe it won't always be like this but that's how it is now. And that's how we can put up with so much: the hunger, the trekking, the danger, the frostbite, the chilblains and the blistered feet. We do it for each other. Taking the war to the enemy is only part of it; the more important part is the sense of belonging, the comradeship. I tell you something: that in the whole history of Ireland there has never been anything so extraordinary as what we've been doing here under Hurley over the past twelve months.'

They walked on and on like that, their feet sinking in the mud and melting snow, discussing the permutations of the revolution and the possibilities for peace, crossing field after field, climbing ditches and occasionally checking that the bolts of their rifles were open so that they wouldn't shoot one another by accident. Eventually, after what seemed an age in which they felt they had moved like tired ghosts through a land of mist and trees disguised as hoary scarecrows, they reached the hamlet known as Clonmult.

'The place we're going to is up here around the corner,' Josie Ahern said. 'Over there, beyond the church.'

They walked beyond the church and up a slight incline and turned left into a narrow lane. The house they were looking for was on high ground, facing south, with a small wood behind it; it had a commanding view of the countryside on three sides. On a clear day the enemy could be seen coming for miles away. It reminded Dinny of home: another long low farmhouse with a thatched roof, a cowshed adjoining it at a right angle and a few trees to the front. The owner, a local farmer, had recently vacated the house to move to another on his land so it wasn't in too dilapidated a state. With a fire lighting in the grate it would be comfortable enough. For the next six weeks this would be the home for the East Cork column, where they would train and drill and learn the trade of the military which, though clothed in ceremony and protocol, was in Dinny's opinion still just a slightly more glamorous word for the trade of killing.

'Well, here we are at last,' Joe Morrissey said. 'Home sweet home.'

32

Over the next six weeks he learned what it was like to be part of a flying column. He learned how to shoot, even if he did not shoot very straight. He learned how to cope with boredom, for they were cooped up a lot of the time in the low farmhouse with little to do except drilling and marching and going on excursions to gather food or other provisions.

He got to know the other members of the column: a clutch of Aherns and Desmonds, Sonny Leary, Dick Hegarty, Christy Sullivan and their younger followers, all of them Na Fianna members who were there as much for the fun as for the patriotism. He found the leaders and their side-kicks to be a group apart, solemn men with their own idea of what soldiering was about. They took themselves seriously, like footballers in long winter's training for some big game and, like a football team, they stuck together. The leaders saw themselves as an elite, above the concerns of mere civilians. Civilians didn't matter a damn; like the Volunteers, they were just fodder to be used in the fight against England.

But civilians did count. It struck Dinny that ordinary people gained nothing from a war. It was just the worst possible kind of inconvenience. Ordinary people just wanted to get on with their lives, and who could blame them? War wasn't what they wanted. They were tired of war. They just wanted to be left alone. Country people, people like his father, people like the farmer who brought him over the snow bound hills north of Midleton, saw it in simple enough terms: politicians made wars and politicians destroyed lives, whether it was the Kaiser or Churchill or de Valera or Dan Donohoe down at the polling booth. They walked all over the people for their own ends and there was no end to the pain they caused.

As a result, by the time his first month with the column had passed, Dinny found he was drawn more to the boys on the periphery of the group than to those at the centre. On a number of occasions he accompanied the younger lads to the local farms where racehorses were bred and they'd spend their time helping the farmers run the horses out in the mornings and break in colts in the afternoons.

In particular, he became friendly with the bespectacled John Joe Joyce and got to know him well. The days evolved into their own routine around the sound of the Youghal train, the Angelus bells from the chapel half a mile away, the gradual thawing of the frost every morning, the movement of the clouds, the songs of the first thrushes of spring and the barks of young foxes rasping through the night.

Dinny found he was able to lose himself in the day-to-day business of the column. The way the country was now, it was safer being a military man, holed up in a flying column, in territory where there were no military, waiting for action. It was a lot more difficult being a civilian in a town like Cork or Midleton, standing behind a counter or trying to do a day's work while watching the world descend into savagery.

Up here, among the low hills, he could drill and chat to the men and say the Rosary and wind the clock and watch the time roll out. To pass the long evenings, Joe Morrissey gave him John Mitchel's Jail Journal to re-read and he woke one morning after a night in which he dreamt that he walked through an Ireland free. But there was one problem and that was that Dan Donohoe was running the country and lording it over everyone. Yet despite this, his spirit calmed and the agitation began to leave him and the memories of the Rea began to fade.

That was until Ash Wednesday morning when he was going to the village and he met a man leaving the chapel with ashes on his forehead. At the sight of the ashes like a hole in the middle of the man's forehead Dinny's mind suddenly began to whirl and he felt the return of the weakness in his stomach that always accompanied the visions of the Rea. He leaned against a lichen-covered wall and, though he was standing there in the spring sunlight, in his mind he was back in the graveyard.

For some reason he remembered one night when a prisoner was waiting to be executed there. He was the only prisoner to be killed in the actual cemetery itself. He was a well-dressed man in a suit. Nobody knew where he came from, though Dinny surmised he must have come from the city seeing as he was brought by Mick Twomey and his men. He was tied to the railings of a tomb. Twomey, who was a bit of a trickster, knew that Donohoe had no gun on him so he decided he would have a little fun at his expense.

'What are we going to do,' he said. 'I've no revolver on me. You have your Mauser?'

''Tis below in a rabbit hole at home.'

'That's a good place for it. You're going to have to get it.'

'I will like hell.'

And all this within earshot of the prisoner.

'You expect me to walk three miles home and three miles back when we can shove this fellow in there,' he pointed to the vault, 'and finish the job tomorrow night?'

'Well, I'm the boss here and this fellow is a very important prisoner and has to be executed as soon as possible. You catch my drift?'

'There's only one thing for it so. We'll be back in ten minutes.' Donohoe said.

Donohoe and Ned Murphy made their way out of the graveyard. A high moon shone pale as a skull and everything was as clear to Dinny as if it were the middle of the day. The prisoner shook and began to make muffled sounds. He looked like an official of some kind; he had a soft felt hat on his head and a white rag tied around his eyes, though the word was that he was some kind of senior RIC officer.

'You're luck might be in,' Twomey said to the prisoner, you might get what they call in legal circles a stay of execution.'

The man continued struggling but said nothing.

A few minutes later Donohoe and Ned Murphy returned. Ned Murphy was carrying a sledge hammer from the forge.

'This'll do the job, just like my one would have done the job on Mr Pearson. One flake from this,' Donohoe laughed, 'and problem solved.'

'I know you would not let us down. Daneen. You see,' Twomey said to the prisoner who could see nothing but had probably figured out what was going on, 'we are not as well equipped as you fellows. So we have to make do.'

'Bring him over here,' Donohoe said to Dinny and Ned Murphy, 'and put his head down on that headstone – we'll use it for the purpose it's intended.'

Reluctantly Dinny rose to untie the man full in the knowledge that they were going to kill him by smashing his head over a gravestone. When he was untied, he struggled and Dinny and Ned Murphy had to work hard to bring him across several hillocks to where Donohoe stood.

'Now, tie him down there.'

They strapped the man to the gravestone. Donohoe picked up the sledgehammer and made his way across the stones. He was standing over the prisoner and was about to raise the hammer when Twomey pulled his revolver out of his pocket and waved it at Donohoe with a grin on his face that was clearly visible in the moonlight. Donohoe dropped the sledgehammer on the grass.

'You fucker!' He said. You would have me ...'

'And you would have done it too. You're some hoor, boy.' And they all laughed as if this was some kind of music hall joke or a Punch and Judy show staged for adults. Dinny was ashamed to admit he even laughed a little himself at Donohoe's discomfort.

'Enough of the fun.' Twomey stood up and walked calmly over to the prisoner and, without a moment's hesitation, shot him through the back of the head. The man's brains and blood exploded and he slumped over the gravestone.

Dinny remembered the laughter dying in him and he started to get sick, shaking and staggering against the headstones. He leaned forward and puked into the gravel of one of the graves beside the jerking feet of the dying man as Mick Twomey wiped his boots on the grass.

'Are you a man at all?' Dan Donohoe growled, transferring his annoyance onto Dinny. 'Are you a fucking ninny or what?'

'Leave him alone.' Mick Twomey said. 'He'll get over it.'

After that, Dinny knew that whatever had bound him to Dan Donohoe and the Company was severed forever. This was the end of the road for him. This was the moment that he decided to get as far as he could from the area of the Rea and Knockraha. After that moment there would be no going back.

'Now, bury the bastard in somebody's grave,' Mick Twomey said as he and the other Cork men quietly headed off out the avenue from the graveyard. 'And make it fast.'

Dinny and Ned Murphy opened the freshly dug grave of an old woman and threw the RIC man in on top of her coffin. Her name was Nan Dinan and she had died a week earlier of old age.

'She wouldn't have expected this kind of a neighbour in on top of her for the rest of eternity, now would she?' Ned Murphy then said with a grim smile. 'But what must be done, must be done.'

Dinny shook himself and stumbled; he was surprised to find himself slumped by the wall of Clonmult church. It had all been just another of his visions and had taken no more than a minute, because the man with the ashes on his forehead had only barely reached the corner of Clonmult Cross. Dinny felt he was now close to going mad. He held on to the wall and took a few deep breaths before staggering back to the farmhouse where the members of the column were whiling the time away.

Now when he looked at them, he knew that he was different to them, that it was he, not them, who was set apart by what he had seen. Despite their military posturing, the volunteers of the column were somehow quaintly innocent. They had not had to stand in bogs, up to their ankles in bog water, watching people being told to make their peace with God. None of them had stood as close to death as he had. They might have shot and killed and run away, but they had not tied handkerchiefs around the heads of people they had never seen before or stand guard as they soiled themselves or gasped on their last Woodbine before tumbling face down into a peaty grave. None of them had seen what he had seen. The whole thing was like the Wild West to them; they were all Buffalo Bills, with the Tans as Indians. Most of them just pulled triggers and ran like hell.

The experience of having killed someone at close range put a barrier between you and other people that was impossible to overcome. Dinny found it difficult to remember the innocent way he had lived before the killings began. His past was now a foreign place. And if he lived for a hundred years, he would never forget the events in the Rea. It was he, rather than his new comrades, with their talk of Tans and ambushes, who had insight into the true meaning of war. He was a thousand years older than these lads.

His thoughts often came back to one night when he had a long conversation with an ex-soldier being held in Sing Sing. The soldier had told him of how the Tommys had played football with the Hun on a Christmas Day truce in the dim distant past of 1914. He remembered what he had said, word for word, for the soldier was a dreamy sort of chap, a bit like himself.

'The killing began in 1914 and blinded us to the beauty of the world. We asked for death and destruction and both have followed us ever since, for our sins. When you take an eye for an eye, all you end up with is blindness,' he said, as he sat in the vault, holding the thin end of a Woodbine between his fingers.

'I am here among the dead. But I was among the dead many times before, when I sat in the trenches with my comrades rotting and scattered in bits all around me.'

The soldier turned to Dinny and he had a resigned look in his eyes.

'Pray for me,' he said. 'God is the only good man. For what have the rest of us done?' And Dinny had thought at the time that God must indeed be dead, or if not dead, then blind to allow such killing to go on. The soldier told him that he also had such thoughts at the Somme, when so many lives were turned into mud, when humanity was at its most powerless. That this was the low point in the history of civilization, he said. Yet he went on to say that the spring always comes back and the birds start singing and the little white and yellow flowers return in the shade of the ditches. In that place called the Somme, the soldier said, it was a yellow weed called corn kale that grew in summer and the poppies were mixed in with it and they all bloomed together in the churned earth.

'You have never seen destruction like what I have seen,' he said. 'And isn't it amazing to have survived years of fighting the Hun only to have to face being killed by someone like you, a nice boy, in my own place, in my own country, a few miles from my own home? Doesn't life pull the strangest tricks on you, all the same?'

Dinny said he didn't want to kill him but that was the way it was; he was the enemy now.

'Am I your enemy, Dinny?' the soldier asked. Spillane was his name. He had been in the Canadian army and was picked up while working for a farmer outside Midleton. His crime was that he had written to the authorities for a passport to leave the country on account of his declining health. Now he was one of the vanished men of Cork, a man who died twice because his name died with him. For the death of one's name increases the totality of death itself.

'I don't know who my enemy is,' Dinny replied. 'All I know is that he is everywhere.'

33

It snowed again in early February and the roads were once again impassable and remained so for ten days. Nobody came or went to the camp in Clonmult and there were no IRA activities in the area as a result of the snow. The land was waking: hedges dreeped, the drains filled with brown rushing water and the day was made of the soft runny sound of melting snow. The countryside turned to mottled white as the thaw set in, until by the middle of the month all that remained were long streaks of white under the shadows of north-facing ditches.

Dinny was drilling with his new comrades, using a hurley in lieu of a rifle, when Joe Morrissey called him saying there was a message from the watch-post by the church that he was wanted in the village. He blew on his hands that were raw from the cold, pulled his coat around him and walked with his long strides as quickly as he could down the hill to the village.

As he walked, Dinny warmed up and dreamt about the coming of spring, for he was tired of waking up every morning in the tumble-down farmhouse, his feet frozen with the cold. The men were good company but they were kept warm only by their dreams of a republic and Dinny realized very quickly from his time observing them that the fanatic heart is never frozen.

By now the Government of Ireland Act was in place and Ireland was, nominally at least, split into two countries. Dinny thought that this split form of Home Rule, though full of obvious flaws, was the best that Ireland could expect. The others, though, were still full of their dreams; they were blind Samsons fighting on, full of passion, despite the length of time they had been on the run. Too many nights had been spent struggling and marching and lining the sides of ditches for ambushes that never happened for them to stop now. Too much time had been spent in the wind and rain, in muddy drains and behind fallen trees, to even think that there could be anything less than a full republic at the end of it. To suffer the way they had suffered only for the King's writ to still run over all the land? These men would never accept that. They were driven by their dreams, while Dinny, with the knowledge gained in the Rea of the limits of the human imagination, was full of fear. Looked at logically, the Irish would still have to go to Scotland to pick potatoes, to England to build roads and bridges, to America to work the mills and run the politics of Boston and the Bronx.

So much time and energy and spirit had been expended, so much goodness in the souls of the young men who died and would keep on dying. It was on a tiny scale, of course, compared to the pointless carnage of the Western Front, but for the families of those involved it came down to the same thing. You died for the dream but the dream did not die with you, rather it kept on making martyrs.

Dinny walked down between sodden hedges as drains gurgled and leaves were carried away to block the culverts. There was no movement in the countryside, except for a farmer who was forking cut turnips into a butt. The farmer, his boots sinking in the wet soil, saluted Dinny as he passed. The road was an inch deep track of mud, Dinny tried to avoid the puddles but it was impossible. By the time he reached the village, his boots were covered with brown muck up to the ankles.

Clonmult was quiet. It was a village only in name; in reality it was little more than a crossroads with a few houses and a public house at the corner. Today it was silent as a town after a fair day. An advertisement for Sweet Afton missing two letters hung from the side of a deserted shop. The metal road sign pointing towards Midleton had been pockmarked by a shotgun blast. South-facing roofs dripped from melting ice. And there, seated on a horse and trap by the wall of the pub and looking like he was frozen to the bone, sat his father. Doll shook her traces with recognition as Dinny approached.

His father seemed smaller and older and more hunched than he had remembered him. Perhaps it was the cold or the month's absence or the unfamiliar setting. His face was redder than usual and his nose ran. He was dressed in his warmest coat, with his hat pulled down over his ears. He had two jute bags, one on his knees to keep his legs warm and another over his shoulders, so that he looked like a badly filled sack of potatoes perched on the seat. Odd grains of oats still stuck to the bags as if they had only recently been used or if they had sprouted within.

'Well?'

'Well?' His father tried to smile but it was too cold for smiling. Still, he seemed glad to see Dinny and had his usual mischievous twinkle in his eye. It was often like that between them, especially when they were alone, say when they were snagging turnips in the middle of winter. His father, normally so voluble, would become inarticulate, just spitting and grumbling as he lifted the turnips and cut the tops off them. In such days in the middle of winter they could go for hours and say little more than 'well' to each other and both would be content enough with the silence.

'Well? How are you?'

'Not too bad, I suppose, considering. They're good at home?'

'Your mother sends her regards. Bina put this together for you.' The father handed Dinny a basket. 'It contains bits and pieces. I'm sure there's some nice tasties in there and maybe a sup of poteen to keep you warm. You're mother said you're to heat up that soup and get it into you. You have to stay healthy, she says. She prays for you every night, you know. There are Rosaries going at home to beat the band.'

'You didn't come here just to give me that soup,' Dinny said suspiciously.

'I was going to Midleton, so I said I'd call up.'

234

'How did you find me here?'

'Somebody told me that you stayed at Murphy's in Walshtown on the night you left home. I took it from there. It was easy enough. I only had to ask directions twice after that.'

'But this is supposed to be a secret camp.'

'Well, if it is, the whole country knows the secret. But the thing is: I'd another reason to come down to see you, boy. I've a bit of news for you.'

'You have news?' Dinny repeated what his father said, sceptical of his explanations. While his father could simply have come just to see him, Dinny thought there must be some other motive. He felt sure he was about come up with some excuse to get him to go home with him. Dinny looked into his father's shrewd eyes but they gave nothing away.

'Well, cough it up. What's the news?'

'Well, the news is that Pat Hackett passed away, God be good to him.'

'You came all the way down here to tell me that? Sure Pat Hackett must have been ninety.'

'That's what I came down to tell you.'

'You mean to tell me you came all the way here, in frost and snow in the middle of winter, to tell me Pat Hackett died?' Dinny looked at his father incredulously. It was twenty miles in a horse and trap. He had travelled twenty miles to tell him that an old neighbour had died. His father was only fifty five; he was a bit young to be going soft in the head. Pat Hackett had died. So what? Dinny had known Pat all his life; he had often as a youngster milked Pat's four cows when Pat was no longer able to do so himself. Then Pat sold off the cows. So apart from bringing him a butt load of turf every winter, Dinny had not had much contact with the man for four or five years, and none at all since he had got involved in the Cause. Certainly not enough to warrant his father driving twenty miles on a horse and trap to tell him he had died.

'Well, I'm not finished yet, am I?' His father grunted and stared off into the middle distance. 'Ye see, a few days after Pat was buried, God rest him, I got this letter from a solicitor, a Mr W.A.H. Hungerford, in big fancy writing, instructed by Wynne and Wynne, Solicitors in Cork telling me that I was to call in to see him "at my earliest convenience". Well, there was a lot of snow around, so "my earliest convenience" had to wait ten days. This fellow had his office in the South Mall. I had fierce trouble in getting there. There was smoke and ruins everywhere and people hawking things around the street. Cork is gone to the dogs since it was burnt. People are trying to make a living out of the ashes. That's what you brought down on this misfortunate country with your fighting for Irish freedom. By the time ye get this republic you're looking for, there'll be nothing left to govern.'

Well, at least his father hadn't changed his political views. There was no point in trying to explain to him that it was the Black and Tans, not the IRA, who had burnt Cork, no point in telling him that the newspapers carried a whole pile of propaganda, no point in telling him, for instance, that one English newspaper had moved Cork City Hall across the River Lee so that it looked as though it were burnt along with Patrick Street, instead of being a second, completely separate, act of arson. The Tans had been burning every night on the run up to Christmas. But to Dinny's father, the Tans and the IRA were two sides of the same coin.

'The city was alive with soldiers and policemen. I was waiting an hour to get across Patrick's Bridge. They were searching everybody. When I did get through, I was stopped again at the top of the Mall. A District Inspector had been shot that very day. To make a long story short, I got there eventually. There was this big grey limestone house with a lot of steps up to the front door. Army lorries were flying all round the place and frightening the horses. I had trouble trying to find a place to tie up Doll and the trap outside.'

Dinny smiled at his father's explanations. He was so rarely in Cork that, when he did go there, or anywhere else for that matter, you got all the details. 'You get the giblets and all' was how his mother liked to put it, after listening to some long-winded dissertation about attendance at a fair or a hurling match.

'The poor old devil was nervous. I don't blame him. Even I heard gunshots going off two or three times. I thought he's jump under the table at one point. People are terrified. He was a funny kind of an old geezer though, a nice sort of fellow. I'd say he was a Protestant. All the Protestants are nervous. I read in the Examiner how a fellow from Cork cut his own throat on the train from Fishguard to London the other day. He'd got a letter saying he'd be shot. He got that from you fellows. "They won't get me," he said. Imagine that! Slicing his own throat, so that fellows like Donohoe wouldn't get him. Doesn't that take the biscuit, hah? What has the country come to at all, that's what I'd like to know.'

'They were not my fellows.'

'Well, it happened, didn't it? Anyway, to get back to Mr. Hungerford, my solicitor, or rather Pat Hackett's solicitor. Doesn't he pull this sheet of paper out of a metal drawer. What is it only Pat Hackett's will. He reads it out with his old glasses perched on his nose. Imagine the surprise I got when he tells me that Pat Hackett had left his place to you!'

'To me?' Dinny did not know what to say.'Pat Hackett left his farm to me?'

'I can tell you, I was as surprised as you are. Obviously, he must have liked you.'

'But what did I do to deserve this? I thought he had a sister in America?'

'He has. And he left his money – he had a nice few bob put away, believe it or not – to her. But he left the farm to you.'

'Jesus, Mary and Joseph!'

'There's forty five acres there, and it's all good. It's better than the place at home. I often heard my father say that you could manure our place with the soil from Pat Hackett's. I always thought it was a pity he didn't marry and settle down.'

Dinny was lost for words. The last thing he expected was to inherit a farm. He had long since resigned himself to the role of second son: the one who would have to leave because there was a living for only the son who inherited the family farm. And it had long since been decided that Bill would be the farmer and Dinny the carpenter. It might have meant he was following the ways of Christ but, given a choice, he would prefer to be a farmer. If nothing else, farming was largely out of doors and there was variety in the work. His mind raced at the possibilities placed before him, though he knew he would not take up farming again until he was done with the column.

Inheriting Pat Hackett's farm, he knew, opened up all kinds of avenues to him. For a start, it was over a mile and a half from home and did not face the Rea. He could live there without having to look upon the death bogs every day and night. When cleaned up, Hackett's farm would make no bad place for him to live. He had never much thought about his future and had long since resigned himself to going to America as soon as the 'war' was over, whatever the result. Now this changed everything. He could, perhaps, even find a nice girl and settle down.

'But why did he leave it to me? Surely there must have been someone else. I never thought…'

'Obviously, you must have done something right.' His father laughed. 'You're not the worst of them, you know.' Dinny knew this was as close to a compliment as he would ever get from his father. 'We must all have done something right, I suppose, in our own bumbling way.'

Dinny could see that his father was wrestling with feelings of pride in his son and annoyance at the way he was now living his life – 'the bleddy politics'.

'Do you know, when you have children, and, with God's help, you'll know this when you'll have your own, sometimes you don't know whether you're doing the right thing or the wrong thing. You just muddle along as best as you can. Sometimes you think you make fierce mistakes. I was often sorry I did not leave the place at home to you, rather than Bill.

There's nothing wrong with Bill, don't get me wrong. But I often thought you'd have made a better fist of it. You've more get-up-and-go. Ah, Bill will survive. He'll never go hungry. But you'd have made more of it. Still, once a decision is made, a decision is made. I told Bill many years ago that it was his. You were no more than ten or twelve at the time. Now it doesn't matter.'

'Ah, come on, Bill was the man for the home place. You know that as well as I do.'

'I think your mother thought you'd become a priest or a Brother. Then of course you discovered your own cause, fighting for Ireland. I didn't agree with it. I didn't think Ireland is worth killing for, let alone dying for. I still don't. But you're entitled to your opinion and you're entitled to your views. You're no less of an honest man because you go out by night with Dan Donohoe.'

'How are things there? Any news of Donohoe?'

'I heard they bought land again. His family, I mean. Two hundred and fifty acres and a big house. He hasn't been seen at home since long before you left. I suppose he's busy getting into scrapes. There's a lot of murdering going on. I'd imagine he has a hand in some of it. So, what will you do?'

Dinny patted Doll's nuzzle.

'I don't know, to be honest with you.'

'Well, think about it – the farm, I mean.'

'Yea, I will.'

'If you're going to work Pat's place for the coming year, you're going to have to come back by the end of March to start the ploughing, you do know that.'

'That's a month away.'

'You're going to have to think about what you'll sow. You can't leave the place go fallow.'

'I know.'

'Can I ask you something? When the weather starts to dry out, will I start a bit of ploughing there or get Bill to do it? He said in a way that suggested it was the most important thing he ever said in his life.

'I guess so.' Dinny was not exactly used to being the proprietor of a farm and making decisions about the coming year's tillage.

'We'd make a start, anyway.'

'I suppose so.'

'Listen, I'd better be getting along. The days are short this time of year. And it's not safe to travel the roads by night.'

'Right.'

'Right so.' Dinny's father lifted the reins and tapped Doll in the back with them. 'Go on, girl. Hup, there.'

Doll began to walk, the tackle tinkled; the trap began to roll.

'Hey, say thanks to Mam and Bina for this. Tell Bill, I'll be ploughing for him by mid-March.' He held the basket up. 'I'll heat the soup. I'll share it out. The lads will like it.'

'Don't be too generous. I don't want to think I reared a fooleen.' His father pulled his hat down over his forehead and grinned. 'I forgot to tell you they told me you were not to lose that basket.'

'Tell them not to worry. I never lose anything.'

His father laughed as he headed off in the direction of Midleton. Dinny watched him for a minute or two as his father's sack-covered back vanished into the gloom. When he reached the far bend of the road, he waved back. Then he went around the bend in the road and Dinny could no longer see him. As he walked back the rainy lane towards the camp, Dinny was smiling at his good fortune. But he would never see his father again.

34

By late-February 1921 it was becoming clear what was being planned. Information had been received from the city that an armed convoy of British troops was to travel by train from Cork to Queenstown, or Cobh as it was now called, on Tuesday, February 22nd. The column was to ambush a convoy of troops at Cobh Junction. This would be Dinny's first piece of real action and he was hoping he would be given a rifle.

On the Sunday morning before the attack, the leaders: Hurley, Josie Ahern and Paddy Whelan left to select a suitable position for the ambush and the men were given orders to pack up their possessions and follow after them in the late afternoon.

Dinny had gone alone to first Mass that morning. The other members of the column, who had been to Confession in Dungourney the previous evening, were under instructions to go to church in ones and twos and disperse among the people. They were not to bring their weapons into church or alarm the locals. At Mass, Dinny prayed that the visions that had begun to plague him again since Ash Wednesday would go away. He liked being in this particular church, perhaps because it was in the Diocese of Cloyne and not directly under the control of Bishop Coholan.

As he knelt in the little chapel of Clonmult, he made the decision to go back home as soon as he could after the ambush and do his best to take over the running of Pat Hackett's farm. After partaking in such a daring feat as the ambush, his IRA credentials would be beyond question and he would then, he decided, refuse point blank to do any more of Dan Donohoe's dirty work for him. Besides, there were rumours of peace, of de Valera talking to Lloyd George to bring about a truce. Perhaps the whole thing might be over before the sowing season. The men had by now been at the house for a total of six weeks and were glad to be getting away. They were bored with drilling and playing chess and cards and were getting on one another's nerves. These were men itching for action and, once they had been told what the next 'stunt' would be, they looked forward to the possibility of ambushing an entire trainload of military. It would be by far the most daring ambush ever carried out by the column.

After Mass, Dinny was sent on sentry duty on the hill behind the house. Sentries had been also deployed to ring the church bell on the approach of the enemy from the south or the east. Dinny's vantage point at the back of the house took in the entire north and west. But today was the column's last day in Clonmult and the other sentries, local young lads, had already gone off to Stacks to help break in horses.

Dinny leaned against a ditch, his revolver in his pocket, gazing at the countryside, lost in thought and many of his thoughts were ones he would have preferred not to have. The birds were singing with the inevitability of spring; the sun was attempting to shine through the mist. Dinny tried to steer his brain into the siding of the ordinary by thinking about his home and family and planning what he would do once he got going in Pat Hackett's place.

So there wasn't a sound, bar the gurgling of a drain or two. Dampness reigned, as if dew had immobilized the entire country. Two crows, like flakes of soot, flew over his head as he blew on his hands and hugged his chest with his arms and stamped his feet to keep warm. He was walking around in short circles when he noticed a figure creeping along the ditch in his direction. It was Con Foley. He looked like he was in a hurry.

'Tis no day to be out today, Fitzy,' he said. 'Why don't we go up to Cuddy's for a quick one? That'd warm us up. A fella would need some kind of a lift on a day like this.'

'On a Sunday morning?' Dinny was incredulous. 'And what about our orders? Are we not supposed to stay here on sentry duty?'

'Sunday morning is the best time in the week for a jar. As for orders: shag the orders. Sure Hurley and Josie are gone off to Cobh Junction. We're free as birds now, boy.'

'And what if the military turn up, or the Tans?'

'The Tans? Find us up here, is it? Is it the Tans, on a Sunday? The Tans don't work of a Sunday. Sure, there hasn't been a policeman in this part of the country for years. Anyway, you'd see 'em coming ten miles away.'

Dinny looked at Foley and considered this for a while. 'I suppose you're right.'

'Christ, I am right!' Foley laughed out loudly if he was letting Dinny into some big secret. 'I'm right as rain, boy.'

Dinny did some calculations. If he went to the pub with Con Foley for just half an hour to an hour, he would get enough whiskey in his system to dull his mind. He would be back in time to eat some lunch and pack his bag and be ready to go at two o'clock. He would avoid the boredom of being up on the hillside with nothing in his head but negativity. So he went to the pub with Foley, mostly to help him stop thinking about the Rea.

They found a number of the locals there, getting tanked up, filling the dead hours between Mass and dinnertime. The conversation was the usual desultory stuff of pubs: local men steeped in solitude but forced to say something to each other, if only to cancel out the ticking of the clock. The barman shone glasses and looked at his customers as they lazily kicked a few words around between them while managing to say nothing of any significance.

Dinny stayed longer than he'd intended to. He had three whiskeys and after an hour and a half, feeling guilty about having deserted his post, he finally left. He went back to the hill where Con Foley said he'd relieve him in an hour and resumed his sentry duties.

He sat on the ditch again, dizzy from the alcohol, staring bleary-eyed and yawning into the grey drizzle that had by now begun to fall. The whiskey was like a fire blanket, asbestos for the soul, it doused the pain in his mind and reined in his galloping thoughts. It was better than being asleep, for there were no dreams, no nightmares; it was better than a pill.

By one o'clock he realized that if he were to make the march, he would have to get back to the house to eat and pack up his things. There was still no sign of Foley coming to relieve him. The countryside, like his brain, languished in Sunday torpor. He was in a dilemma. If he obeyed orders and stayed where he was, waiting for Foley, who was unlikely to return, then he'd miss the column's move to Cobh Junction. On the other hand, if he wanted to be with the column, he'd have to be packed up and ready to leave within half an hour. He made his decision: he went back to the house, where the men had eaten and were all set for departure. He told nobody where Foley was, in case this got him into trouble.

By three o'clock they were ready to go; Dinny had eaten a quick meal of boiled potatoes and buttermilk, brought in by one of the local Cumann girls from the village. And still Con Foley had still not returned from the pub.

'Dammit,' Paddy Higgins said, 'I guess we'll have to go without the little scut.'

The last job to be carried out before their departure was the filling of water bottles for the column. Dinny and John Joe Joyce were detailed to do this and they gathered up the empty bottles from the men and made their way to a spring about forty yards away.

'Are you nervous about Tuesday, John Joe?'

'A little bit. But God is good; we'll have the element of surprise.'

'Still, after what happened in Clogheen and the boys surrounded in White's Cross...' In the previous two weeks the British Army had rounded up and arrested a couple of active service units in the Cork area. At Clogheen they had shot several Volunteers. It was hailed in the papers as a victory for the forces of law and order.

'That's different. They were given away most likely by locals. Cobh Junction is fifteen miles away, the locals don't even know we're there yet. We'll have come and gone before they even get wind of it.'

'I hope you're right.'

Dinny filled the bottles as John Joe passed them down to him. The spring was still and the water cold; stones glistened on the bottom of the well like tarnished coins. He pushed the bottles against the invisible pressure of the water. Several times he had to blow on his hands to warm them. They had the bottles capped and were about to stand up to return to the house when John Joe Joyce whispered; 'Jesus, look.'

'What?'

'Shhh. Look,' he hesitated. 'Over by the side of the ditch.' Dinny looked in the direction in which John Joe was pointing. There, leaning against the ditch and hidden from the house crouched a British soldier. He was wearing a khaki uniform, a tin helmet, and he had a rifle with a bayonet in his hands.

'I don't think he's seen us,' Dinny whispered. He looked up again. About ten yards further along the ditch from where the soldier lay he could make out another pair of boots.

'There's another one.'

'And I can see a third one behind us. Oh, good Christ, I think we're surrounded. How did this happen? Why did nobody ring the church bell?'

'Maybe they came from the other side?'

'Who's supposed to be on lookout over there?'

'Foley.'

'Foley! Christ. I bet he's gone up to the pub.'

Dinny didn't reply.

'We've got to warn the boys. We've got to run back to the house and warn them. Get out your revolver and shout and roar as you go. When I say 'go', run as fast as you can in the direction of the house. And run crooked so as to give them a difficult target. Remember the snipe.'

Just as they were about to emerge from behind the bushes and run back towards the yard, the front door of the house at the top of the land opened and Michael Desmond sauntered casually out and came down the lane in their direction. It was like a scene from a dream; clearly the soldiers could also see him, yet they let him walk on, and on he came, swinging his arms, singing the slow air, 'Teddy O'Neill', as he strolled along.

Dinny got out his revolver. He never expected he'd have to use it in these circumstances.

'Okay, one, two, three, go.' John Joe stood up and let off a few shots into the air and started to run, shouting. 'Michael, Michael, we're surrounded. Get back into the house. Get back, Michael,' he roared. 'All of you, get back. We're surrounded.'

As they began to run towards the house, crouching as low as possible, the first shots rang out from the military. Michael Desmond looked up in surprise. He smiled as he saw the two men running towards him, thinking this was some kind of prank. Suddenly he spun around as he was hit in the chest by the first fusillade. He staggered and hit the ground with a look of amazement on his face.

As Dinny ran, he could see John Joe's heels flying in front of him. Several bullets crashed through the briars over his head. Something glinted and flashed across his eye line. It was John Joe Joyce's glasses. He felt them crunch under his left boot.

'Oh, shite.'

Then suddenly John Joe was hit and stumbled and fell right across Dinny's path. Dinny tripped over him, landing in a clump of weeds.

'I'm hit, Dinny. Christ, I'm hit, Oh Jesus,' he moaned, 'right through the belly. Jesus, Mary and Joseph, the pain is desperate.' There was a hole in his shirt and blood was beginning to soak through it.

'Can you make it to the house?' Without his glasses John Joe's eyes looked myopic, their gaze turning inwards from the pain he was suffering.

'I doubt it,' he grimaced.

'I'll carry you,' Dinny said.

'Don't. Try to save yourself. I'll never make it.' John Joe gasped.

'I'll say an Act of Contrition for you.'

'Don't, Dinny. I can say it myself. Go, for the love of God, go, while you're still able.'

Dinny suddenly wanted to scream at the injustice of the world. Instead, he gently lowered John Joe's head to the ground, stood half-upright and ran until he reached the small grove of trees at the edge of the haggard. Just as he entered the clump of birches he felt something like a hot iron go through his thigh. He fell over. The pain was so fierce he felt himself get sick. He looked down. Blood was seeping through his trousers. He clutched his leg. His hand was sticky. He wiped it. It became sticky again. He tried to stand up but the leg wouldn't support him.

The house was now only ten yards away and he managed to drag himself across the cobbled yard until he reached the gable end. He slowly inched round to the back of the house where there was a passageway between a low wall and the house itself. There, under a window ledge, he tore the sleeve off his shirt and tried to stanch the blood. He was able to talk to the men inside the house.

'We're surrounded, lads. Completely, as far as I can see,' he gasped.

'Where's John Joe?' Joe Morrissey called out from inside the house.

'Shot. Badly injured. And, unless I'm greatly mistaken, Michael is dead out the front of the yard.'

'Jesus, the bastards. Can you get in here?'

'I can't stand.'

'Are they Tans?'

'Well, the ones I saw were soldiers.'

'Hobson's choice.'

He gritted his teeth.

Then the firing began in earnest. Bullets cracked off the walls of the house, whizzed into the trees and ricocheted off ditches and stones as the yard turned into a fairground shooting gallery. The window over his head shattered, and glass fell like jagged hail all over him. He groaned and tried to take deep breaths. He felt he was about to faint. He could hear Jack O'Connell inside giving the order for the men to load their rifles. Suddenly the sound of rifle fire came from the house as the IRA fired back in the general direction of the soldiers outside. At least now, Dinny thought, the fight was not completely one-sided.

'Can you stop the bleeding?' Joe Morrissey asked.

'I'm trying. Maybe if I had a bandage or something, I could.'

A few minutes later a hand was stuck out the window and a piece of sheet dropped down to him.

He ripped his trousers and began bandaging his leg in earnest. From what he could see there were two wounds, a small entry wound and a larger exit wound. Because the bottom half of the leg hung loose like a piece of butcher's meat he reckoned his thigh bone must be broken.

As he lay there, pursing his lips, trying to breathe evenly, he could hear everything that was going on in the house and he could see into the yard from where the shooting was coming.

For fifteen minutes the firing continued on both sides. Bullets clattered off stones and drilled holes in slates; bits of masonry fell around him. The ceramic pot on the chimney got a hit and shattered into a hundred pieces which slid down the roof and fell around Dinny. Then as suddenly as it had started, the firing from the British stopped and from beyond the yard a crisp English officer's voice could be heard calling.

'This is the British Army. You are completely surrounded. Further resistance is useless. You have no escape. Come out with your hands up. '

By way of response, the men in the house began singing The Soldier's Song, their voices loud in defiance. Suddenly, the front door burst open; the IRA began firing again and Jack O'Connell and four others rushed out and ran in opposite directions. Immediately, the military returned fire.

Mick Hallahan went down at the door, Dick Hegarty was shot as he tried to climb the fence in front of the house, Sonny Leary ran across the yard and was shot in the arm. Realizing his chances of escape were limited, he managed while ducking and weaving to get back to the house. Jack O'Connell and Seamus Ahern managed to get out of the yard but Seamus Ahern was shot dead as he climbed over the ditch at the far side of the first field. He went down like a sack of corn. Only Jack O'Connell escaped.

Dinny could hear the roars from inside.

'They've all gone down. God help us all.'

'No, they haven't,' Dinny said, gritting his teeth. 'I think Jack O'Connell got away.'

'He'll have to try and reach Conna and get the North East Column to relieve us,' somebody said. 'And that's a tall order'

'We'll fight on. Jack O'Connell won't let us down.'

At that point, though his wound seemed to have stopped bleeding, Dinny propped himself against the stone wall, leaned his face against the lichen covered sandstone and passed out cold.

The siege lasted for another hour, with occasional shots being fired by both sides. Jack O'Connell tried to get help but it was too late. Such reinforcements as did arrive, came in the form of two lorry loads of Black and Tans from Midleton. The men in the house heard a volley of rifle fire in the distance and cheered, believing it was the North East Column. But then someone else said, 'it's the Tans, lads. We're finished.'

Dinny regained consciousness as the smell of smoke reached his nostrils. Just before the Tans arrived, the military had somehow managed to get a man in close enough to pour petrol on the thatch and set it alight. This was the reverse of half a dozen sieges that the column had participated in over the previous year. They were used to being on the outside, shooting and burning their way in. The besiegers were now the besieged.

He opened his eyes. Flame was licking at the thatch roof. Clouds of smoke slung low around the yard. Dinny could see the Black and Tan lorries come up the lane and park out of range of the house. A dozen or so men got out.

The army stopped firing again. Dinny could hear the crackling and feel the heat. Pieces of burning thatch dropped around him like dozens of smoking cigarettes as the roof went up in flames with an angry roar.

By his reckoning, there were still fourteen or fifteen men inside the house. He could hear them choking in the smoke. Suddenly he heard a noise beside him and he dragged himself slowly and painfully to the corner of the house. Stones were being knocked out of the gable end at the back of the fireplace. Two heads appeared. Sonny Leary and 'Fintan Lalor' Glavin tried to crawl through the hole they had made in the wall. The firing started again, this time from the right hand side of the house. Bullets ricocheted around the corner, hitting the wall over his head. Sonny Leary was hit again, this time in the forehead and he collapsed and tried to get up but vanished as someone grabbed him by the legs and pulled him back inside. Glavin also disappeared back into the house.

The firing stopped again. Silence hung in the air as the smoke swirled and draughts were being sucked in through the broken windows to feed the flames. As the roof crackled and sagged over their heads, Dinny could hear the men in the house begin to get nauseated from the smoke. There was the sound of gagging and spluttering. Then he heard the voice of Paddy

Higgins shouting across the yard for terms of surrender from the British and the reply from the officer in charge of the military, the same voice that had requested their surrender at the outset.

'If you break up your arms and throw them into the fire and come out with your hands up, you will be spared.' The two voices were as clear over the crackling of the fire as if they were the voices of friends talking to one another across a ditch on a fine summer's evening.

'And if we don't?'

'If you don't, you'll be burnt to death. That is your decision.'

'How do we know we can trust you?' Paddy Higgins half-spoke, half-coughed the words.

'You don't have a choice. But I give you my word of honour as a British officer that if you surrender and come out unarmed you will be treated as prisoners and not ill-treated in any way.'

There followed the muttering of hurried consultation and a short argument in the house.

'Okay,' Paddy Higgins called out again, 'we agree to that. Give us a few minutes to get rid of the guns.'

'You've got two minutes. But just remember; if there's any monkey business, you'll be shot on sight. Dinny crawled back to the window. He could hear the sound of the rifles and shotguns being broken and tossed into the flames inside the house. He took his own revolver out of his pocket and threw it over the wall. Then he heard Paddy Higgins say; 'We'll say an Act of Contrition now, just in case we get the other version of British justice, for God knows what they'll do to us when they get us into Cork jail.'

Dinny said the Act to himself. 'O my God, I am heartily sorry for having offended Thee, and I detest my sins above all other evil...' He thought of the men in the bog – that was the great stain on his own soul - and prayed for those strangers just as he prayed for himself... who in thy infinite goodness art so deserving of all my love...

'Now one verse of Amhrán na bhFíann and then we go out.' Paddy Higgins's voice was shaking. He made a white flag out of a torn piece of sheet and tied it to the stock of a rifle and stuck it out the window. The men sang one verse of their anthem and opened the front door. One by one, they marched out of the smoking house with their hands in the air.

There was a strange silence in the yard, almost a sort of longing, the uneasy quiet at the end of battle. It hung in the air like the low smoke and swirled uneasily as if it had the actual weight of impending doom. The officer in charge stood up to accept the surrender. He had a revolver in his hand that he used to signal to his troops that they were not to fire. Dinny could see the helmets of the soldiers. They remained where they were, brown mushrooms growing out of the ditches, still aiming their rifles in the direction of the house.

The officer had taken three strides in the direction of the IRA men and was about to accept their surrender when there was a shout from the rear of the troops.

'There's Ahern and Desmond,' an Irish voice suddenly shouted. It was an RIC man, an Irish Black and Tan. Suddenly shots rang out. The Tans, who up to now had taken no part in the shooting, began to break ranks from behind the troops and ran towards the surrendering men firing as they went.

Liam Ahern was hit in the face and the back of his head was blown out. Dave Desmond spun about as rifle fire went into his chest and he went down as well.

'And there's another one of those Aherns,' one of the Tans shouted. 'Get the dirty Sinn Fein bastard.' A group of five or six Black and Tans rushed through the cordon of troops, some firing carbines, others firing revolvers and shouting as they went.

'Now take a bit of yeer own fucking medicine, ye dirty hoors,' the first one roared, firing his revolver into the line of emerging IRA men. 'We've been waiting a long time for this,'

'This one is for poor old Martin Mullen,' the second RIC man screamed as he ran with the others. 'Ye left his poor family to starve.'

'And this one is for Thorpe and Dray,' a Tan with an English accent shouted as he fired two or three rounds into Jer Ahern who had turned around and was trying to make his way back into the house against the stream of stumbling men trying to avoid the flames.

'We'll kill every last one of you filthy Fenian bastards.' English and Irish accents combined in the assault. The soldiers stayed where they were, taking no part in the melee, but allowing the Tans to keep on shooting.

Joe Morrissey and 'Fintan Lalor' Glavin were the last to come out and they began firing again at the onrushing policemen. One policeman was hit in the shoulder and spun around. Another clutched his leg. While trying to make a lunge at the first Black and Tan, 'Fintan Lalor' Glavin tripped over the writhing form of Christy Sullivan, who had just fallen in front of him. The Black and Tan emptied his revolver into Glavin's back where he lay. By now Donie Dennehy was crawling around on his hands and knees, coughing blood. Two Tans were on him in an instant, kicking him in the belly and turning him over while another Tan ran a bayonet through his belly and up under his sternum. Joe Morrissey ran along the wall but was hit as he reached the edge of the haggard where he fell on his face, lurching and jerking in the dirt.

The policemen, their ammunition now spent, dragged the remaining men from the house, kicking and rifle butting everybody they came across.

It was only when Moss Moore and Paddy Sullivan emerged, doing their best to drag the unconscious Sonny Leary on a stretcher over a pile of bodies, that the officer in charge of the troops ordered his men to fire into the air to stop the carnage.

The whole massacre had taken only a minute. The scene was now one of utter chaos. The yard resembled an abattoir, with gore everywhere and smoke swirling and men writhing and crying in the mud or moaning in pain, their blood flowing into the gullies.

The Tans now lined the survivors up against the wall of the cow shed and began to search them. Any money, watches or items of value they found, they pocketed. Had the army officer not ordered them to back off, they would most likely have killed all the remaining column members.

'What are these then?' the Tan with the English accent said, holding in his hand the contents of one man's pockets.

'Rosary beads and a Sacred Heart scapular,' Edmund Terry one of the young lads stammered.

'Holy pictures is it? Fuck these then.' He began to rip up the little badge of the Sacred Heart. 'A lot of fucking good your scapulars are to you now. You should have thought of these,' he caught a Rosary beads, 'when you murdered Mullen and Dray and Thorpe at Christmas.' He held them up in front of young Terry's face and pulled them apart. The beads flew in all directions and landed in the mud and blood at Terry's feet. For good measure, he smashed the crucifix in two and stamped on it.

'You are holy people all right,' he screamed, 'holy murderous fucking bastards.'

They continued searching the dead and dying men; ripping up any other religious items they found, till the ground became a strange litter of holy detritus, Miraculous Medals in the mud, pictures of Christ and the saints and the Virgin being blown about in the breeze.

All this time, Dinny was lying at the back of the house, not sure exactly what was going on. So far, he had not been spotted by the troops or the Tans. He could hear the melee from the front of the house and knew from the shouting and moaning that some kind of killing was going on. He considered his options and knew that he didn't have any. If he crawled out of the shadow of the house he would be seen. In fact if he tried to move in any direction he would probably be shot. So he stayed where he was and he prayed.

Meanwhile, the military remained where they were and left all the work of searching and intimidation to the Tans. Eventually, the Tans rounded up the survivors and those who were not too badly wounded and marched them off across the fields to the roadside where their lorries were parked. Unknown to them, they were being observed by two men; Jack O'Connell, still vainly waiting for reinforcements to arrive from Conna, and Con Foley, who had been making his way back from the pub after his day's drinking, only to encounter the troop lorries blocking his path. He stayed where he was and crept into the bushes and watched as the troops led the seven or eight survivors of the column to the lorries. He hadn't heard the early firing and the ructions at the farmhouse and, even if he had, he was too drunk to realize what was going on. But he would go to his grave with the lives of his comrades on his limited conscience and he would never drink whiskey again. And he would survive the war, though not for long.

He crept away and prayed that the survivors of the column would never be let out of jail so that he could avoid their revenge. He slipped back home. Too days later he caught a train to Belfast where he boarded a liner for New York. However, he did not leave his wild ways behind him: he got caught up in bootlegging in the Bronx a few years later and was shot dead on a subway train in New York and the proceeds of a truck load of illegal whiskey stolen from him.

Dinny Fitzgibbon was still lying on the ground at the back of the house, drifting in and out of consciousness. The cobbles beneath him were cold and wet and he felt the chill from the stones climbing through him as if it was some rising damp. In spite of that he was sweating from the pain in his leg as he lay in his own stench.

As he listened to the departing soldiers, he reckoned that he had a reasonable chance of survival. His leg was ruined but he could put up with that. He would not be ploughing Pat Hackett's with a leg like that. The village was less than half a mile away. The villagers would come, Jack O'Connell would come back; someone would call a doctor.

But nobody arrived from the village. The locals stayed away, they were too frightened of the soldiers and the Tans. Instead, when all the prisoners had been piled into the lorries and the troops had left, some of the Tans came back to finish off the wounded. They bayoneted all the men lying on the ground, some dead, some unconscious, some barely conscious and moaning quietly from their wounds. They nailed a scrawled notice to the gatepost to the effect that if any of the dead were moved before they returned they would burn the village to the ground.

It was now gone five o'clock and almost dark. Their last task before they left was to burn the ricks of hay and straw in the haggard behind the house. As one of them came around the corner carrying a can of petrol he saw Dinny lying in the passageway. Dinny noticed him approaching and immediately feigned death.

'There's another one here,' the Tan called out. 'We missed one of the buggers.'

The Tan lowered the petrol can to the ground near where Dinny lay and studied him, with his rifle lowered, bayonet at the ready.

'Is he alive?' someone called out.

'I don't know.'

Dinny could hear the second Tan's footsteps on the cobbles. He tried to pray. 'Receive me into Thy hands, O Lord...'

Then he felt something rip his belly and a burning feeling ran across his stomach. Instinctively, his hands moved to hold in his innards that he could feel were now spilling out on the ground like a bag of warm eels.

'He's alive all right,' the Tan said. 'But he won't be alive for much longer.' He could hear the policeman talking beside him, his heavy breathing, the cigarette rasp in his voice. Then he felt the bayonet push hard against his chest and heard a crunching sound like someone grinding mangolds as it went between his ribs. A hot liquid came up his throat and he coughed and choked and lost consciousness, smothered in his own blood.

The last thing he saw as his eyes closed, smelling the earth on the cobbles beneath him, was a single daffodil about ten feet from where he lay. It swayed, nodding in the smoke, a bell tolling silently for all the men who had died, for all the pain and suffering that is brought on by war and violence and the depravity it leads to. The Tan walked towards it, went around the corner of the house and disappeared, and Dinny, an unlikely martyr, became the latest in the long list of Irish martyrs. An hour later the villagers arrived, led by Jack O'Connell, and all that was left for them to do was place sheets over the bodies of the dead.

4573460R00145

Printed in Great Britain
by Amazon.co.uk, Ltd.,
Marston Gate.